FINAL JUDGMENT

FINAL JUDGMENT

A JERICHO NOVEL

TONY ACREE

Cover photo by Bill Noel

ISBN: 978-1-958414-36-1

Enigma House Press

Goshen, Kentucky 40026

www.enigmahousepress.com

ALSO BY TONY ACREE

<u>Victor McCain Thrillers</u>

The Hand of God

The Watchers

The Speaker

Revenge

<u>Victor McCain Short Stories</u>

Nightmare

Back to Hell

Lonnie, Me and the Hand of God (written with Marian Allen)

<u>Samantha Tyler Thrillers</u>

Vengeance

Absolution

<u>Paige Aldridge and Victor McCain Thrillers</u>

The Devil's Mark

Dead Man's Flood: A Charlie Powell Short Story

<u>Non-fiction</u>

Tell Me More

For Mary, my first muse.

1

I sat in my chair, feet on the windowsill, and watched a Paducah Barge Company tugboat push several barges loaded with coal down the Ohio River toward the McAlpine Locks and Dam. Two American flags whipped from side to side in the late spring breeze on the front of the tug, showing both their patriotism and helping the captain navigate the river from the tower which rose three stories above the deck.

My office was on the top floor of an old whiskey distillery converted to office space on Main Street in downtown Louisville. I got it at a bargain discount rate due to the thanks of a former client whose daughter struggled with a stalker the police were unable to dissuade. I convinced the young man a second visit from me would lead to an increase in the use of his medical insurance and he left her alone. Her father showed his gratitude by offering the place at a cost that fit my budget.

My reverie was broken when my office door opened, and a man entered without knocking. I swiveled my chair around and dropped my feet to the ground, the gun in my hand pointed more or less in his direction. Definitely more.

"I told you if you showed up here, I'd kill you," I said.

The man nodded and closed the door behind him. He crossed the office and sat in one of my two leather client chairs, then placed a tan Ferragamo briefcase on his lap.

I leaned forward, resting my gun hand on the desk. I was aiming for intimidating. He ignored the gun, flipped the locks on his briefcase, slid out a manila folder, and tossed it on my desk. Guess I needed to work on my intimidation.

"His name was Greg Chambers. Twenty-eight years old and he worked as an electrician for Lear's Electric."

Several 8 x 10 glossies slid out of the folder, but I kept my eyes on Justin Roman. He's a defense lawyer. Never take your eyes off a defense lawyer. Besides, I have great peripheral vision, and I could see enough to tell the top of Mr. Chambers' skull had been bashed to a bloody pulp.

In contrast to my six-foot-one and two-hundred pound stature, Roman was whipsaw thin, with most of his brown hair galloping off the back of his head. He was of average height and wore a dark blue Armani pinstriped suit which probably cost more than all my office furniture combined. Then again, so would most bikinis.

"I told you on the phone I wasn't interested in playing detective for you, Justin," I said. "I'm on vacation."

"Look, Jericho, I need you on this one. Besides, when do you ever turn down business?"

"I haven't had a vacation in almost two years. I just caught a guy wanted by an insurance company, an Indiana bails bondsman, and a soon to be ex-wife for skipping out on all three of them with a boatload of cash. The insurance company and bailsman paid me enough to take several weeks off, and I plan on heading to Hawaii for some fun and sun."

"And the ex-wife? What did she pay you?"

I smiled. "Homemade cookies with benefits."

I put the gun away in the top drawer of my desk and Roman closed the briefcase and sat it on the floor beside his chair. "You'd really turn down the chance to work a murder case?"

I shrugged. "Who's your client?"

"One of your old buddies, Robert King."

I laughed, but not with pleasure. King was one of Louisville's top crime bosses. Loan sharking was his main trade, but rumor says he dabbled in rackets, gambling, and prostitution. The rumors, however, have not stopped him from being a major player in county politics. Hell, he was even voted Rotarian of the Year.

"Going to school together back in the day doesn't make us buddies, Roman. I'd nail his ass to the wall given half the chance. A choir boy he's not. Bobby would off his own mother if she owed him two nickels and didn't pay up."

"He says he didn't do it."

"All your clients say that."

Roman crossed one leg over another. "He's willing to pay you well."

"The cops have been busting their balls to nail Bobby for years. Now you're telling me they have him on a murder rap? I plan to celebrate by donating to the Policemen's Benevolent Society."

"There's nothing I can do to change your mind?" he asked.

"Nope, it's a matter of principle."

"I will pay you double your normal hourly rate; double the retainer and you can claim nearly anything you want as expenses."

I swiveled around to look briefly at the river. The tug had passed under both the new Lincoln and old Kennedy bridges and begun the slow turn to the locks to find its way around the Falls of the Ohio and down river to the Mississippi and maybe all the way to the Gulf of Mexico. I thought for a moment then turned back to Roman. "Okay, I'm in."

I pulled the folder toward me and opened it.

Justin asked, "What about your principles?"

"They're overrated."

2

"**D**id you know F. Scott Fitzgerald wrote *The Great Gatsby* after spending time here at the Seelbach? This is where he met George Remus, a bootlegger out of Cincinnati, and some believe Fitzgerald used him as the inspiration for Gatsby."

Robert King sliced off another hunk of filet mignon and speared it with his fork. He used it to gesture around the Rathskeller, the restaurant in the bowels of the Seelbach Hotel where the two of us were having lunch, before shoving it in his mouth. He chewed loudly for a moment, then continued, "And it's the only room in the world completely covered in Rookwood pottery. Can you believe all these frickin' pelicans on the walls? Some claim they're a nod to the occult."

"You angling for a job as a tour guide when you get out of prison, Bobby?"

He pointed his fork at me and said, "Kiss my ass, Jericho. I ain't going to prison. You're going to see to that."

King makes a Sumo wrestler seem small by comparison. He had to have weighed at least four-hundred pounds. Dressed in a dark blue suit, gray shirt, and tie, he sported a flat top haircut with the sides cut short. A Bellarmine University ring large enough to blind you if it caught the light just right clung to a meaty finger on his left hand.

I opted for the Kentucky carp and snow creek mussels washed down with two fingers of Woodford Reserve Double Oak bourbon. I sipped the whiskey. "Why don't you start by telling me how you knew Chambers?"

"The man comes to me a few months ago and tells me he needed a loan. Short term kind of deal. I was happy to help out."

"For a small double-digit percentage, I'm sure. How much was he into you?"

King wiped his mouth with a napkin and shifted in his seat. I swore I could hear a plea for mercy from the chair. "Couple grand. He had been paying real regular, then he skipped a week and I stopped by to remind him of his obligations."

"I thought you had people to do that kind of thing for you. Why didn't you use them?"

"Pure chance. I happened to be in the area after playing a

round of golf at Valhalla when I got a call from my accountant who told me he'd been late, going into week number two. He lives a few blocks off Shelbyville Road in a patio home development. I figured I'd stop by and have a chat."

"And things got out of hand? That what happened, Bobby?"

He tossed the steak-stained napkin on the table. "I told you. I didn't do it. I didn't go over to hurt him. If I wanted him roughed up, then you're right. I'm not an idiot, I'd send one of my guys over to make him pay up. Break a leg if needed."

"Like you used to do back in school? You always had others do your dirty work."

"Christ, Jericho. You still pissed about that? That was, what, third grade? You gotta let it go."

"You sent John Sterling and Roger Bryant to shake me down for my Air Jordans. I loved those shoes. When I beat the crap out of the two of them for trying, they suspended me for a week and my father tanned my hide and took my shoes away as punishment. You bet your ass I hold a grudge."

We sat staring across the table at each other for a few more minutes. Bobby broke the silence first. "And that's why I wanted you on the case. You hate my guts. I know it and so does everyone else, including the cops. When you prove I didn't do it, people will have to listen."

He had a point. Bobby had to know if I found any evidence pointing to his guilt, client privilege or not, I'd use it to bury him. It was the only reason I took the job.

"Okay. Fine. You decide to make an in-home visit. Anyone else know you were going? Any chance this was a setup?"

"Not a soul. I didn't even know I was going to stop by. Pure chance."

"Fair enough. Tell me what happened next."

"I drive by his house and his truck is out front. I know he works for Lear Electric, and I figure he must be home. I park, go to the door, and knock. No answer. I tried the knob and the door's unlocked, so I go in."

"Did you see anyone else before you entered the home?"

He thought for a moment and then shook his head. "Nah, there wasn't anyone around. He lives at the end of a small cul-de-sac and there weren't any cars in the driveways on either side of his."

I motioned for him to keep talking while I ate more of my carp.

"I opened the door and shouted his name. Nothing. I walk into the living room, and I can see there's a body lying on the floor in the kitchen. I walked far enough to be able to see the whole scene and then got the hell out of there. I wiped down the doorknob with my suit coat, jumped into my Audi and hightailed it home."

"If there was no one home at either house, how'd they catch you?"

"Damn busybody in the front of the subdivision. He thought I'd been driving too fast coming into the damn place and took note of my license plate. Reported it to the cops.

When they came to see me, they had a warrant to search my place and they found a spot of Chambers' blood on the bottom of my shoe."

"Thought you said you didn't go into the kitchen?"

"And I didn't. You've seen the crime scene photos, right?"

I nodded.

"Whoever did this had a real hard on for this guy. They beat the ever-lovin' shit out of him. Blood splattered all over the kitchen. Some of it must have reached the living room and I stepped in it. "

I knew from the crime scene report Roman included that Chambers' skull was crushed in by his own hammer. They found his tool belt hanging on a chair by a small Formica table in a breakfast nook, the hammer tossed onto the floor. The thought was Chambers had been gazing out a window over the kitchen sink when he was struck from behind.

"The cops got a good case against you, Bobby. Motive, opportunity, physical evidence. And I promise you, if I prove you really did do this, I'll be the cop's best friend and I'll be there to watch them push the plunger in the gas chamber. "

"I keep telling you. I. Didn't. Do. It. The case is all circumstantial and all pointing to the wrong guy. Time for you to start earning the money I'm paying you, don't you think?"

I caught the waiter's eye and motioned for a to-go box.

3

With the day pleasant and rain free, I dropped the soft top and removed the doors on my forest green Jeep Wrangler and cruised down the Gene Snyder Freeway past horse farms and rolling fields of Kentucky bluegrass until I hit the exit for Shelbyville Road and hung a left. Chambers lived in far eastern Jefferson County, not too far from Middletown.

The patio homes where Chambers lived sprawled just outside the commercial district on the other side of the interstate. There were about three dozen patio homes in the small development, most of them two-bedroom homes like Chambers'. I glanced at the file on the passenger seat as I turned into the subdivision and read the address of the busybody who turned in King. Stu Conley lived a few houses from the entrance to the subdivision on the main drag. I eased into the concrete driveway and parked next to a late 90's red Buick Skylark.

He lived in a well taken care of home with white vinyl siding and maroon shutters. The sweet smell of freshly mowed grass filled the late May air, and a row of purple coneflowers lined the stepping stone sidewalk to the front door. I barely turned off the engine when the front door swung open, and a small elderly man stood watching me approach. He appeared to be north of seventy-years-old and wore a sleeveless white T-shirt, tan slacks, and bedroom slippers. Gray hair stuck out at wild angles on the top of his head. I guess combs were optional in his home.

"Can I help you, Mister?" he asked.

Clear, suspicious green eyes stared out from under bushy eyebrows that nearly met in a unibrow. I offered my hand and introduced myself. He grasped the offered hand and shook it, but not with any enthusiasm.

I told him my name and why I was there.

"Yeah, that lawyer feller told me you might be stopping by. Come on in. We can set out on the deck and chew the fat a bit."

He led me through a house as neat on the inside as the out. In the kitchen he asked if I wanted coffee.

"Yes, please. A splash of milk if you have it."

He grunted and fixed two cups of Dunkin Donuts medium roast from a silver Keurig sitting on a gray granite countertop, and then I followed him out a sliding glass door onto a mahogany deck which ran the length of the rear of the home. A large, tiled patio table sat to one side with an even larger forest green umbrella providing shade from the early afternoon sun.

He sat in a padded deck chair, and I sat opposite him. He sipped his coffee and then put the cup on the table. "So, you're working for the scum-bucket who murdered Greg Chambers. That right?"

"The scum-bucket says he didn't do it."

"Yeah, yeah, yeah. They all say that right up until the time they flip the switch on the electric chair and fry their asses."

"We don't use Old Sparky anymore in Kentucky. They go to the gas chamber. It's a more humane way to kill the damned and saves on the electric bill."

"You some kind of smart ass, boy?"

"Every kind."

He waved me off. "Well, I don't care if they juice 'em or gas 'em. As long as they get what they got coming, it's all the same to me."

Over his shoulder I watched a doe and two fawns eat grass at the edge of Conley's property, not a care in the world. There was a time when deer wouldn't come anywhere near a yard if there were people in sight. Now, with most natural predators gone, they ignored us like we were part of the patio furniture.

"The police report says you saw King speeding in the subdivision. That right?" I asked.

"Yes, sir. I seen that man fly out of here in a bright blue foreign jobbie like Satan himself was chasin' him, and that's after being above the limit comin' in. We have a fifteen mile an hour limit and he had to be doing twice that. A lot of people like to walk their dogs around here and when pricks like him fly through here it's dangerous. I try and keep an eye out and make sure people pay a price for reckless driving."

"A regular Dale Earnhardt Jr. Did you see anyone else coming or going that afternoon?"

"Yep. Like I told the police, I noticed Greg come home about three that afternoon. I was out front working in the yard. The damned crabgrass keeps popping up and this place takes a bit of upkeep. I lost my wife a few years ago and now I got all the chores to do."

"Anyone else?"

"Pizza guy about a half hour later. That one done got two tickets for speeding through here. He flipped me the bird when he drove by. I saw him leave a few minutes later and I flipped him one back."

I nodded. "And no one else?"

"Nah. Not a soul. Just them."

"How well did you know Chambers?"

He shrugged. "Ain't like we were drinking buddies. I knew him to look at him, that's about it."

"He ever cause any problems?"

"Not since the little blonde lead foot of his stopped coming around."

"Girlfriend?"

"I'm guessin' so. She came round real regular for quite some time. Then a month or two ago, she quit coming. She drove one of them little red Mazda sports cars. What do you call 'em?

"A Miata," I suggested.

He snapped his thin boney fingers, the sound loud enough to make the deer at least glance our way. "That's the one. I had to yell at her more than once to slow her ass down driving through here. Didn't hurt my feelings when she stopped buzzin' down to his place."

"Was it one month or two months ago?"

He stared up at the sky for a moment and gave it some thought. "Two. She had a Cardinal sticker on her bumper, and I remember thinking she had to be ticked U of L didn't even make the NCAA tournament back in March. Haven't seen her since."

About the same time Chambers borrowed the money from King. "Know her name?"

"Like I told you, Greg and I weren't drinking buddies. No clue what her name might be."

"You still have her plate number?"

"Very funny. Give me a sec."

Conley disappeared inside the house while I sat and watched the deer eat. He returned a moment later with a green post-it note. In neat, precise handwriting, a six-digit tag number filled the space.

"There ya go. Now if you don't mind, I've got a bit of work to get done and I ain't getting any younger."

I thanked him, returned to the Jeep, and drove down to Chambers' home at the far end of the subdivision, the last home at the end of a dead-end street. I nosed the Wrangler into the driveway and parked next to a Lear Electric panel truck, surprised the company had yet to reclaim their truck. I sat in the Jeep for a moment and glanced around the quiet street.

The cul-de-sac sat at the edge of a field leading up to Floyds Fork Creek, the grass and weeds nearly waist high. A stand of locust trees bordered the creek. I knew from looking at a Google map of the area there was nothing between here and the creek but more field until you hit a dirt service road the utility company used to access the power lines which filled the horizon and marched off into the distance.

The police had interviewed all the neighbors and checked alibis but none of them were home when Chambers was murdered. And if Conley was right, no one else drove in that afternoon. Which meant the murderer most likely parked on the access road and crossed the field to get to Chambers' place.

I hopped out of the Jeep and tried the chrome handle of the Lear truck, but it was locked. I peeked inside but saw only empty Styrofoam coffee cups and discarded McDonald's bags which filled the passenger side floorboard. Won't the Lear folks be happy. With nothing else to see, I hiked down the sidewalk to the front door.

The only thing Chambers' and Conley's places had in common was the floor plan. Where Conley maintained his property with obvious love and a huge amount of sweat equity, it was clear Chambers' skill with electricity did not transfer to home maintenance. The vinyl siding was overdue for a meeting with a power washer and there were more yellow dandelions in the front yard than there were blades of grass. Tiny maple saplings were growing in the grimy gutters and a large wasp nest clung to one of the dingy white window frames, huge red wasps flying back and forth.

The faux wood door featured a keypad lock mechanism tied into the alarm system. I checked my phone for the text from Roman with the code, tapped in the numbers, pressed the asterisk key, then heard the locking mechanism disengage and the deadbolt slide free.

The day Chambers died the alarm company reported he turned off the alarm at 3:09 p.m. and did not re-arm the system. King showed up around seven. Either Chambers knew the killer and let him into the house, or the person slipped in once the alarm had been disarmed like Bobby had done.

I turned the brass knob and entered, then stood in the front entry way for a moment and listened. The alarm panel next to the front door remained quiet, having never been turned back on. Empty houses have a different vibe from those where someone is home. Perhaps our senses pick up the subtle vibrations of people walking across the floor. Maybe we can feel the smallest movement of air a person moving from one room to the next creates. Who knows? On this day, Chambers' home felt completely empty.

The front entry gave way to a spacious living room and featured a gathering of mismatched furniture. A green sofa filled up one wall with an off-brown recliner to one side separated by a floor lamp which might have been left over from the '60s. Magazines covered a beat all to hell cherry coffee table in front of the sofa. A few *Guns and Ammo* mixed with a few *Maxim* issues in a pile in the middle of the table.

On the green carpeted floor at the far end of the living room a sixty-inch Samsung TV sat on an overmatched entertainment center. DVDs were stacked on either side, many of them out of their cases. I stood in the middle of the room and turned around in place seeing if anything caught my eye. Nothing did.

Directly to my left, the living room gave way to a breakfast nook and an arch to the kitchen. I retraced the path Bobby would have walked. A pizza box sat open next to the sink with a pie going stale with a couple of slices of pepperoni and sausage missing. Blood, mixed with the tomato sauce, covered a large portion of the rest of the box, along with the window over the sink and blue and white checkered tile used as a backsplash. In this case, it caught more than grease.

The crime tech geeks determined Chambers had been standing in front of the kitchen sink when the first blow from the hammer cracked his skull wide open. In a bit of irony, the hammer used to murder the electrician was a Dead On Death Stick, a twenty-one-ounce hammer popular with younger carpenters and electricians because of the cool name. According to the crime scene geeks, to figure the force of the blows when they struck Chambers' skull, you multiply the hammer mass by its acceleration. All I knew was his head never had a chance.

Chambers stood five-feet-eight-inches tall, and the assailant was likely a few inches taller due to the angle of the blood pattern from the blows. When Chambers fell forward, the murderer held him down over the sink and struck him repeatedly, an estimated fourteen times. It was easy to see how King stepped on a spot of blood which stretched from the sink to the ceiling to the living room. The murderer had to have been covered in blood.

The savagery of fourteen blows suggested he'd royally pissed off someone. The question was, over what? Perhaps an angry ex-boyfriend? Money he borrowed from someone else? I believed Bobby when he said he didn't do it because it's hard to get money from a corpse. Perhaps Chambers needed the money to pay off a predator even more vicious than Robert King. One scary proposition.

I searched the rest of the house, starting with the master bath where I found a box of feminine hygiene products stashed in the vanity and two different toothbrushes in a holder on the sink. If Chambers and the girl had split, he had yet to toss out her toiletries. Wishful thinking for a happy return?

A search of the master bedroom itself and a guest bedroom turned up nothing other than the man's lack of home maintenance which was matched only by his lack of housekeeping. In the master, clothes were piled in a corner next to an unused clothes hamper and the bed clothes were tossed to the side in a heap.

He did not seem to have a landline which meant there was no easy way to check his most recent caller ID list. I made a mental note to ask Roman to subpoena his cell phone provider for the information. We might get it during discovery from the prosecution, but only if the other side deemed it exculpatory, and I didn't want to wait that long.

I went through all the drawers in his dresser but, again, I struck out. Chambers led a singularly normal, if slovenly, life and there were no guns to be found, smoking or otherwise.

The cops also never found Chambers' cell phone. The murderer likely took it with them. The cops also found no laptop or computer in the house and only a true luddite went without a computer these days, meaning the bad guy took it as well.

I heard a car stop outside and made it to a front window in time to see the mailman toss some mail into his box and shut the flap. Apparently, the United States Postal Service was unaware of the fact their customer no longer needed the latest Kroger supplement.

I waited until the mailman made his turn around and disappeared up the street and then went out to the box, flipped down the lid and glanced through a stack of bills and ads. The only thing of real interest was a green return receipt from the post office where Chambers sent a parcel to a woman named Amelia Hedley who lived on Herbert Avenue in Louisville. The zip code put her in the south end of town out near Dixie Highway, an area known as Lively Shively.

Chambers mailed her the parcel two days before his murder, and she didn't sign for it until three days after. The receipt did not list the size or contents.

After taking a close look around to make sure no one was watching me, I returned the rest of the mail to the box, while palming the return receipt and folding it in half. After I closed the box, I slipped the receipt into a pants pocket and walked casually to my Wrangler and left. Stealing mail, even from a dead man, is a federal offense with up to five years in jail if you're caught. When you're a smooth operator like me, that's not really a concern.

It was likely the lead would go nowhere, but it at least gave me an angle to follow, a path to someone Chambers knew well enough to mail a package. Perhaps she drove a red Miata. You never know what piece of information might lead to something else, and now I at least possessed something the cops didn't. Yay me.

I fired up the Jeep and started for my office. When I swung out onto the highway, I caught a glimpse of a red Ford Mustang Shelby GT350 as it pulled away from the curb and fell in behind me a few cars back. I remembered seeing the same Mustang behind me when I left my meeting with King. I occasionally go through car envy and stopped by to look at a blue one a few months ago at a Ford dealership in Louisville. Hard to miss a sweet ride like the Shelby.

To make sure the car was tailing me, and it wasn't my imagination, I turned quickly down a side street and accelerated about half a block and then came to a stop. In my rearview mirror I watched the Mustang start to turn down the same street, see me stopped, and then change their mind and continue straight. I quickly made the block and when I hit the main drag, I could see the Mustang turn onto the interstate. I pushed the Jeep hard and made the ramp a few seconds behind them, but they must have seen me closing the gap and when they hit the interstate the driver put their foot into it and the Shelby, one of the fastest cars on four wheels, shot away like a rocket.

Trying to keep pace was pointless so I eased up and settled into my normal five over the limit pace. Interesting. I felt a bit of personal disappointment for not managing to get the license plate, but it happens, even to those of us who are the very best at what we do. It wouldn't happen a second time.

4

I slid a yellow notepad from my desk drawer and jotted down a few notes about my interview with Stu Conley and noted Amelia Hedley's address and the reminder to ask Roman to try and get Chambers' cell phone records. I then turned on my computer and searched social media for Greg Chambers. I have Facebook, Twitter, and Instagram accounts under an assumed name, using a picture I downloaded off a free picture site, and use it to search for people I might be investigating. Some people make keeping track of their movements unbelievably easy through social media.

Greg Chambers was not one of them, with only a Facebook account he rarely posted to and didn't even bother to upload a profile picture, instead leaving the gray placeholder silhouette. In today's world, most people are all over social media. Chambers appeared not to be a fan. His profile page said he was single, his birthday was in July, and he had a brother named Patrick.

I trolled his friends list, which consisted of eighty-seven friends, and found Amelia Hedley halfway down. A visit to her page showed an attractive blonde with an upturned nose and cross tattoo on her neck. Her page was set to private so I couldn't get any of her personal information, but she appeared to be the same age as Chambers. I sent her a friend request and then checked for her on the other social media sites. I found an Instagram page, also set to private, and sent a follow request there as well.

Before I could do anything else, my office door opened and Dean Monroe, like Roman before him, walked in without knocking.

"There is an old tradition," I said, "where one takes one's knuckles and then uses them to rap upon yonder door frame before entering the residence of another."

A bit over six feet tall, Deano wore a crisp denim shirt, jeans with a pressed crease, brown Tony Lama cowboy boots, and a black Stetson. He hooked a chair with a foot, dragged it closer to my desk, plopped down, and then rested the heels of his boots on the corner while pushing the Stetson up a bit with one long index finger. And I'll be damned if he wasn't chewing on a toothpick.

"The donut boys in blue aren't happy with you, my friend. No sir, not even a little bit," he said in a slow southern drawl.

"Kentucky cowboy? Really? You were born in Madison,

Wisconsin and went to school at U Dub. I thought you guys wore Cheese-heads, not Stetsons."

He shrugged. Deano and I had been friends for several years having crossed paths on a job for a local debutante. I'd been working security at a Derby party she hosted in a mansion overlooking the Ohio River, and he'd been working the debutante.

Deano is the type of man women fall over themselves trying to land. In this case, the debutante gave it her best shot, but he ended up spending most of the night talking shop with me, much to the young lady's chagrin. Deano owned a security firm and frequently spent time with the bluest of Louisville blue bloods.

"You can hide a lot of cheese in a Stetson." He removed the toothpick from his mouth and pointed it at me. "Word on the street is you're working for Robert King. That true?"

"Yep. And you know what that means?"

He nodded. "If he hired you, he didn't do it. You'd fry his ass quicker than bacon at a Weight Watchers convention. Still, it doesn't make the cops any happier. They think you've gone over to the dark side."

"I have to admit, it feels the same to me. But if he didn't do it..."

"Then someone else did and now you're going to find out who and save Robert King's ass. What's the world coming to? Your life won't be getting any easier. Did you hear who they assigned to the case?"

"Not yet. Who?"

"Augustine Tugbe and Emit Brown. The cops I know say Tugbe doesn't like private dicks in general, and you in particular. What'd you ever do to piss him off?"

"Do you remember me telling you about Newt Porcher?"

Deano thought for a second and then barked a short laugh. "You mean that short fat little prick who used to be a private investigator here in town? Vaguely. Whatever happened to him?"

"Dead. Newt was on a job trying to get pictures of a guy and his mistress through a bedroom window and the guy shot him claiming he thought Newt was a prowler. Most suspected it was straight out murder, but the prosecutor couldn't, or wouldn't, pursue the case. Newt wasn't exactly a lovable guy.

"Sounds about right."

"Newt gave me my first job in the business. Early in Tugbe's career as a wet behind the ear's detective, Newt screwed up one of his cases by tipping off a suspect in a robbery-homicide Tugbe was interested in. The guy skipped town and they never caught him. After that, Newt and anyone associated with him was persona non-grata as far as Tugbe was concerned."

"Sins of the father, so to speak."

"Yep. And you're right. I'll have to step lightly around Tugbe. Good detective, though. I don't know much about Brown, which makes me wonder why they charged King. All their evidence is circumstantial and Roman won't break a sweat tearing their case apart."

Deano shrugged. "It wasn't his call. The local Commonwealth's Attorney was all hot and bothered about charging King, sooner rather than later. Called a press conference to make the announcement before the ink was dry on the big guy's thumb print at booking."

"Alexandra Cutter? She's always been a publicity hound. Still, you'd think she'd want an airtight case against King before moving."

"What can I tell you? She's both a lawyer and a politician. I don't pretend to understand her motivations. What's next, Sherlock?"

"I'm going to get some dinner, then track down the brother and talk to him. Want to join me?"

Deano dropped his boots back to the floor. "Nope. I only stopped by to give you the heads up the cops aren't going to be letting you out of any speeding tickets. I've got plans tonight."

"What, you going to the rodeo?"

"Not a public one, but there's a certain cowgirl who might need some bronco riding tonight."

"That's a visual I could have lived without."

"Yippee ki-yay."

5
————

Divots is a golf themed floating bar on the Ohio River in Goshen and an easy walk from my condo. Since I cook an edible meal about as well as I do brain surgery, I'm a regular. I slipped into my favorite booth with a view of the river, the front door, and one of the docks. Call me paranoid if you want, but I like to see what's coming. Even when it's not. The fact boats tie up to get grub and some of those boats have beautiful women in bikinis has nothing to do with my choice of views.

Photos of famous golfers and courses covered the walls, and over my booth a photo of Ben Hogan and Arnold Palmer smoking at the 1966 Masters hung in a beautiful cherry wood frame. Interesting, since you aren't allowed to smoke in most bars in the Louisville metro area.

The place was quiet for a Monday night. One of two

reasons I was a regular approached my table. Mary McGill placed an Old Fashioned made with Woodford Reserve Double Oak bourbon in front of me without me saying a word. In her mid-twenties, Mary tended bar and waited tables at Divots while finishing her degree at the University of Louisville's Louis D. Brandeis School of Law. Tonight, her shoulder length blonde hair was pulled into a ponytail, and she wore a black polo shirt and khaki shorts which passed for a uniform at the restaurant.

Tall and with the figure of a mythical Amazon, we'd struck up a flirtatious relationship over bourbon and beef. The steaks were reason number two for my regular patronage. I love a good steak and Divots were the best in town.

"You want the usual for dinner?" she asked.

"Yes'em. That's why it's called the usual."

"Smart ass. Don't you ever feel the urge to try something else?"

I offered her one of my best smiles. "There are some things I never want to change."

She laughed, gave me a wink, and went to the kitchen to place my order. I watched her go, contemplating the advantages of a woman with both youth and beauty when the opposite of both slid into the booth across from me.

Theodore "Teddy" Ferguson, owner of Divots, wore a red golf shirt, red and white checkered pants, and a haircut this side of a dead raccoon. His face featured a nose two sizes too big and was covered in a patchwork of veins from an obvious life of heavy drinking. Bushy, snow white, eyebrows topped eyelids which stayed at half-mast over a pair of watery blue eyes.

Teddy bought out the previous owner who operated a hamburger joint, renovated the place with a golf motif, and opened a year ago to rave reviews. Over the past year, we'd become something close to friends. As close as Teddy ever came to friends at any rate. To say he had the charm of a pissed off pitbull would be an understatement. He was an acquired taste.

"Please tell me you're wearing those pants because you lost a bet," I said.

"Screw you, asshole. These pants happen to be the height of fashion."

"In 1960, maybe. You're a man fifty-years behind the times, Teddy. Thank God someone else dresses the staff."

"Again, screw you. I'm not here to enjoy your witty banter. I'm here to try and save your backside. A little birdie told me you are working for Robert King. Is that true, Jericho?"

Seems little birds were flying all over town. "Started today."

"Jesus H. Christ on a stick. And here I thought you were a Kentucky hick with at least some common sense. Are you fuckin' nuts? Why in hell would you go to work for him? You know he's a made man, right?"

I nodded. "He says he didn't do it."

Teddy rolled his eyes, not a pretty sight. "And I bet he told you he loved baby seals, too. And puppies. He tell you that, too? You know about my past, Jericho?"

"You've never been much to talk about your time in Boston, Teddy, but rumor among those who would know says you were a former high-ranking member of the Irish Mafia in Beantown."

He shrugged his shoulders. "Alleged member."

"Rumor also has it you accomplished the near impossible and left the Family business on both good terms with the Family and the police, retiring to live a life on the straight and narrow in the great Commonwealth of Kentucky."

"Look, Jericho, whatever I may or may not have done in the past up in Boston, I keep my nose clean down here. I moved to be near my little girl. She's a doctor over at Kosair Children's Hospital."

"She's a bone doc, right?"

We were interrupted for a moment when Mary brought my Caesar Salad for me to eat while I waited on my ribeye and baked potato with extra sour cream. She asked Teddy if he needed anything, and he waved her away. She gave me another wink and left.

"Yeah, she fixes up kids who fall down and go boom. She's the light of my life and it's because of her I got out of the family business. You know what I mean?"

"Alleged life."

"That's right. Alleged. But it don't mean I don't still have contacts from back in the day. And when I moved here, I knew all about King and the things that fat bastard has his hands into. He's bad news, Jericho. The worst of the worst. You don't need to be working with him."

Mary wiped down the counter with a towel and I noticed her more than once glancing my way but trying hard not to be caught doing it.

"Look, I appreciate the concern, but as strange as it seems, I believe him when he says he didn't do it. Heaven forgive me, but I do. And with the cops looking to pin this one on him and not considering anyone else, it means a murderer might go free."

"Life's tough. Finding who did it, that's the cops' job. They don't get it right, tough shit. That's on them. Not you. Guilty or not guilty, you hitch your little red wagon to his crap train, and you will carry the same stink. You don't need that. Get out now while you can."

"I'm touched, Teddy. You really care."

He shoved his way out of the booth and stood. "Care? Hey, dumb ass, if you get caught up in this King thing and something happens to you, I could lose one of my best customers. You pay half the wages of the staff with all the money you spend in this joint. I'm watching my bottom line."

I pointed to the way his stomach hung over his belt and said, "You better watch your belt line."

"Always a fucking comic. Eat your salad, wise ass."

And I did.

6

Patrick Chambers walked into the Raven in St. Matthews around 9:00 p.m. The Raven sits in the heart of St. Matthews in eastern Louisville and serves the best lamb shank this side of a Blarney stone. When I finally got hold of Patrick, he agreed to meet me, and when I found out he lived a few blocks away on Wallace Avenue, I suggested we meet there for a late drink.

He agreed despite not being happy I called. I asked him how I would recognize him, and he said he would be the tired one. I changed into a blue University of Kentucky polo shirt, black jeans, and deck shoes. I felt chipper.

When a bald man around thirty-years-old pushed through the doors, I knew I had found my man. He wore a rumpled brown suit, a sickly beige tie, and scuffed black patent leather shoes. I lifted a hand, and he shuffled my direction.

He slid onto the stool next to me and ordered a Guinness. I'd beat him there by a few minutes and nursed a glass of Red Breast 24-year Irish whiskey. I extended my hand, but he didn't take it. His expression said he put me in the same category as lepers. Maybe a handsome leper.

"Let's get something straight: I'm only here so you won't bother my mother. She's suffered enough with Greg's murder, and I don't want you showing up on her doorstep to make things worse. Ask me what you need and then get the hell out of our lives."

"I love take-charge guys who are direct. Fair enough. Let's see if we can make this short. Can you tell me why Greg borrowed money from Robert King?"

"No clue. I work at the Humana building downtown in claims. I've managed to stash a bit away and mom's not hurting for anything either since dad died and left her some life insurance and his pension, but he didn't ask either one of us for help. Why he went to the shylock is beyond us."

I sipped the whiskey. A woman with hair the color of a setting sun pulled into a tight ponytail and a freckled nose sat two stools down from me wearing a hunter green pantsuit. She was reading the Wall Street Journal while eating shepherd's pie. She glanced my way and I smiled. She shook her head with a half-smile and returned her eyes to her paper. You win some, you lose some. I returned my attention to Greg's brother.

"I will buy with you, sell with you, talk with you, walk with you, and so following; but I will not eat with you, drink with you, nor pray with you."

Patrick paused with the Guinness halfway to his lips. "What the hell?"

"A rose by any other name?"

"What's wrong with you?"

"Only the Bard knows. Never mind. Had Greg ever asked you for money in the past? Maybe he needed more and was embarrassed to hit the well again."

"No, Greg led a simple life. You've been to his place?" When I nodded, he continued, "Look like a man living high on the hog to you? Greg didn't make much, but he didn't spend much either. He never asked me for money and mom said he'd never ever asked her for any either."

"Yet instead of coming to either of you, he borrowed nearly two-grand from a man who enjoys pulling the wings off butterflies. I have to ask: any drugs, alcohol or gambling problems?"

Patrick muttered for a moment under his breath, and I thought he might take a swing at me with his bottle. "You bastards plan to use character assassination against my brother to try and get that asshole off, aren't you?"

"For the record, the asshole says he didn't do it. And for what it's worth, I believe him. If he didn't, then someone else did. Don't you want the monster who did to pay for it? I'm not interested in trashing your brother, but there's no doubt he borrowed the money, and he didn't come to you guys to get it. Seems to me he didn't want to tell you why. In my experience as an investigator, when someone is between a rock and a hard place and doesn't come to his family for help, it usually means he was into one of the two: drugs or gambling debts. And the people who run in those worlds have no problems being violent. Did your brother like the ponies?"

Patrick placed the Guinness on the counter and twirled it between his fingers. While not mollified, he at least didn't look like he planned to rip my head off. "No. And I don't think he did drugs either. I've seen people who are hooked on drugs and there are signs, you know? Not Greg. And I know for sure he doesn't gamble."

"How's that?"

"Last summer a bunch of us went out to the Horseshoe Casino, the one across the river in Indiana. Greg gave me grief for wasting money at the poker table. According to him, gambling for real money was stupid. That's why none of this makes sense."

"Who's Amelia Hedley?"

"Who?"

"Pretty blonde friend of your brother's. She may have visited him a lot at his place. Thought they might be an item."

The redhead finished her dinner, removed a pen from a purse, and wrote something on the edge of the front page. She got up and laid the paper next to my beer and left.

I glanced at the paper and read in incredibly neat handwriting: *Would smell as sweet. Call any time. Chelsey Meredith* and a phone number. The Bard scores again. I moved her into the win column.

We both took a moment to watch her leave, along with every other red-blooded American male in the pub and admired how the pantsuit fit well in all the right places, the ponytail bouncing from side to side as she walked. When she was gone, he said, "I know he was dating a gal for a while, but never met her. It was kind of a December to May romance which never made it to May. He didn't bring her to any of the holiday stuff. What about her? Think she had a jealous boyfriend or something?"

"Just asking. Not even sure she's the girl I'm searching for." I switched gears. "Greg piss anyone else off you know of? Maybe this has nothing to do with the loan shark stuff."

"Like I told you, he lived a simple life and kept his nose clean. I've never heard of him having a beef with anyone. Nobody would want to hurt my brother."

I stared at him for a few moments letting the obvious hang there. He sighed, pulled out a wallet as battered as his suit, dropped a ten on the counter to pay for his beer, and left. I finished mine and picked up the Wall Street Journal for reading later. Yay team.

7

L ear Electric sat in the middle of a brick strip mall built alongside what used to be a bowling alley in Crestwood, Kentucky. It was flanked by a furniture store, auto repair shop, and an old-fashioned shoe repair shop.

My shoes were not in need of their service as my cap-toed Oxford rip offs were bright and shiny, to go along with a spiffy navy blazer, white button-down shirt, and gray slacks. I have no doubt GQ will be calling any minute for me to grace the cover of their private detective issue.

I pushed open the glass and metal door as a small bell dinged to announce my arrival. A counter with a faux white marble top took up about three-quarters of the front room, and several racks of electrical equipment filled the rest. Row after neat row of electrical outlets, covers, switches, and a ton of other stuff I didn't recognize filled the shelves. I know as much about doing electric work as I do nuclear physics.

An elderly woman waddled out from between two of the stacks. Plump to the point of being almost completely round, her perfectly quaffed hair offered up a slight blue tinge. It reminded me of the coloring my grandmother used to dye her hair to hide the fact it had begun to turn yellow. Most women these days opted for their original hair color, and it made me smile to see one keeping the old traditions alive.

"May I help you?"

"Yes. I'm investigating the death of Greg Chambers and I'd like to speak to his supervisor."

"Well, that'd be the owner, Charlie Lear. One second."

She disappeared the way she had come and returned a few moments later with a middle-aged man with salt and pepper hair and a Van Dyke beard. His arms nearly busted the seams on his long-sleeved shirt. Charlie Lear was stitched in red cursive thread above his left shirt pocket.

He stuck out a hand and I shook it. The grip was as firm as his arms were bulging. I tried not to show any weakness and returned it in kind, my macho ego still intact.

"I thought Detectives Tugbe and Brown were investigating Greg's murder. Who are you?"

I told him my name and said, "They are, but I wanted to do a follow up interview to see if you remembered anything since you spoke to them. Sometimes if you answer the same questions at a later date you remember things you forgot the first time. "

He shrugged. "I don't think I forgot anything but go ahead. Ask away."

"What type of employee was Greg?"

"He could be a pain in my derriere, if you want to know the honest truth. Don't get me wrong, he was a good worker when he showed. His problem was the showing up part. I had to sit him down a couple of times and read him the riot act, but he was okay."

"Boozer? Too many late nights stretching into the next morning?"

"I don't think beer or whiskey was his problem. He had an ongoing love affair with his pillow. The man could take a nap any time of the day. A regular Rip Van Winkle."

"We all need our beauty sleep. In the weeks before his death, how did he act? Anything out of the ordinary?"

Lear scratched his Van Dyke. "Not really. Same old Greg. Sorry."

The blue-haired woman cut in, "I can tell you he was in a pretty good mood the day he was killed. That I can tell you for sure."

Lear shot her a surprised look. "How so, Evelyn?"

"He'd just got back from Mr. Montez's place. I saw him out in the parking lot on his phone and when he hung up, he gave a fist pump like he'd scored the winning touchdown. He came in whistling and singing and when I asked him what'd gotten into him, he kissed me on the cheek and said, 'Evie, when it's your lucky day, it's your lucky day.' He always called me Evie. Not so lucky when you consider the poor thing was dead a few hours later."

Lear shook his head, disgust on his face. "That's the perfect example of another one of Greg's occasional problems. I sent him over to Damon Montez's to put in a new breaker box, but he left the job early, never finished it. He cut out early and went home."

"Aha," I said.

"Aha?" Evelyn asked.

"That's what we in the detective business call a clue."

Lear rested his meaty fists on his hips. "It's what I call a pain in my ass. I had to send another guy out there to finish the job and offer Mr. Montez a discount. And, if you think about it, if he'd just done what he was supposed to do, he might still be alive. He should have been on the Montez job until after six p.m."

"Did he have any other jobs that day?" I asked.

Evelyn said, "He did a job for Mrs. Scott over in Pewee Valley before he went to put in the Montez breaker."

I asked for the addresses of Scott and Montez. After consulting a computer, Evelyn wrote them down on a scrap sheet of paper and handed it to me.

"Do you think he'd still be alive if he hadn't quit early?" she asked.

Before I could respond with a silique on fate and the spiritual nature of life and death, the door opened. The bell dinged, and a black man wearing a gray suit, white shirt, and snazzy maroon tie with purple ducks strode in. To accessorize the outfit, he had a gun on one hip and his detective first grade badge clipped to his belt.

He wore his dark hair cropped close and the hint of a mustache showed above his upper lip. Hard brown eyes locked on mine, and I thought I detected the slightest clenching of his jaw.

Lear quickly offered Detective Augustine Tugbe his hand and Tugbe shook it, but the policeman never broke eye contact with me. Lear picked up on the tension and swallowed hard. "We were just going back over things with Detective Jericho here. You two work together, right?"

Tugbe asked, "You introduce yourself as a police detective, Jericho?"

"Not even once. I told them I was investigating the death of Greg Chambers. They only asked my name, not who I was with."

Lear balled his fists again, but this time they weren't on his hips. "You son-of-a-bitch. You led us to believe you were with the police. I ought to kick your ass from here to Sunday."

I shrugged. "You know what they say, when you assume you make an ass out of you and me." I paused a beat, then continued, "And you might want to make sure your health insurance policy is fully paid up before your mouth makes threats your fists can't back up."

Lear took one long step in my direction, but Tugbe stepped smoothly between us, put a hand on his chest, and the electrician pulled up short.

"I'm sure it's all a misunderstanding, Mr. Lear. I'll handle it." He nodded toward the door, and I followed him outside. Once outside, he leaned against the bumper of a silver Dodge Charger and slipped a pack of Extra Spearmint gum from his inside jacket pocket. He removed a stick and held the gum out to me. I accepted the offer, thanked him, unwrapped the gum, and popped it into my mouth and he did the same.

"With the sharing of bubble gum, are we bros now?" I asked.

His jaws worked the gum like a jackhammer. "When I heard you were working for King, I thought your name sounded familiar and dug into you a bit. Everybody tells me you two can't stand each other, yet you're now on his payroll."

"You should see the retirement benefits package he offered."

"So just like Newt, you can be bought?"

"Are you judging me by the sins of the father, Tugbe?"

"I'll match your cliché for cliché: apples don't fall far from the tree. You worked for Newt, and I can only imagine the bad habits you picked up. Answer the question."

I shrugged. "I'm on the team, but I made it clear to King if

I found out he did it, I'd bury him. He wanted to hire me anyway."

"What about attorney client privilege? "

"If I find evidence he's guilty, you will have a new friend going by Unnamed Source. But I won't find anything. He knows I'd never keep quiet and yet here I am. When King says he didn't do it, I believe him. Which means you have a problem. You know it too, that's why you're out here still digging. Where's your partner?"

Tugbe breathed in deep, let it out slowly, and pushed off the Dodge. "He's busy. And maybe I'm still digging because I'm thorough."

"I know you're thorough. I'm not the only one with a rep. Which makes the fact you charged him so quickly curious. Why the rush?"

"Not my call. All politics, man. You know Alexandra Cutter?"

"The Commonwealth's Attorney? Long, blonde hair and legs which go all day? Know of her, but not personally."

"Rumor has it she plans to run for the 4th Congressional House seat next year and mounting King's fat ass on the wall would be a great way to kick off her campaign. We told her our case was thin, but she couldn't wait to get her photo op and had King indicted."

"Sucks to be you guys. Good luck with that."

Tugbe circled to the driver's door and opened it but leaned on the roof of the Charger instead of getting behind the wheel. "If you mess with my case, I'll put your balls in a vice and crush them. You hear me?"

"If you do, I'll be able to reach my goal of singing all the high parts in Phantom of the Opera."

He shook his head, but I thought I caught the barest glimpse of a smile. "I'm going to watch you leave now."

I thought about reciting the Constitution of the United States or pointing out I was standing in a public parking lot, but I'd learned all I was going to learn from the fine folks at Lear Electric and I could let Tugbe win this one."

I slid behind the wheel and started the Jeep and drove away singing "Music of the Night."

Tugbe didn't clap.

8

Originally known as Smith Station, Pewee Valley was established in 1852 as a stop on the Louisville and Frankfort Railroad. The name change had nothing to do with the town's small size and everything to do with a type of small bird named a Pewee. Add to it that the town sat on a ridge and not in a valley and the name change is more than strange.

The town is also known for The Little Colonel Playhouse with a red train caboose out front, as well as the Little Colonel children's books of Annie Fellows Johnston. My mom owned a set. I never read them.

Winifred Scott lived on the west side of town in an old plantation style manor in the middle of what appeared to be over five-hundred acres of land. Huge wrought iron gates, a keypad, and call box off to one side stood wide open. I passed

by oaks and maples which lined each side of the long gravel
drive ending in a circular driveway.

One of the old growth trees lay toppled next to the drive,
and an elderly man worked a chainsaw and log splitter with
a stack of wood large enough to show he had been at it for
some time.

He stood well over six feet tall and was what my family
called "country big," with broad shoulders and huge hands. I
waved as I drove by and got a short wave and glare in return.
Must be my aftershave.

I parked in front of a long porch lined with tall white
columns which disappeared around each side of the two-
story clapboard house and made my way to the huge green
front door. Both the door and the rest of the house had seen
better days.

I used the brass knocker in the shape of a lion's head to
announce my presence. I imagined the door opening to
reveal a man wearing a white suit, black bowtie, and a
carrying a bucket of chicken. Instead, a skinny black woman
in a gray maid's uniform answered. I told her who I was and
why I was there, and she invited me inside.

"You wait here a moment and I'll see if Miss Winnie is
seeing anyone today," she said.

She left me standing in a large open area with rooms off
to either side, a wide staircase leading to the second floor
and a hallway which must have led to the rear of the house
where the maid disappeared. A portrait hung on one side of

the hallway of a man in Army military greens and he appeared to be a younger version of Mr. Happy outside with the chainsaw. His chest was covered with ribbons and a colonel's insignia showed his rank.

On the opposite side of the hallway was a portrait of a young lady wearing a flowing silver gown and playing a grand piano. She was thin with long fingers and a beautiful smile.

The room on my right appeared to be a study with floor to ceiling bookcases filling up one whole wall. The room on my left looked to be a sitting room. In both rooms sat a baby grand piano. The place smelled musty; the way large older homes do when most of the rooms go unused.

The maid returned and said, "Miss Winnie says it's okay for you to come on back."

I pointed to the portrait. "Did I see him outside on the way up the drive cutting up the tree?"

"No, sir. This is Colonel Samuel Scott. He died some time ago over in Africa. The man outside working is his brother, Jacob. He kind of takes care of the grounds for Miss Winnie. That's her over there." She pointed to the portrait of the woman playing piano.

I held out my hand. "And you are?"

She gave my hand a quick shake. "Agatha. I'm the house-keeper. Nice meeting you. Follow me."

We walked down the hallway. "Kind of takes care of?"

She waved one slender hand back and forth. "He does

when he gets a mind to, but there's a lot of things on his To Do list which don't ever seem to get moved to the Done List."

"Leads to job security. Were you here when the Lear Electric guy was working?"

"I was. I made the man a turkey sandwich. He ended up needing two of them. Why do you ask?"

"He's the man I want to talk to Mrs. Scott about. He was murdered Monday night."

Agatha stopped and put a hand to her chest. "That's terrible. Do they have any idea who did it?"

"Not yet but we're trying to find out. Did you talk to him?"

"Not much past asking what he wanted for lunch. He was polite enough, but I really didn't talk to him."

We walked to the end of the hall where there were three wooden doors. The one straight ahead was open and I could see a huge kitchen with another door leading outside. The one to the right was closed. Still shaking her head about Chambers, Agatha knocked on the left-hand door and, without waiting for a response, opened it.

The chandelier hanging overhead told me this had likely been used as the dining room when the home was originally built. Now it had been converted to a bedroom.

A king-sized bed sat on the far side next to a bay window overlooking the side yard. A set of chest of drawers, nightstand, and a small table were off to one side. On the other side crouched a huge whirlpool tub, seemingly out of place.

In the middle of the bed lay a woman who may have

been in her eighties. Thin to the point of making me wonder if she was suffering some sort of illness, long white hair framed her head against the pillow. Dressed in a faded pink robe she sat propped up with several pillows and a comforter pulled up to her waist. A copy of The New York Times lay open on the comforter and a pair of reading glasses perched on the end of her nose. I could see the ghost of a resemblance to the young lady in the portrait.

Agatha introduced me, "Miss Winnie, this is Mr. Jericho. He's a private detective."

"Thank you, Agatha." Then to me, she said, "Would you like some coffee or something to eat, Mr. Jericho?"

"No, I'm good, thanks."

"Very well. That will be all, Agatha."

The housekeeper left the room, closing the door behind her and Mrs. Scott took off her reading glasses and laid them atop her paper. "What can I do for you, Mr. Jericho? I assume you are here about Mr. Chambers?"

"Yes, ma'am. It turns out you were one of the last people to see Greg Chambers alive. Can you tell me why he was here? What type of work did you need him to do?"

She pointed a slender finger at the whirlpool. "My health has gotten worse in the last six months, and I rarely leave my room. My latest doctor thought it might be good for me to have that monstrosity to help ease my back pain. This house was built around 1850 and, unfortunately, the outlets in this room are not strong enough to handle the tub's electrical needs. I don't understand all the electrical mumbo-jumbo. The young man had to run new lines strong enough to carry all the power, or so I was told."

"The 1850's? Family place?"

She nodded. "My late husband's family, yes. For generations, each of the men in the family all served in the military, most all of them reaching the rank of general. His sixth great-grandfather served with Washington in the Revolutionary War and afterwards he was given several thousand acres here in Kentucky in a land grant. This farm is all that's left."

"The house is lovely," I said.

"And that's a load of horse manure. This place is falling to pieces, a lot like my body. Everyday something new breaks down. After I die, I've told my son to sell it and be done with it. I don't have a lot longer and next year he's considering running for the Kentucky Supreme Court. He doesn't need the headache."

I paused for a moment, with a light bulb popping in my brain. "Your son is Judge Ransford Scott? Judge 'Hang'em High' Scott?"

She smiled with about as much warmth as an ice cube down the back of your shirt. "That's right. We don't believe much in parole in this family. It's why crime is so high. Other judges sentence these hoodlums to light sentences, and they are out almost as soon as they go to prison. Ransford sees to it they stay there as long as possible."

"If you do the crime, you should do the time."

She snapped two dust dry fingers and then pointed at me. "Now you're talking. Once he's on the Supreme Court, he will be able to do even more to change things in this state."

"I'll be sure to vote for him. About Greg Chambers, what type of mood was he in? Good mood, bad mood?"

She shrugged bony shoulders. "Mr. Jericho, I really don't know. I'm not in the habit of interacting with workers. They do their job and then leave. I enjoy my privacy."

"If you don't leave your room much you must have been here the day he installed the electric. Even if you didn't talk to each other, you must have seen him working. What about his body language? Did he whistle while he worked?"

"He seemed neither in a good mood nor bad mood. He worked efficiently and left in a hurry. He had another job to get to and was anxious to leave."

"Yet he took the time to have lunch? He couldn't have been in that big of a hurry."

She stared at me for a moment, and it was obvious she wasn't used to being challenged. "I offered him something to eat just as I did you, young man, and, unlike you, he accepted. He ate his food, did his job, and left."

"Good for him. Well, not too good, as it turns out. I couldn't help but notice you have a piano in both front rooms, as well as the one in the portrait hanging in the hallway. I'm guessing you loved to play?"

"Mr. Jericho, I played in some of the greatest music halls around the world. I've been blessed to perform for Queen

Elizabeth and other monarchs who love someone of real talent. Arthritis forced me to quit performing professionally years ago, but I still love to play on the days when I can get out of this bed."

The bedroom door swung open, and Jacob Scott entered the room covered in sawdust, his shirt drenched in sweat. He did not appear any happier to see me.

"And you are?" he asked.

"Would you believe the second coming of Sam Spade?" His eyes narrowed and his scowl deepened. "I guess not."

"Winnie, has this man been bothering you?" Jacob asked.

She waved him off. "Jacob, our conversation has been quite pleasant, but I believe Mr. Jericho and I are done."

"Actually, I was wondering if it was too late to take you up on lunch?" When neither one responded I said, "No? Well, then."

I removed a business card from my pocket and set it on the nightstand next to Winifred's bed. "If you can think of anything else, please don't hesitate to call me."

She said, "I wouldn't hold my breath, young man."

Jacob opened the door and nodded for me to leave. I thanked them and told them I would see myself out.

Jacob said, "I'll see you to the door."

"No need."

"I insist."

I shrugged and fell in next to him. I asked, "Were you here when Greg Chambers was working for Mrs. Scott?"

"The electrician? Yes, but not here at the house. I was mending a broken fence near the back of the property. I was out there all day. He was here and gone before I returned to the house. You must be the guy I was told has been working to get his killer off."

"Your nephew talked to you about it?"

"He spoke to Winnie and me, yes. Nasty business and you work for a nasty man."

"You'll get no argument from me on both accounts. Robert King is a nasty man, and this is a nasty business. But I'm now convinced, more than ever, he didn't do it."

We reached the door, and he opened it for me. "Says you," he said. "Shows you're not much of a detective, if you ask me."

"Now who's being nasty?" I asked.

He responded by shutting the door in my face. I guess he showed me.

9

Damon Montez lived in a two-story brick house in the Grand Dell subdivision in Crestwood set on about an acre of land with a three-car garage and a pool large enough to host the Summer Olympics. I pulled in behind a BMW X-5 and shut off the engine. The Beamer's license plate read GLFPRO.

I rang the ivory doorbell and a tall man swung the door open, and he matched the license plate. He sported a golf visor, sandy brown hair sticking up behind it like an untrimmed bush, a pink Polo shirt, and khakis. A brown belt with dogs every couple of inches circled a trim waist.

I introduced myself and he invited me inside. His bitching started the moment he closed the door behind us. He talked over his shoulder as he led me down a hallway. "I can tell you the guy really ticked me off. Our house got struck by lightning the day before, the day with all the storms, and it fried our breaker box. The whole damn thing turned black. We called Lear and they said they would send a guy out the next day. I took the day off to be here. My wife works for UPS and she's out of town on business and couldn't be here. To start, he was two hours late. Then, once he got here, he spent more time checking his phone than he did working on the damn box."

I followed him into a spacious living room with a leather sectional and a seventy-inch flat screen on the wall. He gestured for me to sit, and we did. Several oil paintings by Michael Prather were scattered on the walls, along with a photo of Montez and a woman I assumed to be his wife embracing on a beach. A patio door provided a view of the inground pool, the water reflecting a glint of sunlight.

"Any idea who he was talking to?" I asked.

"Not a frickin' clue. What I can tell you is he lied to me. He looked over the box and then told me he needed a part from their shop. Said he didn't have the right size replacement on his truck and told me he'd run there and be right back. Said he'd have me up and running in no time. Never saw him again. I waited another hour and then called Lear. When I found out he went home, I blew a gasket. They cost me a whole day. I reamed the guy who runs the place a new one and they sent out another guy and gave me a discount on the work. It should have been free after all the hassle."

"I'm going to hazard a guess and say you work for a golf course."

"I'm a teaching pro out at Oldham County Country Club. You're lucky you caught me. I'm headed out to a tournament for teaching pros down in Nashville. Another couple of minutes and you'd have missed me."

"And a few hours away from the course cost you that much money? After all, don't you guys get paid to play in the sun?"

He stared at me for a moment. "Let me tell you something. You try and straighten out the slice of an amateur golfer who thinks he knows more about a golf swing than you do and can't do what you tell them from one swing to the next. I earn every penny."

"Wasn't it Mark Twain who said golf is a good walk spoiled?"

He offered a wolf grin. "Depends on who you're walking with."

I conceded the point. "You said Chambers was checking his phone. Any idea what he was doing? Was he texting? Reading email?"

"No clue. I saw him typing a couple of times, so maybe a reply to one or the other? How the hell should I know?"

Before I could respond, a woman a few years younger than Montez entered wearing a near sheer one-piece bathing suit showing off the body of an athlete. She wore her long brunette hair pinned up in a bun and sported the kind of tanned body earned by many hours laying poolside.

She stopped when she saw me, a look of surprise creasing her brow." Oh. I'm sorry, honey. I didn't know someone was here."

I stood and introduced myself.

She gave me the kind of smile which would make a lesser man's knees get weak. Thank goodness I was made of heartier stock. To me she said, "I'm Sidney." And to Montez, "Damon, you didn't tell me you were expecting company."

He mumbled something under his breath, his nervousness cranking up a few degrees. "You were supposed to be getting ready."

She bent and kissed him on the top of the head. "I'm going to take a quick dip in the pool before we leave. I've been cooped up inside all day and I need to stretch out a bit."

She waved to me and slipped out the patio doors to the pool. Undoing the pins in her hair, she let it fall about her shoulders, dropped the pins onto the ground, and dove in, making strong strokes to the other end and then back again.

Montez watched me watching her and his face turned red. I made a pointed glance at the picture of who I assumed was his wife and then back to him. "Wow. She's changed quite a bit."

"Look, it's not like that. Sidney is one of my students and she wanted to tag along to the tournament in Nashville to see what it's like. She has real potential. I think she can even play on the tour one day."

"I noticed. Was Sidney here when Chambers worked on the breaker box?"

"I don't see how that's any of your business."

I nodded and stood up. "I get that a lot. I'll go ask Sidney. She seems the talkative type."

He jumped up from the couch and moved between me and the patio doors, his hands up in front of him. "Wait. Fine. Whatever. Yeah, she was here. What difference does it make if she was here or not? She spent the entire time by the pool, and they never talked."

"And your wife knows you're giving her, hmm, private lessons?"

He moved up close, invading my private space, the brim of his golf visor nearly touching my forehead, and used a finger to poke me in the chest. "If you breathe a word of this to my wife, I'll make you regret it. Do you hear me?"

"If you poke me in the chest again, I may have to give *you* a private lesson in manners."

He had me by a few inches and about twenty pounds and it was obvious he grew up an alpha male, with women loving him and men being intimidated. Despite my warning, he stabbed a finger in my direction.

The distance between us was short and my shot to his solar plexus didn't carry the amount of power of a full punch. And I used my left hand. After all, I didn't want to cripple the guy.

I rotated my hips slightly, my first turning as I caught him directly below his breastbone. He never saw the punch coming and it doubled him over, his diaphragm spasming from the blow, making it hard for him to catch his breath. I caught him by the shoulders and guided him to the couch where he collapsed onto his side, his eyes closed in pain.

"You need to work on your follow through."

He groaned a reply which I am certain was not a compliment on my teaching style. I glanced up to see Sidney standing outside the patio door, drying her hair with a fuzzy beach towel while she watched me. Her suit became completely transparent with the dip in the pool, and it appeared either she was excited to see me or unusually cold. She bit her lower lip and pressed her breasts even more forward and I swear she batted her eyelashes at me.

I gave her an appreciative look and a wink, then crooked a finger. She slid the patio door open, came inside, moved in close, tossed the towel around my neck, and pulled my face close to hers.

She nodded her head in Montez's direction. "What did you do to him? One moment he was standing and the next he was going down. I swear I never saw you move."

"I toppled him with my rapier wit and intestinal fortitude."

She rubbed the tip of my nose with hers and I felt her

breath, fast and warm. "I think you did more than that. What did he do to make you hit him?"

I glanced at Montez, still moaning on the couch, his eyes closed tight. "He tried to keep the two of us apart. Can you believe it?"

Her eyes sparkled and she pressed her body into mine, her wet bathing suit feeling cool against my own clothes. "You want me?"

I put my lips next to her ear and whispered, "I do. I want you to tell me if you met the electrician when he was here."

The change was instant. She pushed me away and slid the towel from around my neck. "Him? You want to know about him with me here?"

"Unfortunately, yes. Were you?"

She walked away a few feet, twirled the towel between her two hands, and then tried to snap me with one end, biting her lip again. "And if I was?"

I waited patiently. After a few moments, she plopped down onto the couch next to Montez and brushed the hair from his forehead, his visor having slipped to the floor.

"Whatever. Yes. I was here."

"And you two talked?"

She helped Montez to a sitting position, and he bent over his knees while she rubbed his back. He said, "I think I'm going to be sick."

Sidney gave him a disgusted look and scooted a few feet

away. "A bit. He was distracted and wasn't here long. He spent more time on his phone than anything. Kind of cute though."

I was beginning to think Sidney's type of man would be any of them who were breathing. Montez sat up straight and stared me down. "You need to leave. Now."

"Any chance you can tell me why I yank all my putts to the left?"

He clenched his jaw a few times but remained silent.

Guess not.

10

"No Mary tonight?" I asked.

Teddy sat across from me sipping a couple of fingers of twelve-year-old Glenfiddich. Tonight, Teddy wore a white Izod shirt with a blue blazer and tan pants. "Sorry, Ace. She's got a big final tomorrow and she needs the night to study. You may find this hard to believe, but her job in life is not to be here to wait on your beck and call."

I tipped my Old Fashion in his direction, and we clinked glasses. "Here's to good grades and a ticket out of this place."

Teddy slid out of the booth, and, for a moment, I thought he might toss the whiskey into my lap, but even he wouldn't waste twelve-year-old Glenfiddich.

"Eat up and hit the road. And learn some manners."

I laughed and cut into my steak as he walked away. The restaurant was half full, with most of the customers outside at the Tiki Bar enjoying the warm late spring night. From my booth, I watched two women in matching red bathing suits, one blonde the other brunette, hop off a speedboat while a guy tied off a line.

In the middle of my contemplating if they might be able to help my golf swing, a man slid into the spot vacated by Teddy. Thin and boney, he wore a grimy Duke ballcap, green T-shirt and faded jeans. Nicotine stains covered the index and middle fingers of his right hand and his clothes reeked of cigarette smoke.

A blue wooden toothpick hung in one corner of his mouth, bouncing up and down. "Mind if I join you?"

I took a sip of my drink and set it down carefully. "Yes. I do. You're not my type. I like a little meat on my dates."

His eyes narrowed and the toothpick froze for a moment before he snorted and glanced around the bar. "Funny. What's a guy got to do to get a drink in this place?"

He lifted a hand and waved for a waitress to come over. She smiled and walked over with a menu. "Will this gentleman be joining you for dinner, Mr. Jericho?"

Before Slim could answer I said, "No, he won't."

Her brow furrowed and she didn't know what to do next. Slim winked at her. "I don't need a menu, honey. Bring me a Bud Light. I'm watching my weight."

The joke was lost on her as she left to fill the order. I cut off another hunk of steak and kept the knife in my hand, twirling it around. "What do you want? If you're collecting for the American Lung Association, you look like a lost cause."

"Funny man, aren't you?"

"Better than average. What do you want?"

His eyes flitted around the restaurant. "You're working for King." A statement, not a question.

"Gee. Thanks. I was wondering who was paying my bills. That takes a load off my mind. Another mystery solved."

The toothpick began to work overtime, seeming to keep time to some beat in the guy's head only he could hear. "I want to hire you."

We paused for a moment while the waitress sat his beer down in front of him and left. "I appreciate the offer, but I think my dance card is full."

"You haven't even heard what I want you to do."

"Go figure. The truest wisdom is a resolute determination."

Slim leaned into his beer and took a healthy pull of the amber liquid. "Are you fucking nuts?"

"No, but Napoleon might have been." I returned to my steak and ignored him. I stared past his shoulder at the two girls in the red bathing suits who now danced in the light of a tiki torch to music I could faintly hear from inside the bar. The Rolling Stones. I liked the way their hips swayed to the rhythm and knew Mick and Keith would approve.

Slim lifted his beer and took another swig while he glanced over his shoulder at the two women. He returned his gaze to me, his face contorted in a leer, and said, "Nice. But back to business."

"We can't get back to business because we were never in business. Finish your beer and take your Duke ass out of my booth."

I added a bit of menace to my tone, but Slim didn't seem to care. He reached into the back pocket of his jeans, and slid out an envelope and tossed it on the table between us. "There's ten-grand. Want to know what you need to do to earn it?"

"Not particularly. As you pointed out, I have a client. Why don't you go invest it in an iron lung? I think you'll need one sooner than you think."

He continued like I never talked. "What you have to do is nothing. That's it. Not a thing."

I stared at him for a moment. I had to admit I was curious. Not about the money, though ten-grand never hurt. It would pay a lot of bills. The real question was why, though I thought I knew the answer. "Nothing? That's a lot of greenbacks for doing nothing."

He spread his hands wide. "And yet, that's all you need to do. Keep investigating for King. But do nothing. Find nothing. Report nothing."

Bingo. Rather unethical, don't you think?"

Slim waved me off. "I represent a group of people who

have been hurt by King. We want him to spend the rest of his life in prison and we don't want you to muddy the waters and get him off. Word is you might be good enough to do that. And rumor has it you don't even like the guy. It's a win-win for everybody."

"He says he didn't do it."

"And you believe that bull shit? Don't matter. We don't give a rat's ass if he is innocent or guilty. He's done enough to warrant the time in prison. Take the money and make everyone happy."

"As tempting as it sounds, I will have to pass. After all, once I start accepting money for doing nothing, I'll get used to it and all I'll do is sit in my office, play solitaire on my computer, and gain weight. I could get diabetes. You wouldn't want me to get diabetes, would you?"

Slim polished off the rest of his Bud, set the empty bottle on the table, slid the money back across the table, and returned it to his pocket.

He stood and said, "Mister, you're going to regret not doing business with us. You have my word on it."

"I'll add it to the list. It's a long list, so it might be a while before I get to actually regretting it."

Slim offered up a single middle finger salute and left, leaving me to pay for his beer. While I didn't regret turning down the money, I did ponder why they wanted me to lay off the investigation. He might've been telling the truth, though if I was going to pick a point man for trying to convince me to tank the King investigation, I don't think he'd be my first choice.

I finished my steak and drink, paid for my bill and his beer, and spent a few minutes more watching the women dance. They say to dance like nobody's watching. I think they enjoyed dancing knowing everyone was watching. They could add me as a fan.

I slipped out of the booth and headed outside to my car. I wish I could tell you I anticipated what happened next, but I didn't. My belly was full, and my mind still danced with the women out by the Tiki bar. When the attack came, I only had a millisecond to notice. I rounded the rear of a van near my Jeep when my peripheral vision caught motion and I turned my head to look behind me and the baseball bat landed with a sickening thud across my shoulder blades. It drove me down to my knees in the parking lot, and my head hit the bumper of my Jeep.

I tried to stand but another blow in almost the exact same spot sent me to the ground, this time to my stomach. Someone kicked me in the ribs, and I covered my head with my hands while I pulled myself into a fetal position.

"I told you to take the money, asshole. Now we have to deliver the message in a different way," Slim said, with more than a bit of satisfaction in his voice.

Getting my ass handed to me by the Marlboro Man hurt

my pride, almost as much as the pain in my back. Okay, not really, but close. He bent over to say something to me, and I lashed out with a swift kick and drove my foot straight through his kneecap, bending it backwards in a way it was never meant to move. He shrieked and dropped to the ground.

I started to push myself up when my brain registered the fact Slim wasn't holding a baseball bat, and thanks to my great detective mind, I figured out there were two of them. I rolled hard to my right and tried to get under my Jeep when the next blow clipped my shoulder, setting it on fire. It was followed by a swift kick to the head, which I only partially avoided, my world starting to fade to black around the edges.

Slim, who rolled from side to side holding his knee, yelled, "I'm going to kill you, you motherfucker."

I closed my eyes and figured he had a better than average chance of succeeding when I heard someone in the distance start to yell. Slim snarled a few curses my way and told the other guy to help him up. I heard them move away, and shortly thereafter a car started up and peeled out of the parking lot.

Pain seemed to come from every inch of my body, though I knew that was merely a defense mechanism. I tried to move and felt a wave of nausea and decided remaining still might be a better plan of action. In fact, taking a long nap sounded even better.

I heard someone tell me to hang on and lay still while

they got help and I tried to respond, but my lips seemed to not want to move either. Mentally, I agreed to do exactly as they asked, then I thought of the two women dancing at the bar and wondered if they made hospital calls.

I doubted it.

11

Here's the thing about hospitals: they're noisy. The main thing they tell you to do is rest, then they hook up enough beeping machines to run a small nation. All of which keeps you from sleeping. Then the nurse comes in every so often to check your vitals. Awake again.

I kept trying to drift off. It hurt less when my eyes were closed, and I dozed more than I slept. The pain meds certainly did their part to help knock me out. I noticed I was hooked up to a morphine pump. I was pushing the button over and over when a nurse walked in and said, "Honey, those things only work every fifteen minutes."

To which I responded, "I don't want to be late."

I awoke from a nap where I'd been dreaming Sandra Bullock was yelling at me for not paying more attention to my surroundings when I got attacked. I told Sandra that's not why she usually visited me in my dreams, and she informed me it would be from now on. I'll call it a nightmare.

"About damn time you came around. You're missing your fantastic meal of clear Jell-O and pudding. I almost ate it myself."

I turned my head to see Deano sitting in a chair reading a People Magazine with Brad Pitt and Angelina Jolie on the cover. When I moved my head, my back screamed in protest. I tried to sit up and decided laying down wasn't so bad after all.

"How bad?" I asked.

He dropped the magazine onto a side table and stood. He was dressed in a blue blazer, white T-shirt, and jeans. I detected a small bulge from a gun on his hip.

"All things considered; they worked you over pretty good. A likely concussion, major contusions on your back and left shoulder. No broken bones, but you're going to hurt like hell for a while."

I nodded to the gun. "You think I need guarding?"

"Teddy was pissed you got beat down in his parking lot. If his best customer died, he would need to find at least three people to replace you. I'm doing him a favor."

"If you want to do him a favor, then tell him to dump karaoke night."

"And miss hearing drunk middle-aged suburbanites try and sing show tunes? Not a chance." He turned serious and tossed a thumb toward the door. "I know the last thing you want me to do is make your day better, but Brown and Tugbe are waiting to talk to you. Feel up to it?"

"I think cops are better on pain meds. Why not?"

Deano walked to the door and opened it and waved to somebody I couldn't see. A moment later, Detective Tugbe walked in with a folder under one arm, followed by a short spark plug of a man. Where Tugbe was dapper and put together, Detective Emmit Brown was rumpled and slovenly. He sported a two-day growth of beard, and his suit was wrinkled. He wore a perpetual smirk and offered the demeanor of a pitbull with gas. Brown closed the door. Just the four of us.

Deano sat back down, crossed one leg over the other, and this time picked up a National Enquirer from the stack on the table. According to the cover, Hilary Clinton was on her deathbed. Again.

"Hit the road, Monroe. We got things to talk over with choirboy here and you're not invited," Brown snarled.

Deano licked a finger and flipped another page in the Enquirer before turning his gaze on Brown. "Good to see you too, Emmit. I'm not done reading my magazine and I want to see if Cher really is a dude and has been pretending all these years. I'll need to hang out a bit longer."

Brown balled his fists but kept them at his side. "That wasn't a request, asshole. When I tell you to leave, you leave. Otherwise, I'll arrest you for obstruction of justice."

Tugbe put a hand on Brown's arm. "Ease up. We aren't arresting anyone for anything."

Deano laughed. "I hear Detective Brown has made a career of not arresting anyone."

Brown took a step in Deano's direction and Tugbe put a hand on his chest to stop him. The rumpled detective pulled a hand back as if to take a swing at Tugbe, then thought better of it. "Fine," he snarled. "Let him stay. He's probably involved and I'm going to nail him, too."

Tugbe let out a small sigh and turned to me. "Ferguson told us a man visited you while you were at Divots. What did he want?"

"He wanted to hire me to work the King case. His idea of working it was throwing it."

"And he offered you money?"

"Yes. Ten-grand. I turned him down."

Brown snickered. "What? He didn't offer enough, and you tried to shake him down? Is that what happened, Jericho? And then your would-be partners decided to take it out of your hide?"

"They actually offered me the money to help buy you a new wardrobe, but I told them no amount of money would make you look good."

Brown lost the smile and began toward the head of the bed. Deano dropped the National Enquirer on the table with a thud and rested his hands on the arms of the chair, his gaze intent on Brown. Brown pulled up short, then slid a glance his way and swallowed hard, his nostrils flaring. Tugbe rolled his eyes.

"That's it," he said. "Brown, wait for me outside."

When the little detective started to protest, Tugbe went to him and bent to whisper something in his ear. Brown's face turned pale, and he turned and left the room, opening the door with a bang as he stormed out. When the door closed, Deano picked up the news rag and started reading again.

Tugbe watched him go and shook his head before turning to me. "I'm not making excuses for my partner, but this case is getting to him. He and King have a history and he thinks you're trying to get him off."

I nodded. "And he's right. If he didn't do it, I am trying to get him off so you guys can get the real killer."

"The man at Divots really offered you ten-thousand dollars?"

"He did. But I didn't like his sales pitch and refused."

Tugbe seemed to consider this for a moment, and I noticed the smallest of nods. He opened the file folder and removed a sheet of paper. When he flipped it around, I saw a printout of six photos arranged in two rows of three.

"Any of these guys the man who offered you the money?"

I glanced at the photos and without hesitation pointed to the third picture in the top row. "That's him. He's a bit older now, but that's him."

Tugbe returned the paper to the folder and tucked the folder under his arm. "Reginald Davis. He used to work for

King. Fancies himself a player in the local crime world. Sounds like Reggie wants to make a play for King's business if King goes away."

"And he wanted me to help make sure it happens? Still think King's your guy?"

"Yes, I do," he replied, though his eyes said he didn't believe it.

Deano slipped a phone out of his pocket and started typing.

To Tugbe I said, "I managed to rearrange Davis' kneecap before one of his flunkies beat me down. I'd check the area hospitals."

"I'll do that. And, Jericho?"

"Yes, Detective Tugbe?"

"You let us handle this, you hear? I'll take care of Davis. And despite what you think, Brown will come around. He's a good man."

I didn't reply and Tugbe left the room, albeit quieter than Brown did. I turned to Deano, the pain now muted with the name Reginald Davis. "Anything?"

"I've already got people looking for him. We'll find Davis, and with any luck, before the cops do."

I laid back and closed my eyes. "I want in on it when you do."

I can't be sure, but as I drifted off to sleep, I thought I heard Deano whistling "Bad to the Bone."

12

The hospital cut me loose late the following morning and Deano dropped me off at my condo while he went to help in the search for Reginald Davis, the would-be kingpin.

There were muscles hurting I never even knew existed and I made my way to the shower where I stayed under the hot water until the water started to run cold. I carefully worked on each part of my body that hurt, which meant every part.

I toweled off and shrugged into a UK T-shirt and some gym shorts. I was in the kitchen trying to figure out what to have for dinner when my doorbell rang.

I snagged my gun from the kitchen counter and held it behind my back while I glanced out the window next to the front door. Mary McGill stood there holding a large paper bag. I tucked the gun into the waistband of my shorts and opened the door.

Mary wore her Divots polo shirt and khaki shorts. Her long blonde hair, normally in a ponytail, was loose and fell around her shoulders.

"Hi. Teddy felt bad you were mugged at his place, and he knew you weren't likely to be coming out tonight. And he worried if you tried to fix yourself dinner you might hurt yourself even worse, so he sent me to bring you dinner. On the house."

She held out the bag to me and I opened the door wider, motioning for her to come in. She did and glanced around while I went into the kitchen and started to unload the bag, finding two steak dinners instead of one. I put the gun on the counter.

"Are you joining me for dinner?" I asked.

"If you don't mind. I'd like that."

"It sure beats the hell out of eating with Teddy."

I stretched to set the bottle of wine to the side and winced in pain. A frown creased Mary's face. "I hear you took quite the beating."

"I feel like someone ran over me with a TARC bus and then hit reverse and did it again."

"Then I think I can help. I originally wanted to be a physical therapist and learned how to do deep tissue massage. Dinner can wait. Let me see what I can do to loosen you up."

"That's not an offer I'm going to turn down. One sec."

I set the oven to two-hundred degrees and slid the steaks onto a warmer pan and then put it on the middle rack and closed the oven door.

"Where do you want to do this?" I asked.

"Let's find a bed where you can stretch out."

I nodded and led the way down the hallway to my bedroom. I thanked the Lord I'd made the bed and picked up the underwear off the floor yesterday morning.

"Take off your shirt and lay down on your stomach."

I did as she asked and removing the shirt caused me to offer up a small groan. I crawled onto the bed and lowered myself down gently. I heard her gasp.

"That bad?" I asked.

"When those bruises are another day or so old, you will have every color of the rainbow on your back, I think."

I dragged a pillow close and wrapped my arms around it and rested my chin on it for support. "Have at it."

She climbed onto the bed and then straddled me, her strong fingers beginning to work the tight muscles of my upper shoulders and neck. I did my best to act macho and not scream in pain as she worked, but the occasional wince escaped.

I closed my eyes and tried to put my mind in neutral. After a while, the pain went from intense, to a dull roar, then to only mildly there. Her fingers were doing wonders and I told her so.

"Thank you. Feeling better?"

"Are you kidding? I haven't felt this good in I don't know how long."

Not a total lie. Having a beautiful woman give me a back massage, no matter the pain, always feels good. I heard the rustling of clothes and then she leaned down close, her bare breasts on my back. She placed her ear next to my ear. "Let's see just how good I can make you feel."

I rolled over and she bent down and kissed me, first softly, then longer, harder. I wrapped my arms around her and pulled her close. She felt a lot better than the pillow.

We got completely undressed and made love for most of the rest of the afternoon, dinner now on hold for a bit longer. When we finished, I stroked the hair out of her eyes, and she unconsciously tucked the wayward curl behind her ear.

She kissed me again. "Mind if I ask you a personal question?"

I shook my head. "Don't mind you asking, doesn't mean I'll answer. What's your question?"

"Teddy told me you were married once before but got a divorce. Why did you two split up?"

"I ended it because she drank too much, smoked too much, and swore too much."

She furrowed her brows. "Then why did you get married in the first place if she did all those things?"

"Because she didn't start doing all those things until we got married. I tend to have that effect on people."

She let out a laugh more beautiful than the chiming of

church bells on Christmas morning. "Sounds like you're a challenge."

"More than a little."

13

The next morning, I went to my office and spent the first part of the day answering mail, reading about the newest recruits signed by the UK basketball team, and managing to see how long my body would hold out. By later afternoon, I found the pain holding at a manageable level and decided it was time to hit the field.

I found the return receipt I'd taken from Chambers' mailbox. My thoughts drifted more than a few times to Mary who spent the night, leaving early to head back to her place to do homework. Perhaps my reduction in pain was due to her massages. Perhaps.

I punched the address into my phone GPS and headed to Lively Shively. The town started on the old Louisville and Nashville stagecoach line in the early 1800s. It earned its Lively nickname during World War II when adult entertainment businesses sprung up around an old Army base located off 7th Street.

The home I wanted was off Bonnie Lea Court. The house, a tiny tan brick ranch, sat near the street with a carport and two cars in the driveway, an older model Ford Taurus and a red Miata. Bingo. I parked in the grass along the street and walked to the door.

I pressed the doorbell and waited. A few moments later the door cracked open a bit, revealing a short attractive woman with olive colored skin and short cropped black hair. She wore a white T-shirt and gray sweatpants.

"Can I help you?" she asked.

"Are you Amelia Hedley?"

"Who's asking?"

I fished my private detective's badge out of my blue sports coat I wore with a black shirt and jeans and held it up for her to see. "I'm investigating the death of Greg Chambers. Are you Amelia?"

"No. I'm not."

A woman of few words. "Is she here? I'd like to talk to her for a moment."

"She's not here."

Her eyes shifted quickly to the right when she said this and I tried to look past her into the house, but with the door only open a fraction, all I could see was the part of what looked to be the living room.

"Do you know when she will be back...I'm sorry, I don't think I got your name."

"You didn't get it because I didn't give it. Amelia is gone and I'm not sure when she'll be back. It could be days."

I pulled out a business card and offered it through the small opening. "If she gets back soon, please have her call me. It's important."

The woman stared for a moment, then snatched the card from my fingers and closed the door, throwing the deadbolt. I stood there for a few seconds lamenting in my mind the lack of both civility and trust in the new modern world.

I walked back to my Jeep and noticed a car parked on the street at the corner and I thought the man was watching me, though from this distance I wasn't sure. After being taken by surprise once, I wasn't about to let it happen again. Only one way to find out for sure.

I started down the sidewalk toward the car. I'd only made it a few steps when the car accelerated down the side street out of sight. I made a note: blue Suburban, newer model. Too far to get a plate but close enough I'd recognize it if I saw it again.

I returned to the Jeep and circled the block, parking in the same spot as the Suburban and watched Amelia's house. I turned the satellite radio to a blues channel and settled in.

I cracked open one of two Diet Dr. Peppers I kept in a small cooler on the floorboard and watched the day go by. A kid rode passed on his ten-speed bike twice looking at me. I reached into the back seat and grabbed the latest Lee Child novel and lost myself in the newest Jack Reacher thriller while keeping an eye on the house.

I made it through about a third of the book when Amelia walked out the front door to her Miata. She was dressed in a white buttoned-down shirt, black slacks, and flats. She carried a small matching black purse. She got in her car, started it up, reversed out of the driveway and headed my way. I lowered the sun visor to obscure my face and watched as she went by me. She coasted to a stop at the stop sign, and then turned left.

I gave her a block and then pulled out behind her in a loose tail. I passed the kid on the ten-speed and waved at him. I got a squint stare in response. Amelia cut through the subdivision, and we ended up cruising down Taylor Boulevard.

A few blocks later she turned into the parking lot for the Toy Tiger, a gentlemen's club. I hit the Wendy's across the street and parked with a view of the Tiger. Amelia got out of her car, and I figured her for a bartender and not a dancer.

I let her get inside and then waited another half hour to make sure she was clocked in and working before I crossed the street, parked, and went inside.

I pushed the door open wondering how many singles I had in my wallet.

14

The interior was dark enough to hide the wear and tear on the tables and the age of the dancers, both those too old and too young. A guy wearing a stretch black T and jeans greeted me the moment I cleared the doors. His bulging arms attested to long hours in the gym and perhaps the use of performance enhancing drugs.

"There's a ten-dollar cover."

I slipped out my wallet and handed over a ten, while nodding at the muscles. "Your mother must be proud."

His brows furrowed while he wondered if I was insulting him or paying him a compliment. He gave up and said, "You don't touch the girls. You don't proposition the girls. You don't take pictures of the girls. Got it?"

"Am I allowed to look at them?"

"If you tip them, sure. Look all you want. If you touch, you'll be dealing with me."

I'm not sure but I think he managed to puff out his arms even more. "I bet you can crack walnuts with your underarms."

I got more furrowed brows as I walked further into the club. There were tables arranged around an L-shaped stage. A young brunette twirled around a dancer's pole with all the enthusiasm of a visit to the DMV.

To the right were a series of rooms where patrons went to get private lap dances, the entrances covered with hanging beads. A long black lacquered bar filled the wall to the left. Row upon row of bourbons, whiskeys, and other spirits fronted a mirror.

I was one of only three people here this early on a Sunday. Two men who looked old enough to be my grandfather waved folded-up ones to the brunette who spun off the pole and onto all fours. She crawled up to them and allowed the men to stuff the ones down her bra. Once they did, she returned to the pole and her slow spins.

Amelia stood behind the bar washing down the top with a towel. I went over and pulled up a stool. Up close she was a beautiful woman with tired eyes. The kind who has seen more of the hard knocks of life than she should at her age, which I put in her mid-twenties. Her blonde hair fell about her shoulders and baby blues glanced my way.

"What will you have?" she asked.

"If I order an Old Fashioned, will I get change for a twenty?"

"Depends on how well you tip." She stared at me for a moment then continued, "That's an old man's drink. You're what? Thirty? Do you really want one?"

I nodded. "Thirty-two, but I'm an old soul."

She went about fixing my drink. She dropped a sugar cube in a glass, added bitters, a couple of ounces of Four Roses, and began mixing the ingredients. I gave her a moment then asked, "You were Greg Chambers' girlfriend, right?"

There was the briefest pause in her stirring and a quick glance my way. "I'm sorry. I don't know who you're talking about."

I slipped the return receipt out of my pocket and laid it on the counter between us. "Want to try again? Greg sent you this package a few days before he was murdered. What did he send you?"

Amelia shot a look at Muscles, her look pleading. I glanced over my shoulder and saw him start in our direction. I returned the mailing receipt to my coat pocket. "Amelia, I'm not the guy who murdered Greg and I'm not the cops. But if you don't talk to me, I'll have to tell the cops about you. Then life will get more difficult."

Muscles crowded in close. "Amelia, is this guy causing trouble?"

He stood close enough for me to smell Old Spice aftershave, the kind my father wore. Talk about an old soul. "Amelia and I were talking about a friend we both have in common, weren't we?"

"He's lying, Todd. He was trying to proposition me. When I told him no, he kept at it. He's scaring me."

Her story was a lie, but I could tell the fear in her voice was real. She was scared and who could blame her. Her boyfriend was dead and a stranger showing up first at her house and then at work put her on edge.

Todd laid a beefy hand on my shoulder. "I warned you, asshole, mess with the girls and you get to deal with me."

"Be still my beating heart. Whatever will I do?"

This time there was no doubt my words were meant as an insult. He balled his fist and aimed a devastating right to my jaw. Unfortunately for Todd, I leaned back on my stool and his punch sailed past my head. I snatched his wrist and yanked him off balance. When he started to fall, I grabbed a handful of hair and smashed his face onto the bar counter.

When his nose hit the hardwood, it exploded in a shower of blood all over the counter, ruining Amelia's hard work. She stood there frozen and watched as her would-be savior slid to the ground, unconscious.

I leaned across the bar and slid a hand into the ice chest to get a couple of cubes, dropped them into the glass, and drank my Old Fashioned. I checked the stage and found the two old men and the dancer staring at me. I raised a glass in salute and the geezers waved a hand in response, then returned their attention to the dancer, their interest in my little dust up now over. Sex over violence any day.

The dancer shot a look at the door leading to a backroom and I knew my time at the strip joint would soon be coming to an end. I stood and dropped a twenty on the counter, then checked on Todd. He was breathing and his muscles were still impressive.

"I'm a private detective and I left my card with your roommate. Call me. Whatever Greg was into, I can keep you out of it if you let me help you. If not, then you're going to find the shadows catching up to you. If I could find you, then..."

She said nothing and I stepped around Todd and left. After the beating I took a few days before, it felt good to work out the kinks and prove I could still defend myself. My wounded macho pride felt reinstated.

I fired up the Jeep and wondered if Amelia would call me. I wondered if Todd would still have a job after today. I wondered about a lot of things.

15

I decided to stop by my office and type up the notes of the case so far. It didn't take long. Afterwards, I planned to enjoy a lazy Sunday afternoon. I kicked my feet up on my desk and returned to the Jack Reacher novel. A little decompression helps and, truth be told, my back was none too happy with the beatdown I gave Todd. Getting older is not for sissies.

I made it through a chapter when there was a knock at my door, then it opened, and Commonwealth's Attorney Alexandra Cutter walked in. She closed the door behind her, crossed the room, and sat in one of my chairs, glancing around my office. From the expression on her face, I guessed she was not enamored with my decorating skills.

I shut my book, rested it on my lap, and gave her my best smile. When she glanced at my feet, still on my desk, and frowned, I waited for a beat and placed them on the floor then swiveled my chair to face her.

A handsome woman of about fifty-years-old, she wore a red thigh-length dress cut low enough to show more than a glimpse of her breasts. When she crossed one tanned leg over the other, I didn't stare. That would be rude. Instead, I took several quick glances. She wore her blonde hair shoulder length and carried a Gucci purse.

We stared at each other for a few moments, and I was happy to let the silence stretch a bit. She was easy on the eyes, and I've grown to be quite happy with silence. It was obvious she was waiting on me to start the conversation. She would have to get used to disappointment.

Finally, she said, "You're not exactly what I was expecting."

"Don't let it bother you. I left my Captain America suit at home. I'm off duty."

She gave me the kind of flinty stare I'm sure she reserved for murderers and rapists. I'm neither, so it didn't bother me. "I was thinking you look...normal. I imagined a man who would work for Robert King to be a bit more sleazy."

I covered my heart with my hand. "Wait till you get to know me. I'm sure your opinion will change."

"Detective Brown believes you're on the take, playing both King and Reginald Davis against the other. And when you shook Davis down for more money, he assaulted you. Sounds sleazy enough."

I laughed. "Detective Brown wouldn't be able to find the prize in a box of Cracker Jacks. What does Detective Tugbe think?"

She sat thinking, wondering how much to tell me. In the end, she knew I knew already. "He thinks you're playing it straight and you truly believe King is innocent."

"Counselor, 'innocent' is not a word I'd use with Robert King. He just happens not to be guilty of this particular murder. I'm sure you'll get him eventually. But your case is flimsy, and I think you don't need me to tell you that fact."

"We have a very strong circumstantial case. And I've also been told you've been interfering with our investigation, claiming to be a detective when you're not. I am considering bringing obstruction of justice charges against you."

"And we both know that's bullshit. Come on, Counselor. If you were going to arrest me, it would be Brown here, not you. What do you want?"

She uncrossed then re-crossed her legs to great effect. "What I want is for you to back off. You are complicating things, and I don't want to have to come down on you, but I will. Tell King you're out of it. Make up any excuse you want. You've stepped into the deep end of the pool, Mr. Jericho, and you don't realize someone is about to tie an anchor around your neck."

"I've always been a good swimmer. I find it interesting that both the good guys and bad guys want me to take my ball and go home. I think, deep down inside, you guys both worry I'll find out the truth and you can't let that happen."

"I find that insulting. All I care about is the truth." She even managed to look insulted without moving a muscle. It transitioned to anger when I laughed.

"Counselor, all you care about is running for Congress. You blow this case after arresting King and posing for your photo op you'll be lucky to run for dog catcher and win. That's what you care about."

She stood, the knuckles holding her purse turning white. "You've been warned. I'll bury you if you don't back off. I'll fucking bury you."

I gave her a two-fingered salute, swiveled my chair, and returned my feet to the corner of my desk. I opened my book and began reading. I could hear her teeth grinding before she turned and left, making sure to slam my door.

Who says I don't have a way with women?

16

When the sun began to sink low in the west, I locked up the office and pointed my Jeep in the direction of the home of Damon Montez. I arrived to find the lights on in the house and figured I timed it about right.

I parked, walked to the door, and rang the bell. This time the door was opened by a tall woman, her dark hair gathered in a ponytail, dressed in a white top, jeans, and bare feet. I recognized her from the picture in the living room.

I introduced myself and said, "I'm investigating the death of Greg Chambers, the electrician who showed up to fix your breaker box. I wonder if I could ask you a few questions?"

"I'm sorry, Mr. Jericho. I'm afraid I won't be of much help. I was out of town during all of this. I don't have anything I can tell you. Have a good evening."

She started to shut the door and I asked, "Is your husband a jealous man, Mrs. Montez?"

The door paused in its trajectory. "Why in the world would you ask me that?"

"Any chance we can move this conversation off of your front porch?"

She kept the edge of the door between us, an artificial barrier. "I'd like to see some I.D., if you don't mind."

I took out my wallet and slipped out my PI license and handed it to her. She studied it for a moment, then gave it back. She opened the door all the way and waved me in.

She led me to the living room I'd been in a few days earlier. She offered me a seat on the couch while she sat in a nearby chair. She folded her hands, then rested them in her lap. "I'll repeat the question: why did you ask me if my husband was the jealous type?"

"I talked to your husband earlier this week and he showed a temper. I wondered if he was the type to be jealous."

She barked a short laugh. "I don't know what exactly you're implying, but I told you—I wasn't home when the electrician was here and I'd never met him in the past, so there was no reason for him to be jealous. And what, pray tell, did you do to make him angry?"

"He didn't like it when I wanted to talk to a woman named Sidney, who was here at the time."

Her brows drew down and I noticed the first real signs of

tension. "She is one of his students. She went to the tournament with him. Why in the world would you want to talk to her?"

"Because she was also here when Chambers showed up to fix your breaker box. I wanted her take on what happened that afternoon."

"I'm sure you were mistaken. She had no reason to be here."

I sat there for a moment, saying nothing. Then her eyes narrowed, and her breathing kicked up a notch. "Are you suggesting she'd been here more than the day of the trip?"

"Not suggesting. Declaring. She confirmed she'd talked to Chambers. She said he was cute. In fact, she's quite attractive. I loved the bathing suit she wore for a dip in your pool. Which brings me back to my original question about your husband: Is he the jealous type?"

She glanced over my shoulder to the pool. Her hands went from relaxed to two balled up fists. "That goddamned son-of-a-bitch. I warned him." She stood and continued, "Excuse me for a second."

She left the room and went into the kitchen. She returned a moment later with a knife big enough to carve up an elephant. I prepared to defend myself, but instead of coming at me, she crossed the room to a large, framed picture of Damon with Phil Mickelson hanging on the wall. Mickelson's signature was prominent in the bottom corner. She used the handle of the knife and broke the glass, then reversed it and slashed the picture to shreds, doing so hard enough to gouge the wall behind the picture.

When her fury was spent, she tossed the knife onto the floor, stepped gingerly around the broken glass, returned to her chair, and sat down again, smoothing stray strands of hair back into place let loose during her attack on the photo.

"To be blunt, yes. He's always had a temper and is especially possessive. He can be quite jealous. He also considers himself something of a Casanova. But if he got mad at the electrician, he'd have beat the hell out of him here, not wait until later and murder him. It's all about showing dominance. He'd want his little slut to watch."

"O, beware my lord of jealousy; it is the green-eyed monster which doth mock the meat it feeds on."

She smiled a small, tight smile. "Othello. Appropriate."

I shot a look at the knife thinking the husband was not the only one with a temper. "Mrs. Montez—"

"Debbie. Call me Debbie."

"Debbie, I understand why you're upset. I hope when Damon gets home you will have calmed down enough not to turn him into a eunuch."

She pulled an iPhone out of her pocket. "Oh, he won't be coming home. I can promise you that much."

She furiously texted a quick message and then returned the phone to her pocket. Not a second later, the phone rang, but she ignored it. "I told him weeks ago if I caught him again with his zipper down when it wasn't supposed to be, we were through."

I started to reply when my own phone rang. "Do you mind?"

"Not at all. Feel free. Would you like a glass of wine? I think I will."

I shook my head no, and answered my phone while she returned to the kitchen.

"Where are you?"

"Pleasant evening to you too, Detective Tugbe."

"Where are you?"

So much for small talk. "I'm in Crestwood. Why?"

"I'm going to text you an address. I need you to head this way, right this minute."

He hung up the phone without waiting for me to reply. Debbie Montez returned to her chair, a large glass of red wine in one hand. She'd lost the scrunchy and let her hair spill down upon her shoulders, then folded her legs under her and settled deeper in the chair.

"Are you sure you won't join me?" She practically purred the question.

"As much as I'd love to, I'm afraid duty calls." My phone beeped and I saw an address on the outskirts of Prospect, not far from where I lived. "Literally."

"Your loss."

"Yes. Yes, it is."

17

It wasn't hard to find the address. All I needed to do was drive to the large grouping of red and blue light bars when I got close. I turned down a beat-up paved road with large potholes and more than one batch of weeds growing up through the cracks in the pavement. It ended in the parking lot of a former swim and racket club.

I remembered going with my friends to swim there when we were kids. The deteriorating building now matched the road more than it did my memories. The tennis courts, nets long gone, were full of small sprouting trees. The front of the building showed a sagging roof and windows boarded up by plywood.

A young beat cop waved me to a stop. I gave him my name and he spoke for a moment into a radio attached to his shoulder. Evidently, he got the word I was expected, and he waved me through. I parked at the end of a line of four black and white prowlers and Tugbe's unmarked.

Tugbe stood waiting for me in the open doorway. His face was drawn, and he didn't appear to have gotten much sleep in the past twenty-four hours, his normally clean-shaven chin showing a bit of fuzz.

"This way," he said.

"Who was murdered?" I asked.

He stopped in his tracks. "Who said someone was murdered?"

I shrugged and pointed back the way we came. "You wouldn't have half the force out front for anything less."

Tugbe grunted and we continued deeper into the building. Off to our left I could see several large crime scene lights in what used to be the party room and we turned in its direction. A memory came to mind of a birthday party of a girl I liked. I think she liked me too until I got sick from chocolate ice cream and threw up all over her shoes. Talk about a romance killer.

Tugbe said, "A group of kids snuck into the building to play hide and go sneak. Turns out someone else snuck in before they did."

He waved me into the room. Four bright lights pointed to a spot in the center of the room. There were two CSI techs working while a third photographed the scene. The focus of their examinations was a body tied and duct taped to a stout wooden chair.

The woman's face was unrecognizable, having been beaten to mush and her head pushed back, her mouth open in a silent scream. From where I stood, I saw most of her front teeth were broken. She wore what had been a blue tank top, now stained burgundy with her own blood. I moved a few steps to the side and glanced at her hands. Most of her fingers were bent in directions they were never meant to go. Someone took the time to break each one of them.

The olive skin and cropped short black hair told me who was sitting before me. Hedley's roommate. This morning she'd been alive and now she'd met a horrific death. The part of my brain, deep down where the abnormal thoughts traveled, went cold. I knew I was going to find who did this and return the favor.

Tugbe watched me closely, gauging my reaction. "You knew her." Statement, not a question.

"Obviously you know this, or you wouldn't have ordered me to show. How?" Though I suspected I knew.

He removed an evidence bag from the pocket of his jacket and held it up. Inside I saw my business card, crumpled and distorted. "We found this shoved into her mouth." He gestured to the scene before us. "This was staged for your benefit. You live not far from here, right across the county line in Goshen, right? The person who did this is sending you a message. Who is she?"

I stifled a sigh. "I don't know her name. I was looking for her roommate who used to date Chambers. The roommate's name is Amelia Hedley. She told me Amelia wasn't home, and I left one of my cards with her." I nodded at the body.

"What time was this?"

I told him and turned around and left the room, Tugbe keeping stride. "You talked to Amelia?" I asked.

"Yes. Brown and I interviewed Hedley early on. The roommate, too. Her name is Kaylee Lund." We walked a few steps in silence, then he continued, "Did you see anyone else there?"

I thought of the guy watching me who drove off before I was able to get close enough to see him. I kept him to myself. "No. She was alone as far as I could tell. You checked on Amelia?"

"We tried, but she's not home. We have people watching the house in case whoever did this takes a run at her when she gets home." He paused a moment, thinking over his words. "Whoever murdered Lund beat the hell out of her after torturing her first. They used their fists. The CSI folks found bits of black calfskin leather from a glove in the wounds. I'm guessing he was trying to get information from her she didn't have, and it angered him."

I nodded. "Same kind of rage shown at the Chamber murder scene. Still think King is guilty?"

It was his turn to remain silent a beat more. We stepped outside into the late evening coolness. "It's possible King hired someone to do this. Put us off the right line of investigation."

I stared at him without saying anything. He shook his head in frustration. "Yeah, yeah, yeah. There's more going on here than a simple loan shark beat down."

"Detective Tugbe, for the first time you and I agree. I think you should know Alexandra Cutter visited my office this afternoon."

"She asked you to back off, didn't she?"

Smart man. "Yes, she did. I respectfully declined. Where's Brown?

"He's on his way. Interestingly, he was meeting with Cutter."

We both chewed on this fact for a moment. Tugbe broke the silence first. "You've stirred up a hornet's nest, Jericho. You better watch yourself. Someone is warning you off. Could be Reggie, but I doubt it. Whoever it is knows you are involved, and it might be you next."

"Worried about my wellbeing, Detective Tugbe? I'm touched."

"Hardly. I'm trying to avoid extra work. I don't need another murder case right now."

Too bad, I thought. *When I catch the guy who did this, your count's going up.*

18

Mary raised up on an elbow, the covers slipping down to her waist, revealing a body Michelangelo would be hard pressed to improve. We'd spent the last hour getting to know each other better on quite an intimate level.

"Do you think Tugbe is right, and the murderer is trying to send you a message by killing this woman?"

I ran my fingers through her tousled hair while I rested on my back and stared at the ceiling. "Quite possibly. Stuffing my business card into her mouth is fairly direct. The question is, was he the man I saw when I questioned her at her place?"

"Was he there before you, or did he follow you?"

I thought about it for a moment and then said, "No clue. He might have followed me there. I'm just not sure."

She returned her head to my chest, her fingers tracing slow circles on my skin. "What if he decides to come for you?"

"I pray he does. I'd rather him take a run at me than at someone like Amelia. I'm much better able to handle this kind of thing."

"I'd rather the cops catch him first. We haven't quite got you healed up from the last attack. Any news on that front?"

I shook my head. "Seems Reggie has gone to ground. I've got Deano looking for him. We'll find him, and then I'm going to show him and whoever he had with him the proper way to swing a Louisville Slugger."

Her fingers stopped moving for a moment, then resumed their slow trail across my chest. "Is your world always this violent?"

"No. Usually most of my work is the boring kind. Following people who are trying to pull insurance scams, cheating on their spouses—that kind of thing."

She grew quiet for a bit, and I could feel her heartbeat against my side, slow and steady. I knew she was building up to something and waited for her to say what was on her mind.

"Everyone wants you to quit," she said. "The Commonwealth's Attorney, the cops, even the bad guys. Is there a point where you would consider it?"

I thought about it, but not for long. "No. I wouldn't." I paused a beat, then continued, "The more people push me to drop it, the more convinced I am King didn't do it. Don't you think Chambers deserves to have the real killer brought to justice?"

She shrugged one incredibly smooth shoulder. "I do, but that's why we pay taxes and have a police force." She turned my head toward her and kissed me. "I'd kind of like to keep you around a while with all the right parts working properly."

"Then let's test again to make sure they still do."

And we did.

Sometime later, Mary fell asleep, and I began to drift off myself when I heard my phone buzz on the nightstand. I palmed it and slipped out of bed, careful not to wake her up, and retreated to the living room, shutting the bedroom door behind me.

I glanced at the screen and answered the call. "Calling me at two a.m.? What made you think I'd be up?"

Deano laughed. "If my girlfriend were as hot as yours, I wouldn't be sleeping a wink."

I moved to the front window and nudged the blinds to the side, taking a long look at the street. I didn't see anyone. "You're having me watched?"

"The way you're pissing people off, you bet your ass. I don't have a lot of friends."

I laughed. "For what it's worth, I don't see them."

"They work for me. You won't. Now, as to the reason for

my call. I haven't found Reggie yet, but I may have found Babe Ruth."

I let the blinds fall into place. "Tell me."

"Seems Reggie's been expanding his work force. The most recent addition is a guy named Hunter Pavey; former Marine forced out on a dishonorable discharge for beating the crap out of a private he didn't like. Now he's Reggie's new enforcer."

"Sounds like a sweet guy. You got an address?"

"Yep. Lives over in southern Indiana. I think we should pay him a visit."

"Bet your ass, though let's do it in the morning. As you've pointed out, I have reason not to want to leave now. She's leaving around seven. When she does, perhaps we should give Mr. Pavey a wakeup call he won't soon forget."

"Works for me. I'll bring the bat."

He hung up and I returned to bed, sure I wouldn't be able to sleep a wink. I slipped under the covers and Mary rolled over and draped a slender arm across my chest and snuggled in close, her breathing slow and even. I could smell the scent of her shampoo, a pleasant fruity scent and I closed my eyes and listened to her for a few minutes. And fell fast asleep.

19

The most common car sold in the United States of America? A gray Honda Accord. The kind of car no one gave a second glance, making us almost invisible as we sat in one a block down from Pavey's home. He lived in a gray Craftsman Bungalow on the outskirts of New Albany, a bedroom town across the river from Louisville. I brought a box of a dozen Krispy Kreme donuts and two large coffees, and we'd polished off half the dozen already.

A red Shelby Mustang sat parked in the driveway; one I'd seen on several occasions. I rolled my shoulders, feeling the tightness from the assault. I glanced at the clock on the dash showing it was a quarter after nine. The streets were quiet with most people in the working-class neighborhood already long gone for their daily grind.

I sipped from my coffee and gestured toward the house. "I think it's time for me to go pay Hunter a visit."

Deano did his own subtle look around the area. "Want me to go with you?"

"I think I want to get to know Hunter better on my own."

He nodded and understood. The man who beat me down took something from me when he did. I planned to take it back. *Lex talionis.* The Latin form of an eye for an eye, tooth for a tooth. The phrase is meant to limit the form of retribution to an equal form of punishment. Maybe that's why it's a dead language. I'm not much of a "just get even" kind of guy.

I opened the door and got out of the Honda. I wore black sweats and Nike running shoes. I set off at any easy jog, nothing more than a man getting a little morning exercise. When I got to Pavey's home I turned and ran up the driveway. The home featured a detached one car garage and I slowed to a walk when I reached it. A sidewalk ran down between the garage and the house. I followed it to a white side door. Brown curtains covered the four-paned window, and I kept moving to the rear of the house.

A six-foot privacy fence surrounded Pavey's back yard. I lifted the latch on a slat gate at the end of the sidewalk and found it unlocked. I swung the gate open and passed through like I owned the place. The sidewalk hung a hard left and stopped at a redwood deck. The backyard was about a quarter of an acre with a creek rock fire pit in the middle.

Two cornhole boards were off to one side, red and blue bean bags strewn haphazardly on both. The other side of the yard featured a picnic table and a large charcoal grill.

Thanks to the privacy fence, I didn't have to worry about the neighbors seeing me, and Deano watched the front for any signs of trouble. I removed a pair of gloves from my sweatpants pocket and pulled them on.

I made it to the rear door with no problems and found its window was not covered. I glanced inside to see a mudroom with a washer and dryer squeezed along one side. A pegboard was mounted on the facing wall with coats taking up several pegs. I tried the doorknob. Locked.

I scanned the yard and my eyes stopped on a couple of chipped and worn yard gnomes, both wearing green pants and red shirts, their long white beards turned from snow white to dingy gray. I picked one up and tapped one of the panes of glass, breaking it into several pieces, the sound louder than I would have liked.

I snaked a hand through the opening and unlocked the door, then tossed the gnome into the yard. Without hesitation, I turned the knob and entered the house. I reached under my sweat top and got the gun I tucked in the waistband. I listened for the sound of an alarm system beep but heard none.

I moved from the mudroom into a small kitchen and froze. I caught a whiff of a smell much like rotten fruit. I knew what I would find and considered leaving and then decided what the hell. I walked carefully from the kitchen and into a large living room.

A television took up a spot over the far wall. ESPN's SportsCenter filled the screen, the sound on mute. A leather couch and recliner faced the TV, a cherry coffee table in front of them. From my view behind them, I saw an arm hanging limp down one side of the recliner, a spilled can of Budweiser on the floor.

I inched around to stand in front of the recliner and found Hunter Pavey slumped in his chair, a small caliber bullet wound in his forehead. It would seem Pavey's private investigator bashing days were over. He wore a stained white T-shirt, boxer shorts, and no socks or shoes. From the looks of the body, he was likely shot the night before, though my coroner skills were lacking.

I moved to toss the house when my phone buzzed. I glanced at the screen and Deano sent me a text in all caps: COPS. RUN NOW. I heard several cars come to a screaming halt outside and I launched myself toward the backdoor. I shoved my gun into its holster and made it to the yard when the sounds of feet pounding down the sidewalk made me stop.

There would be no time for me to get over the fence into a neighbor's yard, and being caught fleeing the scene wouldn't be the best of looks. With a sigh, I bent over one of the cornhole boards and picked up the three blue bags. I tossed the first one toward the other board and it slid to a stop next to the hole with the edge of the bag dangled over the side as the cops entered the yard, their guns drawn.

I tossed bag number two and was rewarded with a perfect toss as it slammed into bag number one and they both disappeared into the hole.

One of the cops, a younger man with ginger hair and a chin I was quite sure never needed shaving, and a name tag which read Fuller, yelled, "Freeze."

I raised one empty hand in the air, showed him the remaining bag in my other hand and then tossed it toward the board. Both cops watched it fly and hit the board with a thump and it followed the other two down the hole. I raised my now empty hand to join the other.

Fuller's partner, a gray-haired veteran named Salizar, nodded his head in appreciation. "Nice throw. Too bad they don't have cornhole in prison."

I feigned shock. "Why, Officer, is playing cornhole illegal? If it is, then prison is going to be awfully full."

Fuller sneered. "Cornhole ain't, asshole, but murder is."

Salizar cut him off and said to Fuller, "Go have a look inside, see if the caller was telling the truth. I'll keep an eye on pretty boy here."

I watched Fuller disappear inside, then said, "There's a body in there, alright, but it wasn't me. I also want you to know there's a gun in a pancake holster at the small of my back. I have a permit for it."

Salizar shrugged. "Keep your hands up until my partner confirms the dead body and then we'll move on from there."

I noticed his gun hand remained steady and pointed directly at my heart. I did what he said, and we both waited for Fuller to return. He did in short order, his face a few shades whiter than when he went in. I thought the man would lose his breakfast all over the poor gnomes.

"This douchebag shot him sitting in his recliner. He's deader than a doornail."

I said again, "I didn't shoot him. And isn't deader than a doornail a bit cliched?"

Salizar twirled a finger to motion me to turn around and I did. He said, "That's all the kid knows: give a hundred and ten percent, take'em as they come, what doesn't kill you makes you stronger."

He took hold of each of my arms and handcuffed my hands behind my back, then searched me. He found and removed my gun.

"Well, I have one for him: don't judge a book by its cover. You guys have the wrong man."

Fuller, his face going from white to a shade of red, "You can both kiss my ass. As for you, tough guy, you have the right to remain silent—"

I interrupted, "Better to be thought a fool than to open one's mouth and remove all doubt."

Salizar laughed, then laid a beefy hand on my elbow and led me out down the sidewalk to the driveway and to their car while Fuller fumed behind us. Two more policemen were at the front door, now open, and talked into the radio mic clipped to their uniform collars.

Salizar opened the rear door and slid me inside, making sure not to bump my head on the top of the car, and shut the door. He then went to the driver's side and got in behind the wheel. Fuller got in the passenger side, turned to face me, and finished reading me my Miranda Rights. Deano's car was gone, and I was happy he did the smart thing and left when the police showed up.

I settled into the seat and tried to enjoy my ride to the pokey. Jericho, man of mystery and mayhem. I would have to remember to ask for copies of my mug shot.

20

The interrogation rooms at police headquarters were all taupe. Taupe walls, taupe carpet, and taupe seat covers on the chairs. A study was done which showed blanketing rooms in muted colors tended to calm the savage beast. I guess it worked. It made me sleepy.

They left me handcuffed to a ring on my side of the table for most of the next hour. I was going through my second episode of the *West Wing* in my head when Detectives Tugbe and Brown walked in. Tugbe, now clean shaven and wearing a different suit, sat down with a folder in his hand. Brown, rumpled as ever and sneering from ear to ear, sat next to him.

Tugbe removed a set of keys from his pocket and unlocked the handcuffs and sat them to the side. He then removed a paper from the folder and slid it across to me, along with a pen from his inner suit pocket. "This form states you were properly Mirandized. Please sign at the bottom."

I spent a moment reading the form and Brown growled, "It's a simple form, asshole, sign the damn thing."

I shot Brown a hurt look. "Why, Detective Brown, I wouldn't want to sign something you may have typed up without double-checking your work. After all, what if you made a mistake?"

I heard him grind his teeth and decided to cut the poor guy some slack. I signed with a flourish and pushed the paper across the table to Tugbe.

He returned it to the folder and carefully set the folder to the side, then rested one hand on top of the other on the table. He watched me for a moment, and I returned the gaze, my eyes full of sweetness and innocence. Once again, I thought I detected the slightest hint of a smile.

"I'd ask you why you were there, but we both know why," Tugbe said.

Brown interrupted before I had the chance to respond, "Because he offed the guy, that's why. Right, Jericho?"

"When we are born, we cry that we have come to this stage of fools."

The man exploded out of his chair and leaned across the table, inches from my face. "You calling me a fool? You better watch your mouth, asshole."

Tugbe put a hand on his shoulder and pulled him into

his chair. "Sit down and stay there. I've had about enough of this hyper-aggressiveness."

Brown spun in his chair and poked a finger into Tugbe's chest. "You've been showing this doofus deference since day one. People are taking notice and they aren't likely to forget it, either."

Tugbe's eyes narrowed slightly. "If you touch me again, you will find out what it's like to eat while wearing a cast. Now sit there and shut up or leave."

Brown's face turned a deep scarlet, and he straightened his tie but did not leave. Tugbe turned his attention to me. "Spare me the King Lear and tell me why you were there."

"Would you believe I was selling Girl Scout cookies?"

Tugbe stared me down and I noticed Brown was opening his mouth to speak and I raised my hands in surrender. "I was looking for Hunter Pavey. I suspected he was with Reggie the day I was attacked. I wanted to ask him about it."

Tugbe nodded, already knowing it was true. "I told you we would handle it. How did you find him?"

"I am a detective, Detective. I have my sources."

Brown's sneer returned. "Monroe. I'll make sure to burn him, too."

"I'm guessing they haven't let you play with fire since you were a kid." Before Brown could get started on another rant, I continued, "Look, by now you've gotten forensics on my gun, and you know it wasn't used to kill Pavey. You know it and I know it. I'm also sure the coroner told you he was killed sometime last night. I was there this morning and have an alibi for last night, right, Detective Tugbe?"

Tugbe and Brown shared a look. Brown looked crestfallen.

"Yes, you do," Tugbe agreed. "Let's get back to Pavey. Why do you think he was killed?"

I sat back in my chair. "Honestly? I don't know, and that's the truth. Perhaps Reggie and Pavey were pushing around the wrong people. If they're muscling in on King's territory, he may have taken offense."

"You mean your boss, right, Jericho?" asked Brown.

I switched gears. "Have you found Reggie?"

The detectives shared another look and then Tugbe turned to me. "He's gone missing. No one has seen him since early yesterday. His phone's been turned off and he's not returning messages."

"Hmm," I said, a man of many words.

Brown let loose a long unpleasant laugh. "If King's doing this, that's conspiracy to commit murder for you, Jericho. Maybe the two of you—"

I cut him off. "Dear Lord, give it a rest. You're like an old dog with his last bone. If King had anything to do with Pavey's death, do you think I'd be at his house this morning looking for him? You may not like me, but you know I'm not stupid. You guys and I want the same thing: to find the murderer. If King is involved, fry his ass with my blessing."

For the first time, Brown appeared almost mollified. Almost.

Tugbe stood up and Brown did the same. "Whatever the reason, people around you are dropping dead at an increased rate. You should keep it in mind. You're free to go."

The two detectives left without another word. I sat there for a moment, thinking. Tugbe was right. There were now two people dead who were in some way connected to me, at least tangentially. If Reggie's disappearance remained permanent, it would make three. Was Pavey connected to me, or a random mob underworld fatality? Regardless, Lund's death was no doubt a message to me. But from whom?

Time to find out and send a reply.

21

I texted Deano to let him know I was out of the slammer, then stopped by the office and caught up on some paperwork and bills. When that was done, I fired up the Google Machine. I typed in Golf Tournaments and Nashville and found one for club pros at Hermitage Golf Course. Club pros from all around the Midwest were in town for a four-day tournament. I clicked on a list of the participants and scrolled down until I found Damon Montez's name.

There were no scores listed and I found a phone number for the golf course clubhouse. I punched in the numbers and, after selecting the pro shop, a young woman answered.

"Hermitage Golf Course, how may I help you?"

"Hi, my name is Rupert Shaw and a friend of mine, Damon Montez is playing in your tournament. I am thinking of surprising him with a visit if he made the cut, but you don't list his scores on the website. How's he doing?"

"One second." After the briefest of pauses she returned to the phone. "I'm sorry Mr. Shaw, but Mr. Montez was a no-show."

"Does it say what happened to him? He was fired up about playing down there this weekend."

"I'm sorry, sir, but it doesn't. Is there anything else I can help you with?"

I told her there wasn't and hung up. Interesting. I wanted to eliminate him as a suspect, and if he were in Nashville playing it would be unlikely, he'd be up here killing Kaylee Lund or Hunter Pavey. I would have to take a closer look at Montez. While I found it hard to think jealousy would drive him to murder Chambers after one single visit to his place, I couldn't be sure there wasn't more to it.

What if he caught Sidney and Greg doing the horizontal bop? His anger was easy enough to see when he saw me simply looking at her. And the attack on Chambers was carried out with a rage which fit, though it was unusually thin. Still, he was a suspect until I could rule him out.

I looked up the number for the Oldham County Country Club and dialed their clubhouse and asked for Montez only to be told he was at a tournament in Nashville. I thanked them and hung up. As far as they were concerned, he was out of town. Perhaps he'd flown down to some sunny clime with Sidney. There were worse things.

I texted Deano and asked him to find Damon Montez's cell number and if he would run down Sidney's name and number. I provided as much information on her as I had and got back a thumbs up emoji in return.

I was contemplating my next move when there was a knock on my door. I went and answered it to find Judge Ransford Scott standing there.

"Mr. Jericho?" he asked.

"The one and only. Come inside, Judge."

I waved him to a chair, and he sat while I returned to the chair behind my desk. A man of middle years, he wore a dark suit with a red tie. He crossed one leg over the other and rested a hand on each arm of the chair.

He nodded in my direction. "It's not often people recognize a judge unless you've been in my court, and I don't remember you coming before me."

"Thankfully I've lived a life as pure as it is sedate. I've been a fan of yours for years. What can I do for you, Judge?"

"My mother said you came to see her about the death of the electrician. What was his name again?"

"Greg Chambers."

"That's right. I apologize. I should have remembered. Anyway, it was court scuttlebutt you are working for Robert King. And having an employee of a suspected mob boss and murderer visiting the mother of a Supreme Court candidate..."

He raised his hands in the air in a helpless gesture.

"You are worried about appearances?" I asked. "So, is it official? You're running?"

"Official, no. Running, yes." He uncrossed and then re-crossed his legs. "May I ask how your investigation is going?"

"I'm not at liberty to say, confidentiality and all, but that's never stopped me before. Things are progressing."

He raised an eyebrow. "Do you really think he's innocent?"

"I do. And I think I'll be able to prove it."

"While I think you're wrong and the police have the right man, if you find evidence he is innocent, then let me know if I can be of help. I have quite a bit of pull with the police department. Despite King's unsavory reputation, if he is an innocent man, I want justice done and the true killer behind bars."

I tipped my head in his direction. "And you don't want to have to find a man like King innocent should he end up in your court."

It was his turn to nod. "I would rather it be right the first time, Mr. Jericho, no matter the reason. The offer of help still stands."

"I appreciate it, Judge. As I said before, I've always been a fan."

He stood and I did the same. "Does this mean I can count on your vote next election?"

"You keep being Judge Hang'em High and the answer is yes."

"Excellent."

He extended a hand, and I shook it. "Detective Tugbe told me you were a good man."

"Now I will owe him money."

Scott smiled and said goodbye and left. I watched the door close and sat back down, thinking. If he talked to Tugbe, perhaps Judge Scott knew how fragile the case was against King and wanted to see just how fragile it was. Being handed what many would consider a slam dunk case and being forced to let King off would not play well with the voters and it occurred to me he was worried about a lot more than appearances with me having visited his mother.

At least he knocked.

22

I was getting ready to leave when I got an email telling me Amelia accepted my friend request from my fake Instagram account. I clicked on the link and began to peruse her photos. There were photos of Amelia in a lot of different outfits. The one thing most of them had in common was the actual lack of clothing. It was obvious why Chambers was enamored with her.

My favorite was of her in a small black bikini. Or perhaps the one of her in a short red cocktail dress. Or the one of her in a light blue negligee. So many choices.

I sent her a private message, what the young people called, "sliding into her DMs." I asked to buy her a drink. Who wouldn't want to have a drink with fake me?

I also noticed she posed in multiple photos with a girl who went by the name @HotTopicMisses. I checked out her profile and, surprise surprise, found out she worked at Hot Topic at the Mall St. Matthews.

I worked at a toy store in Mall St. Matthews when I was a young man. The only thing I remember was the security guards were the same size as the Santas who worked during the holidays. I went down to my Jeep and pointed it in the direction of teenyboppers and senior citizens walking in the air conditioning.

Hot Topic was sandwiched between an Express store and a Starbucks near the food court. I snagged a coffee and wandered over to a group of small wooden tables with a view inside the store. From where I sat, I saw rows and rows of T-shirts, each featuring a different pop culture reference. The ones closest to me were all Marvel shirts. I thought about buying one with Captain America on the front but figured it would be redundant.

After a few minutes, I saw @HotTopicMisses folding a huge pile of shirts on a side table. My lucky day. A sign on the table read "Two Shirts for Ten Dollars." Her hands flew with a practiced rhythm and the pile was going down quickly.

She was somewhere in her mid-twenties, short with spiky blue hair. She wore a Hello Kitty dressed as the Devil T-shirt, jeans, and combat boots. I caught the glint of about half a dozen eyebrow piercings and, upon getting closer, two in her lip. A magnet would not be her friend.

To say I looked out of place would be an understatement.

The store was filled with young girls, some with their mothers. The only other dude in the store was a guy working behind the counter who was the spitting image of Charlie Brown. I hoped he'd learned not to fall for the football trick.

I stopped near her table and glanced at a Star Wars Sith Lord shirt. She noticed me and smiled. I smiled back, then gestured her way with my Starbucks cup.

"Hey, aren't you Amelia's friend?" I asked.

She kept her smile and managed to frown all at the same time. Quite a talent. I think her eyebrow rings clinked together. "Yes, I am. Have we met?"

"Not yet. My name is Jericho and I'm investigating the death of her friend, Greg."

The smile fell away. "Oh, that guy."

I sipped my coffee, Mr. Nonchalant. "Not a fan?"

She snatched another shirt from the pile and folded it like a pro. "Not overly. What a loser."

"How so?" I'm also a great conversationalist.

She glanced around and then lowered her voice. "You know about her getting knocked up, right?"

I didn't, but said, "Common knowledge."

"I know, right? Instead of stepping up and being a real man, he talks her into getting an abortion, and then begs her to pay for it. Can you believe that shit?"

"The age of chivalry is past. Bores have succeeded to dragons."

"Sounds cool. Did you come up with that one?"

"Nah. A guy named Dickens."

"Think he'd mind if we put that on a T-shirt?"

"I don't think he'd put up much of a fuss. You don't sound too torn up about his death," I said.

"Look, I know it sounds harsh, but I told Amelia he was a loser, and she was wasting her time on the guy."

"Did it work? Did he convince her to pay for the abortion?"

She flip folded another shirt and stole a glance at Charlie Brown to see if he was watching us. He wasn't. He was watching two girls arguing over which Game of Thrones earrings to buy. They were out of his league.

"No. In the end, he came up with the money. I can tell you, though, she wishes she'd kept the baby. She's been depressed about it. Then he goes out and gets himself killed. Can you believe it?"

"I'm pretty sure it wasn't on his to-do list. How long did they date after the abortion?"

She folded the last of the shirts, a Sailor Moon pastel print. "It ended that day. She grabbed her things at his place and never went back. Oh, he begged her not to leave, but she was over the relationship."

"Young love is so fragile."

"For sure.

I slipped a card out of my wallet and handed it to her. "Would you please ask Amelia to call me?"

She leaned her hip against the table and bit her lip. "You haven't talked to her?"

I put my wallet away. "What's your name?

"Emily. Amelia and I have been besties since grade school."

"Emily, I tried to talk to her at work, but they don't like interruptions at the Toy Tiger."

"Ah. Sounds like you met Troy."

"More like Troy met me." I smiled and I must have melted every heart in the room.

Emily laughed. "Alright, Mr. Tough Guy. I'll pass along the message. But no promises. OK?"

"Fair enough. Thanks for taking the time to talk to me."

"Are you kidding? I've never talked to a real private detective before. Do you have a gun?"

I lifted the edge of my jacket and showed her the gun on my hip.

"That is so cool. Ever shoot anyone?"

"On purpose? Not yet. But I remain ever hopeful."

I thanked her again and left. It would seem fake Instagram me scored again. I now had a good idea why Chambers needed the money. He was trying to keep his family from finding out about the abortion and I thought I knew why he did that, too.

I pulled out my phone and called Greg's brother, Pat.

He answered on the second ring. "I thought we agreed we were through."

I walked through the parking lot to my Jeep and caught movement out of the corner of my eye. Someone was following me and ducked down behind a Chevy Tahoe trying to keep out of sight.

"One quick question. Are you guys Catholic?"

I pretended to drop my key fob and bent over to pick it up. I crouched low behind an SUV and ran to the end of the car and waited.

"Why the hell would you want to know that? Never mind. Yes. We're Catholic."

He hung up and I slipped the phone into my pocket. I heard footsteps coming fast and I timed it perfectly. A man with a baseball bat walked by where I was hiding, and I stepped up and hit him hard with a kidney shot to the small of his back. He fell to his knees, and I wrenched the baseball bat out of his hand as he fell.

Damon Montez rolled onto his side, the pain intense. He lay there making a growling noise. I rotated the bat until I could see the logo: a Louisville Slugger. I dropped the bat to my side and tapped it against my leg.

Through clenched teeth he said, "I'm going to kill you, you motherfucker."

"I seriously doubt it. I certainly hope you're better at golf than you are at stalking someone. You might wind up seriously hurt this way."

"You ruined my life, you son of a bitch."

"Come on, Damon. Make up your mind, am I a son of a

bitch or a motherfucker? Pick an insult and go with it. And I didn't ruin your life. You did it all by yourself. Where did you go this weekend?"

"I'm not telling you anything."

I sighed. "Damon, Damon, Damon." I gently tapped the bat against his right knee. "This is the knee where you load up your swing, right?"

For the first time I saw actual fear in his eyes.

"If I let loose with this Louisville Slugger, the only golf you'll be playing will be on a computer."

"Man, you can't. Please. No."

"You were going to attack me from behind with a baseball bat. I've experienced that lately. I didn't like it. And you just said you were going to kill me. So, when you say I can't, I most certainly can and will, and you should know, I was an all-star baseball player in high school. I hit over three hundred my senior year. No? Suit yourself."

I wound up with the bat and he screamed, "No. I'll talk."

I lowered the bat. "Where were you this weekend? And don't say Nashville. We both know you weren't."

He laid flat on his back, all the anger gone and replaced by resignation. "Sidney and I went for the weekend to Tybee Island. I have a condo there on the beach. That's where I was when my wife texted. She told me you ratted me out."

"I ratted you out because you lied to me. I don't like it when people lie to me. Of course, in your case, I probably would have ratted you out anyway. Anyone see you there?"

"Yeah. I rented a couple of boards at High Tide Surf Shop. I know the guy who owns it. He always bugs me to help with his golf swing."

I tossed the bat down next to him. "Lucky for you, if your story checks out, you just alibied out of a murder or two."

Resignation now gave way to shock as he sat up, ignoring the pain. "What? Who? Debbie?"

"Your wife is fine. Doesn't matter who it is. If you were on Tybee Island, it puts you in the clear."

I started to walk away and then turned back to him. "And if I ever see you again, I'll put you in a wheelchair for the rest of your life. Get over it and move on."

I left him sitting there, got in my Jeep, and took off. At a stop light, I Googled the number, called the High Tide Surf Shop, and confirmed Damon rented two boards for the weekend, but returned them after one day due to a family emergency. I hung up and thought about things.

Thanks to his macho attempt at bashing in my skull, I could mark him off the super-duper suspect list. The only real problem with removing him from the list, there was no one to take his place. I desperately needed to talk to Amelia. Knowing she aborted a pregnancy at least opened another line of inquiry. Did a new boyfriend find out about the abortion and that Chambers' pressured to go through with it? Did this person then go to Chambers' house and beat the crap out of his head with a hammer?

Possible, but not likely. If I were Chambers and I let a guy into my house who was angry with me, I don't think I'd turn my back on said person for even a minute. The evidence suggested Chambers' was eating a slice of pizza and gazing out his window when the attack started. This suggested a more casual conversation.

The clock on the dash was approaching dinner time. Time for some casual conversation of my own.

23

Mary and I sat in my Jeep outside the Value Market at the Mid City Mall in the Highlands sharing a huge Cuban sandwich picked up at their deli. The night was warm and pleasant, and a string of people stood in line to get into the comedy club at the end of the mall.

"You sure know how to show a girl a good time," Mary said.

"Best sandwich in town and when we're done, I'll splurge and take you to the comedy club."

"You don't think hanging around with you is funny enough?"

She wiped a spot of Dijon mustard from the corner of my mouth with a brown napkin. "I'm sure being with me is every woman's dream. Though I'm only concerned with the thoughts of one."

"Lucky for you, I'm not picky." She took a sip of Ale-8, then continued, "At least you've been able to eliminate Montez as a suspect. That's progress."

"Beats a blank, but it puts me back to square one."

She took another bite and chewed thoughtfully. It was nice to be with a woman who didn't eat like a bird. Mary kept pace with me and maintained a better physique.

"Not quite," she said. "You know Chambers likely borrowed the money to pay for an abortion. You didn't know that before."

I polished off my Diet Dr. Pepper. "Always the optimist. I like that about you. It does give me more information, though I'm not sure how it fits."

"Do you know if Amelia's father is still alive? Any chance Amelia's dad found out about the abortion and Chambers' forcing her to agree to it? You take away a man's grandchild, there's no telling what he might do. And if they'd met before, he might have turned his back on him without giving it a second thought. And if not a father, then perhaps a brother?"

"Good questions, all. And ones to which I don't know the answers, but I will. Let me pull up Ancestory.com and see if there's a family tree to comb through."

A few clicks later and I had the answers. "I managed to find her birth certificate and there's no father listed. The section is blank. As for her family tree..." I did another quick search and found what I was looking for. "She's an only child. Her mother died a few years ago from cancer. Seems she's on her own."

She took another bite of her Cuban, her eyes lost in thought.

"What?" I asked.

"What about Amelia? She had a reason to be upset with Chambers. And he'd surely turn his back on her without thinking about it. Maybe she was bitter about getting the abortion."

"Another good question. At least this time I know the answer. The coroner's report suggested the murderer was nearly six feet tall, judging from the wounds. Amelia is all of five-foot nothing. She's not our killer. Though I will check out the dad angle in case he's returned. Maybe they reconnected after her mother died. No telling."

We finished the sandwich and tossed the napkins and wrapper into the brown bag. We got out of the Jeep and walked toward the comedy club. I threw the brown bag into a trash can with deadly accuracy. I should go pro.

Mary took my arm and we walked casually to the end of the now-dwindling line. The touch of her hand on my arm sent a steady jolt of electricity through me and I said as much.

"Good," she replied.

When we got to the club, I pulled her up short and kissed

her, breathing in the scent of her hair, a mixture of straw-berry and mint. I said, "You know, a guy could get used to this."

"Yes," she said. "He could."

She smiled and once again slipped her arm around mine and we walked into the club. *Yes. Yes, I could.*

24

The next morning, I tried calling Amelia to ask about her father, but the call went straight to voicemail. I slipped on a black T-shirt, jeans, a pair of white New Balance tennis shoes, and a UK windbreaker, and went out to my Jeep. I decided to drive by her house, but it was dark, and her car was not in the driveway. The Toy Tiger wouldn't be open for hours, but I checked there, too, with the same results. I was parked in the parking lot of the Tiger, when I got a text message from an unknown number.

I clicked on it and read, "This is Reggie. We need to clear the air now that Hunter is dead. This is getting out of hand. Meet me at the long run boat dock."

I thought for a moment and then texted a reply, "You

capitalize Long Run Boat Dock. It's a proper noun. And I'll be there. When?"

There was a brief pause, followed by some profanity in all caps, then, "Make it half hour."

I sent a heart emoji and then called Deano. "Reggie Davis wants to meet. You available?"

"For a trap? You betcha. Swing by and pick me up."

I pulled up in front of Deano's house, a two-story brick in Paramount Estates, a former horse farm now a subdivision for those who can afford six-thousand square foot homes, and he hopped into the Jeep. He was dressed in camouflage pants, a black T-shirt, and desert boots.

I asked him, "How many guns do you have on you?"

"Three. And two knives. And a shuriken."

"When did you start throwing ninja stars?"

He started to reply when I held up my hand and said, "Never mind."

We made the drive to Long Run Park, one of the one-hundred Louisville Metro parks spread throughout the city. Long Run Park opened in 1960 and I knew it from years of playing golf there in my youth. If you were willing to walk, you could play all day for seven bucks.

Some of the parks were even designed by Frederick Law Olmstead, the same guy who helped design Central Park in New York City and the park system is one of the most well known in the entire country. Yay us.

The boat ramp sits at the very end of Long Run Park Road. Trees lined either side of the ramp, offering a private hide- away on the lake cordoned off from the golf course, tennis courts, and bike and walking paths. It also allowed someone to hide in the woods and ambush us when we drove up.

I stopped the car a quarter mile from the end of the road leading to the ramp, grabbed the binoculars from the back- seat. Deano and I spent some time scoping out the woods, watching for any movement. Other than the leaves blowing in the wind, nothing moved, either in the woods or on the lake.

I glanced around behind us and there were no other cars to be seen in the parking lot we passed on the way to the ramp. If Reggie was going to meet us, he would be late.

Deano asked, "How do you want to play this?"

I thought for a moment and then said, "I don't see anyone lying in wait for us. And I guess it's possible he has a guy with a rifle on the other side of the lake waiting for us to walk down to the water, but I don't think so. This seems all wrong."

Deano nodded and said, "Why don't I get out and check the woods while you drive on down to the shore? If your phone rings, it means we have trouble."

"Works for me."

Deano opened the door and loped off into the woods to the right of the ramp. Once he was out of sight, I put the Jeep in gear and drove all the way to the end of the ramp, right to the water's edge.

I got out of the car, faced the lake, and felt a shiver go up my spine, realizing how exposed I was to a long gun. The sunshine rippled across the water, the reflected sunlight causing me to squint a bit.

I slipped my phone out of my pocket and checked, but no call from Deano. Clear so far. I continually scanned the far shoreline, watching for a glint of light reflecting off a rifle scope. Nothing. Somehow it didn't make me feel any better.

The only other person in sight was far down on the other end of the lake, a man in a rowboat. I watched him flick his wrist and cast his line about twenty yards out into the lake, his bobber coming to rest on the still water. He reeled in the line slowly and when all the slack was gone, he flicked his wrist again and repeated the process.

I glanced at my watch and saw Reggie was now fifteen minutes late. I sent another text message and waited but got no response. I called the number, and it went straight to voicemail. I put my phone away and was about to get back into my car when I caught a glimpse of something in the water a few feet from shore.

I edged even closer to the water and strained for a better look and felt a rock drop down in the pit of my stomach. A foot or so below the surface I saw what looked to be the top of the tailgate of a black pickup truck. Coincidence? I think not.

I thought about the set up at Pavey's house and I listened for the sounds of sirens. Nothing there either. It was a pretty day, with a light breeze gently moving the tree limbs back and forth, some of them visible on the surface of the water. I glanced once again at the tailgate and knew it hinted at the evil lying just below the surface.

I turned toward the woods and motioned with my hand for Deano to join me. A few minutes later he jogged out of the woods and stood next to me, a questioning expression on his face. I tossed a thumb toward the water, and he moved to the edge and saw what I'd seen, and let out a low whistle.

I asked, "When you were looking into Reggie and Hunter, did you happen to make note of what kind of car Reggie drove?"

"I did. A black Silverado pickup. You thinking what I'm thinking?"

"I am," I replied. "Reggie's not late. He beat us here."

"What do you want to do?"

"What I want to do is get back in the car and get the hell out of here."

Instead, I got my phone out of my pocket, dialed Detective Tugbe and put the phone next to my ear. While it rang, I said, "What I'm going to is what I don't want to do."

Tugbe answered, "Jericho, what do you need?"

"Do you know where the boat ramp is in Long Run Park?"

"I do. Why?"

"I think you need to join me here as soon as you can. And you'll need to bring one of those wreckers you use to tow illegally parked cars. One of the big ones. There's a black truck in the water of Long Run Lake."

There was a pause for a bit, long enough to think my phone dropped the call. Then Tugbe said, "Reginald Davis drives a black truck. What's going on, Jericho?"

"Hell, if I know, Detective. I'll see you in a few."

I hung up the phone, slipped it into my pocket and turned to Deano. "You want to head out?"

He shook his head. "Nah. I'll hang around this time. I'll be your character witness."

"I thought you wanted to help me?"

"I'll lie."

"With friends like mine..."

———

25

A Louisville Metro Police wrecker with the LMPD logo proudly displayed on the door pulled the Silverado out of the lake. The truck's rear end was suspended in the air, water rivulets flowing down and dripping onto the boat ramp pavement, the water making the mad dash back to the lake from whence it came.

Whereas before it was only Deano and me on the scene, we were now joined by Detectives Tugbe and Brown, a full crime scene tech team, and a handful of prowler cars who were keeping the curious at bay.

Deano and I leaned against my Jeep and watched the detectives open the driver's door and glance inside. After a moment, Brown motioned for the wrecker driver to lower the truck's rear wheels to the ground. The man pushed on a lever on the side of the wrecker and the rear of the Silverado was lowered until the wheels were once again on the pavement.

Brown moved to the passenger side door and then Tugbe and Brown spent a few minutes leaning into the truck. It wasn't long before the two of them met at the front of the truck to talk in volume too low for me to hear. From my vantage point, I saw the part of a leg at an angle leaning away from the open driver's door, the knee heavily bandaged, suggesting the rest of the body was slumped to the side. A knee I busted; I was sure.

Once their conversation was over, Tugbe and Brown made their way to us. They shared a quick glance and then Tugbe said, "It's Reginald Davis, alright. He was shot once in the left temple. The truck was in neutral and there's a slight dent and scratches on the tailgate suggesting another large vehicle pushed his truck into the water."

I asked, "Any way to tell how long he'd been there?"

"Not long. My guess is it happened early this morning, before you got the text."

"Unless Jericho here sent the text to himself to try and throw us off track, when it was him and Monroe who offed Davis. No one has a better motive then you, Jericho."

I said nothing and Deano simply shook his head and smiled. Brown knew his reasoning was weak and he looked away toward the lake. I followed his gaze and noticed the guy in the boat was no longer there. Most folks, when seeing all the blue lights, would have rowed closer for a better look.

Maybe the guy simply wanted to avoid being a witness to anything. Maybe.

I returned my gaze to Tugbe. "Did you get any info on the number used to text me?"

I already knew the answer as Deano ran the number through a special app on his phone on the way to the meeting. It was traced to a burner phone. Tugbe confirmed as much.

"Burner phone. Whoever used it has already taken out the battery and it goes straight to a voicemail that's never been set up."

Brown stopped looking at the lake and said to me, "If it's not you, then it seems you have an avenging angel running around taking out your enemies. Any ideas who that might be?"

"That's the first good question you've asked this entire investigation, Detective Brown." I thought for a moment, then said, "But no. As much as I wanted to get payback against Davis and Pavey, I wouldn't kill them. Beat them half to death? Maybe. Kill them? No. And I don't know who would do it on my behalf."

"What about King?" Tugbe asked. "Evidence suggests Davis was trying to take over King's business. He'd have motive to eliminate the competition. Especially once he found out he tried to buy you off."

"Normally I'd agree, and I'd bet good money King was behind this. But if it's the same guy who offed Pavey, they then tried to frame me for it by calling the cops while I was inside. Why would he do that? Unless the call was a coincidence and the BBEG didn't know I was there."

"BBEG?" Brown asked. "What the hell are you talking about."

Deano laughed and said, "Big Bad Evil Guy. It's what the young folks call the villain. Jericho's trying to be hip."

Brown wasn't amused. Tugbe said, "It was no coincidence that they called when you were at Pavey's."

"How do you know?" I asked.

"Because right after you called me this morning, someone called dispatch and said they saw two men push a truck into the water off Long Run Boat Ramp."

"Let me guess," I said, "The caller was anonymous?"

"Yes. And they also called from a burner phone that goes straight to voicemail when you call it."

Deano said, "The text only invited you to the meet, yet they knew two of us were here. That means there *was* someone watching us from somewhere nearby. They were trying to frame us."

I thought about the man in the rowboat. I'd need to ask Deano about it later.

"That makes no sense," Brown said. "On one hand, they are helping you by killing the people who hurt you, then they try and set you up as the fall guy? Explain how that makes any sense at all?"

I thought I knew why, but I wasn't about to tell Brown

what I was thinking. "I don't have a clue, but I'm going to find out."

"No, you're not, asshole. You've already screwed things up royally. Kaylee Lund is dead because of you," Brown snarled.

Deano cleared his throat, knowing I would ignore anything Brown said, and asked Tugbe his own question, "Do you think Reggie's death has anything to do with the death of Kaylee Lund?"

"I don't see how it's not," the detective said. "Considering we found Jericho's card in her mouth and Davis and Pavey attacked him too and are now dead, he's the connection." To me he asked, "And you're sure you never met Chambers? Did he ever work on your townhome?"

"Never. The only electrician to ever work in my place was from Tom Drexler's outfit and it was a guy about sixty years old. It wasn't Chambers."

"Fair enough," Tugbe said. "I'll need you guys to come to the precinct later and do a video statement. Stay around the area in case I need to talk to you some more."

I offered a two-finger salute and then Deano and I got into the Jeep. I reversed beyond the wrecker and the cop cars, then turned around and headed to police head-quarters.

We drove in silence for a moment, then Deano said, "They're right about one thing. You do seem to have a guardian angel, of sorts."

I shook my head. "I don't agree. I don't think he's killing

them to help me. I think he's trying to frame me to get me off the case, or at the very least to slow me down."

Deano nodded. "Could be."

"Did you happen to see the guy in the rowboat on the other end of the lake?"

"I saw him, but he was a good distance away. I know he wasn't catching anything. Why? Do you think he's the guy?"

I shrugged and said, "Someone was watching us, we know that for sure. The text mentioned only me, but the caller knew there were two of us. He might have been the guy, but who knows. Maybe I'm getting a bit paranoid."

"You're not paranoid if they're really after you."

"Truth. It begs the question, though. If the BBEG is willing to kill someone, why not just kill me and be done with it?"

"Maybe he likes you."

"And maybe I'll get to play starting linebacker for the Bengals."

"Well, considering how they've played the last couple of years..."

"I think it's more likely we are getting close, somehow, and killing me might make the cops take what I'm doing more seriously."

"And what are your close to figuring out?"

"No clue."

Deano snicked. "Sherlock Holmes, at his best."

"Indubitably."

26

Even though I did not think King would kill off my enemies and then frame me for the foul deeds, it didn't mean he was clueless. After Deano and I finished our video statements, I dropped him off at his place and then drove over to King Enterprises in the Louisville Riverport Authority on the far west side of the city. It featured everything a growing business might want. Especially when it comes to transporting products as it offers access to both the Ohio River and all the major interstates, all within easy driving distance.

It was rumored for years that King was taking his ill-gotten gains from his various illegal enterprises and then laundering them by moving all manner of things through legit businesses. Do you need a trucking company to transport your widgets from one place to another? King Kentucky Trucking would get the job done.

Want to move freight from the northeast to the Gulf of Mexico? King Kentucky Barge company would float your product the length of the Ohio River and then down the Mississippi River with no problems.

The fact King used his various companies to move illegal products from one place to another was the dirty little secret the authorities knew but had never been able to prove.

King's operation was in the five-hundred block of Cane Run Road, and I eased my Jeep into a slot next to a brand-new Land Rover on one side, and a late model Nissan Pathfinder on the other. I locked up and made my way to the glass front door, King Enterprises stenciled in huge gold leaf letters announcing I was in the right place.

The door opened onto an expansive front area, with black leather seats down both sides of the room, and an expensive looking oriental rug between them, dark blues, reds and purple flowing in patterns that if you stared at them long enough, would make you dizzy.

A huge cherry wood desk sat against the wall opposite the entrance, flanked by stout dark stained wooden doors, each one with a shiny brass handle, one to each side. The only thing on the desk was a phone. Behind the huge desk sat an even larger man, who made the desk seem like a kindergartener's desk. Where King makes one think of a beached whale, this guy more closely resembled a giant from biblical times. I bet David took out one of his great grandpas with a sling and a rock.

He was easily near seven-feet tall with shoulders wide enough to play a Rugby match on them. His blue suit was surely tailored by someone like Brooks Brothers, as there would be no way to find something to fit him on the rack. Hell, there might not be any clothes to fit him anywhere premade on the planet. Any planet.

Large meaty hands, the fingers interlaced, rested on the desk, and the man's eyes tracked me from the moment I came in, eyes in a head about a size too small to fit the body beneath it. The giant's hair was thin and wispy on top and clean shaven on the sides. His eyes, two small black dots, were close together and sat above a razor thin nose and lips.

The weird difference between head size and body size made him seem like a cartoonist's caricature. I'm sure the few people who were brave enough to point this out did so with great bodily risk involved.

"May I help you?" he asked in a high voice, a closer match to head size than body.

"And you are?"

"Arlo."

I let out the smallest of laughs and knew I was on the thinnest of thin ice. Outwardly, there was no change in his face. However, there was some micro expression screaming at me he'd like nothing better than to rip off each of my arms.

I cleared my throat and said, "Tell King Jericho's here to see him."

The giant gently lifted the handle of the phone to his ear and pushed a button. After a moment he said, "A Mr. Jericho to see you."

He listened and then softly set the phone back on its cradle and pointed a finger the size of a bazooka toward a door to the left. "Through that door, all the way down to the door at the end of the hallway. Don't open any other doors. Do you understand?"

"I'm a curious guy. What happens if I open one of the other doors? What if I trip and fall and accidentally fall through one of them?"

"Then I will have to show you the error of your ways. And you don't want me to correct your behavior. As for tripping and falling, I recommend you keep your balance."

I snickered and walked to the door with a kind of saunter to signal he didn't frighten me one bit. It was hard. Though, I figured if it came down to it, there was no way he could keep up with me if I broke into a fast run. If he didn't catch me, I was golden.

The door opened onto a long hallway, with four doors on each side, for a total of eight doors. The carpet was maroon and the walls on the darker side of teal. At the end of the hall was another dark wooden door but this one featured a silver handle, not a brass one. Odd.

I pulled the hallway door closed behind me and noticed

a camera in one corner high and out of reach. I started to make my way to the far door. Along the way, I slowed down enough to listen at each of the doors that lined the hallway. I heard nothing at all behind any of them. I was tempted to open one just to be contrary but decided to be a good boy and leave them alone.

When I reached the far door, I knocked, just to show I was no heathen, then turned the silver handle and swung the door open.

King's office was nothing like I expected. Instead of your standard bigwig office, his resembled a British library. Three of the walls were floor to ceiling bookcases made of Mahogany, a golden ladder and rail circling the three walls, broken only by a huge bay window with a great view of the Ohio River on one side, and a full-sized fireplace on the opposite side.

Every shelf was full of books and while I was not able to read many of the spines, they all looked expensive. On the wall with the door there was rich oak paneling. One side was full of large TV screens, while the other was a wet bar.

Matching mahogany beams crisscrossed the ceiling and dark leather furniture filled the room. King sat in a huge wingback chair, dressed in a black suit with a blue shirt, open at the collar. He was smoking an expensive-looking cigar, holding a book in one hand, a tumbler glass full of brown liquid in the other, a huge spherical ice cube keeping the drink cold.

He glanced my way and gestured to a chair next to his own with a wave of his tumbler. I sat while he took another sip, then set the glass down, slipped an ornate bookmark from the inside flap of the book, marked his place, and dropped the book on a coffee table between our two chairs.

I fingered the book around so I could read the title. *The History of the Most Renowned Don Quixote of Mancha: And his Trusty Squire Pancha*. The book was bound in what looked to be calf leather and appeared to be old. Like older-than-our-country old.

"Don Quixote? What the hell?" I asked.

"An original English first edition, printed in 1687. It cost a pretty penny."

"I'll repeat the question, what the hell?"

King picked up his drink and shrugged while he raised the glass to his lips and took another sip. "People look at me and deduct a hundred IQ points. They think I'm some kind of brute in a suit and tie."

"And you're saying they're wrong?"

"Fuck you, Jericho, and the horse you rode in on. What I'm saying is you, of all people, know you should never judge a book by its cover."

"Come on, Robert. This room is like opening a box of Cracker Jacks and finding a real diamond ring inside." I waved a hand at the room. "An old English style library room inside a warehouse? Do you blame me?"

King got up out of his chair and walked to the wet bar

and made me a drink while refreshing his own. Woodford Double Oak. He returned to his chair and handed me my drink and sat down again.

He was silent for a moment, and I waited him out. "Do you remember my old man?"

I sipped my Woodford and said, "Yeah. I do. Not exactly Mr. Sunshine."

King laughed, but there was no humor in the sound. "My father was a real bastard, no doubt about it. He quit school when he was in sixth grade to go to work and was never much of a reader. Hell, the man could hardly sign his name."

King turned and stared out the window for a moment, and I watched his face run a gamut of emotions from anger to pain and finally to sadness.

"One day," he continued, still looking out the window as if seeing another place and time. "I came home with a book. Ten Little Indians by Agatha Christie. My father looked at the cover, much like you just did with Don Quixote, and asked me if it was about cowboys and Indians."

King took a long pull on his drink, and I kept quiet, never having known the man to be introspective. "When I told him it was a British murder mystery, I did it laughing at the fact he thought it was a Western. It made him angry. Said I thought I was better than him. Smarter than him. And I did. On both accounts but I didn't dare tell him that.

"He picked up my book and tossed it onto the logs we had burning in the fireplace. I was ten years old. I never brought another book home to read if it wasn't for school for fear he'd do it again."

"That's harsh," I said. And for the briefest of moments, I felt sorry for Robert King. "Your dad, didn't he die in a house fire?"

King swiveled his huge head in my direction and leveled his gaze at me, his eyes flat and empty. "After my mother left him, taking me with her, he lived in a little shack of a place. They think he dropped a cigarette after drinking himself into a stupor. The shack went up in minutes. His body was burned beyond recognition."

"If memory serves, didn't the arson investigators suspect an accelerant was used?"

He took another drink of his bourbon. "I wouldn't know anything about that. But when he was gone, I started collecting books and I promised myself, once I got some money, I was going to have a library Agatha Christie would love. And if we are now finished going down fucking memory lane, why are you here?"

I knew most people, at the time of the fire, thought King offed his own dad. He was seventeen and his father was known to beat both King and his mother, so no one shed a tear for the elder King's death or looked deeply into what happened.

I told him about finding Davis and his truck at the bottom of Long Run Lake. "First Pavey, now Davis. You know anything about this?"

King looked genuinely surprised at the news of Davis's death. "Reggie's dead? Drowning?"

I shook my head. "Gunshot to the temple, then his truck was pushed into the lake."

I told him about the two phone calls where someone was trying to set me up to take the fall for the murders. When I was finished, King held up a finger and removed his phone from the inside pocket of his suit coat, pushing a speed dial number. Someone must have answered as he said, "I need you."

He disconnected the call and said, "When it comes to Reggie, a man's got to know his limitations, and he certainly did not."

A moment later, the door opened, and Arlo stepped inside, shutting the door quietly. For such a large man, he seemed to do everything gently. I guess when you are his size, you destroy things if you don't.

King said, "Mr. Jericho tells me Reggie was found murdered this morning. What do you know?"

Arlo glanced at me then said, "The men we hired to find him were not able to do so. They did report we were not the only ones looking for him. The cops stopped by several times and were watching his place from time to time."

"Did they see anyone else looking for him?" I asked.

This time Arlo looked to King who offered a short nod. Arlo said, "Yes. There was another guy watching as well."

"Let me guess. Blue Chevy Suburban?"

There was a brief pause before Arlo replied, "Yes. He drove a blue Suburban."

"Did you get the license plate number?" I asked.

"We did, but when we checked, they were stolen plates. They were registered to a white Honda Civic. And before you ask, no we didn't get a description of the driver. The windows were tinted enough that the guys couldn't get a clear look. At first, they were worried they may have been the Feds, considering it was a Suburban. Once we found out the plates were stolen, we kept an eye out for the guy, but he never showed up again."

King asked me, "How did you know about the Suburban?"

"I've seen one during my investigation. Like your guys, I didn't get close enough to see the driver."

King shook his head. "I thought you were supposed to be good."

"It's only a matter of time until I find out who it is."

"Do you think it's the same guy who murdered Chambers?"

"When I find him, I'll be sure to ask him, though it's hard to see a connection between Reggie and Chambers. Reggie only showed up after you were popped for Chambers' murder. He saw an opening and tried to take it. If anyone wanted Reggie dead, it would be you."

King waved a meaty hand to let Arlo know he could go. Once the big man was gone, King said, "I won't lie to you. I planned some very unsavory things for Reggie once I found him. Now someone has robbed me of the chance to teach him the errors of his ways."

"Can you think of any other rivals who may be weeding out the competition to take your place? Maybe someone else wants to be the last man standing if you go down?"

King shook his head and said, "I let it be known if anyone tried what Reggie tried with you, the repercussions would be swift and permanent."

I drained the last of my Woodford and set the glass on the coffee table and stood. "I'll keep you posted on what I find out."

I made it to the door when King called out to me, "Be careful and watch yourself, Jericho. I need you to stay alive long enough to prove me innocent. After that, feel free to die anytime you like."

He picked up his Don Quixote, and returned to the pages of his book. In the book, Don Quixote tilted at windmills thinking they were dragons. It was my turn to see if I could slay one.

27

On the way home, I flipped over to the Billy Joel channel on SiriusXM and contemplated my next move. While Billy sang *Only the Good Die Young*, I thought about Reggie and how Billy had it wrong. Reggie was relatively young and was as bad as they come, and he was dead.

When it came right down to it, the only people who knew the connection between Reggie and his right-hand man, Hunter, and me—other than Deano—were the cops.

And while cops like Brown didn't like me, there was no way they were going around killing people connected to me and trying to frame me for it. For one, they would do a better job. Cops knew the ins and outs of how killing worked and the frame job would be better constructed. No, this felt more like someone throwing up roadblocks than someone really trying to put me away.

And it still made me wonder: if I was such a pain in the ass to Chambers' killer, why not simply put a bullet into the back of my head? Granted, it would be easier said than done, but still...

These were the thoughts banging around my brain when the phone rang, and the display read Amelia Hedly. I hit the answer button and said, "Jericho."

"Hi. This is Amelia. We need to meet."

I heard the strain in her voice and asked, "Happy to do so. Are you Okay?"

"No, I'm not Okay. Greg's got me messed up in something and it got Kaylee killed and now..."

Her voice trailed off and I said, "Amelia, talk to me. What's going on?"

I heard road noise and could tell she was in her car. She said, "Nothing. For a moment I thought...it doesn't matter. Do you know where Zachary Taylor Cemetery is?"

"Yes, I do. Why?"

"I'll meet you there. I can be there in half an hour. At the end of the turnaround by the President's grave."

She hung up and I stared at my phone for a moment. I've been asked to meet folks at many strange places, but a cemetery? That was a first.

Zachary Taylor National Cemetery is the final resting place of the twelfth president of the United States, along with his wife, Sarah. The land originally belonged to Taylor's father, Richard. He was dug up in the early 90s to test if he was the first President to be assassinated, by poison no less, but they found no traces of the suspected arsenic poisoning.

I swung past the large wrought iron gates and made my way crept past row after row of small white grave markers where soldiers from the Spanish American War, World Wars I and II, the Korean War, Vietnam War and Desert Storm lay at rest. A low stone fence encircled the cemetery, separating it from the residential neighborhoods which grew up around the resting place of the dead.

I saw Amelia's red Miata at the end of the drive, and I parked behind her and got out. The mausoleum holding the bodies of Taylor and the former First Lady sat off to one side, the building made of limestone with a granite base with double glass paned bronze doors, currently closed. A fifty-foot monument with a life-sized statue of the man known as Old Rough and Ready sat next to the mausoleum.

Amelia stood reading the message on the bottom of the monument and I walked up and stood next to her. She looked rough, dressed in gray sweats, her hair needed brushing, her eyes red rimmed, and her arms crossed across her chest.

The message read *Maj. Genrl. Zachary Taylor, 12th President of the United States, Born Nov. 24, 1784 Died July 9 1850.* I raised my eyes to take in the statue of Taylor standing on top of the monument, his left hand resting on his sword hilt.

"Are you a history buff?" I asked.

"No," she replied. "Not really. I remember coming here as a kid on a field trip and it just popped into my head as a place to meet. Kind of out in the open, you know what I mean?"

I nodded but said nothing. The only other people in the cemetery were an elderly couple about fifty yards away, laying flowers at the base of one of the small white gravestones and I wondered: parent or child? I was pulling for father, as the thought of the old couple outliving a son or daughter who died way too early saddened me.

When she continued to stand there without talking, I finally asked, "The last time you saw me, you lied to the hired help and tried to get him to beat me up. What changed?"

She turned to me and the red rimmed eyes flashed anger. "You damn well know why. You got Kaylee killed and now I think they are after me, too. I've been so scared; I've slept the last two nights in my car. I've been too scared to go home."

"What makes you think they're after you, too?" I asked.

"I've seen people watching my house. Somebody is after me, I'm sure of it."

I didn't argue the point as I suspected she was right. Instead, I asked, "Greg borrowed the money from King so you could have an abortion, correct?"

"Emily says she talked to you when you showed up where she works. She says she thinks I can trust you."

"And she's right. I'm not here to jack you up or cause you

trouble. I'm simply trying to find out what happened to Greg. The quicker I find the bad guy, the quicker your life can go back to normal. So, the money. Was it for an abortion?"

Unconsciously, she dropped her hands to her stomach and said, "Yes. God help me, but yes. If I'd just had the baby, none of this would have happened."

"You've got no way to know if that's true or not. I don't think someone is on a rampage over your abortion."

"That guy King killed Greg because he fell behind on his payments. That's what the cops are saying, so yes, it is."

I watched as the old couple walked haltingly to their car, the man's arm around the woman's shoulders as she cried. Son or daughter then, it would seem.

"Amelia, what did Greg mail to you?"

She studied me for a moment, then she slipped a hand into a pocket of her sweats and pulled out a small, folded manila envelope, with a bulge in the middle.

"Greg called to tell me he'd mailed me something that would guarantee our future. He was sure we would get back together even though I told him it would never happen. He thought if he got enough money, I'd be impressed. How this was supposed to make him rich, I have no idea."

She looked up at me and started to hand me the envelope. The breeze picked up and lifted her blonde hair a bit, the cross tattoo visible on her neck. I started to reach out to take the envelope when I noticed a flash of light over her shoulder, a flash near the rear of the cemetery by the stone fence by a large pine tree.

I realized what it was, the reflection of light of a rifle scope, but too late. Before I had time to react, a muffled shot rang out, the result of the rifle most likely using a silencer. Amelia was driven forward into my arms by the shot which entered the back of her head and exited the front.

Blood, bone, and brain matter sprayed across my face as my arms caught her. I twisted and dove to put both of us behind the monument as another shot rang out and a section of the monument was blasted to pieces only inches from where my own head was moments before. I crawled a few feet, dragging Amelia with me, though I knew it was useless. She was gone.

Crimson blood streaked the blonde hair, like a horrific dye job by some macabre hairdresser, the hair falling over the part of her missing face. I scrambled away from her and yanked my gun from its holster. I wiped blood from my eyes, Amelia's blood, and glanced over the monument's pedestal to where I saw the flash of reflected light, but the gunman was gone.

Rage flared inside me, and I screamed something primal and incoherent. I wanted to get up and go after the shooter. And once I caught him, I would take my time in killing him. Yet the rational side of my brain knew going after a man with a rifle with my handgun was beyond stupid. No matter what you see in the movies, a rifle beats a handgun every day that ends in a Y.

I started to get up anyway when I heard someone behind me yell, "Are you alright? You're covered in blood."

It was the old man from earlier. He and his wife were hiding behind their car, a late model Toyota Camry. The sound of his wife crying was the only sound to be heard in the cemetery, other than the traffic whizzing by on Highway 42.

"I'm fine. It's not mine. Call the cops," I shouted back.

"Already did. They are on their way."

With that the two of them ducked down out of sight. I sighed and stared at Amelia for a moment, my brain stuck in a loop of the shooting. Her hand coming up to hand me the envelope, the flash of light, her head exploding, her landing in my arms, falling to the ground...

The envelope...

The envelope. I glanced quickly around and saw it a few feet from her body. I snatched it up and then dropped again behind Taylor's monument, positioning myself so the old folks wouldn't be able to see what I was doing.

I unfolded the flap and dropped the contents into my palm. It was a gold signet ring, the image of a lion prominent on top. I knew there was a time when rings like these were used to seal documents. You would dip the ring in hot wax and press it to the thing you wanted sealed.

While it was gold, the ring did not look overly valuable,

and like Amelia, I could not fathom how Chambers thought this was going to make him rich. Strangely enough, the ring looked familiar, but for the life of me I had no idea why. I closed my eyes and tried to chase the memory, but no matter how I tried, I was not able to pin it down.

In the distance, I heard the sirens of the police drawing near and I dropped the ring into the small envelope, and then folded it and slipped it into the inner pocket of my jacket. I lay flat on my back and stared up at the statue of Taylor.

Taylor served in the Mexican American War in the early 1800s and saw more than his fair share of blood and death. Being a war hero was one of the main reasons he won the presidency.

Now, he looked over the death of another person. One who would never have the chance to be buried in the national cemetery, even though she lost her life there. About halfway up the monument, there was a quote from Taylor: "I have endeavored to do my duty. I am ready to die. My only regret is for the friends I leave behind me."

I knew with certainty Amelia would not agree with him. She was young with decades of life ahead of her. I thought of Emily, the queen of Hot Topic, and wondered what she would think when she found out Amelia was dead.

Someone had declared war on those around me, both the guilty and the innocent. Someone wanted to end my investigation. That meant I was close to finding something. Was it possible the shooter knew what Amelia was going to give me? Was she killed because of the ring? Was it the reason Kaylee Lund was beaten to death, to find the ring?

Tough shit, asshole. If that's the case, the ring was now mine. Come and try and get it. A bullet to the head won't be how you leave this world. Not if I have anything to say about it.

28

"Do you think they followed you or her to the cemetery?"

I stared at Tugbe from the rear seat of his unmarked. Brown sat next to him, this time uncharacteristically quiet.

"I seriously doubt the shooter was following me. I'd only been talking to her for a few minutes when the shot was taken. If they were following me, they would have needed time to scope out the area, find a place to park, find a spot to set up with a rifle and take the shot. There wasn't enough time. They followed her for sure."

Brown asked, "You say she called you to set up the meet. Did she say why?"

"She didn't get that far."

I told them about her confirming that Chambers

borrowed the money to pay for the abortion and how she said she'd been sleeping in her car to try and not be found.

"And yet they found her anyway," Tugbe said. "She had to know something if someone was willing to take a shot in the middle of the afternoon to keep her from talking to you."

I asked, "Did you find anything when you searched her car?"

Brown shook his head. "Not a damn thing. And with her dead, it's likely that what's going on went with her."

Tugbe said, "A guy walking his dog on the street behind the cemetery says he saw a blue Chevy Suburban parked down a side street. It's not far from the pine tree where you said the shooter set up to take out Amelia."

"Any look at the shooter?"

"Negative," Tugbe said. "We have beat cops going door to door asking if anyone saw someone walking. Maybe we'll get lucky."

A blue Chevy Suburban. There was little doubt it was the same person. I thought for a moment and decided to offer them a bone. "She has a friend named Emily. She works at Hot Topic in the mall. If Amelia confided in anybody, it would likely be her."

Brown shook his head again. "You better hope she's still alive, Jericho. Swear to God. You better hope she is."

I didn't respond and the three of us sat there for another moment in silence, which was broken by the ringing of

Tugbe's phone. He answered and listened for a moment, then said thanks and hung up.

Tugbe said, "They've found a blue Chevy Suburban on fire behind an abandoned building off Frankfort Avenue. Buckle up, Jericho. Let's go over and look."

A few minutes later, the three of us were staring at the burned-out hulk of the Suburban. The license plate was run before we got there and sure enough, the plate was stolen, as was the Suburban. The VIN number was the same as a car reported stolen a week ago from a repair shop down off Market Street.

With the news the plate was stolen, I now had personal confirmation it was the same Suburban seen by King's men. It was the right car, though since I never mentioned it to the cops, I wasn't going to confirm they found the right vehicle. But they knew anyway.

Tugbe asked me, "Look familiar?"

"Nope. I don't know anyone who drives one, either."

Brown's own phone rang, and he stepped away to take the call. Tugbe moved up close, almost into my personal space and said, "I know there are things you aren't telling me. I pray for your own sake it didn't get Hedley killed."

"You're right. There are things I'm not telling you. But remember, she called me, not you. For whatever reason, she felt more comfortable speaking to a private dick than a cop."

Before he had a chance to respond, Brown hung up the

call and said to Tugbe, "Let's drop this asshole off at his car. We've got to go."

"Nice to have you back, Detective Brown. I was wondering what happened to the old you."

I heard a string of profanities under his breath as we all got into the unmarked. Nobody said a word the whole way to my car and neither man offered up a goodbye when I got out. They simply drove off. I watched the tail lights as they made the turn onto highway 42 and disappeared.

I glanced again where Amelia's body lay not that long ago. The body was long since removed by the coroner and I saw the crime tech crew over by the wall where the shooter set up.

Knowing there was nothing else I could do here, I got into my Jeep, called Deano, and brought him up to date on the death of Amelia.

"Dude, you truly need to watch your ass. I'm going to assign two guys to watch you for the foreseeable future."

"I'd rather you not. I know your guys are good, but if the person gets even a whiff of them, they may disappear. I need them to make another run at me. It may be the only way I catch who it is."

Deano, doing his best Detective Brown imitation, swore under his breath but then agreed. "Alright. No bodyguards. For now. At least while you are out and about. But at night, I'm having someone watch your place whether you like it or not. No way you can stay up twenty-four-seven."

"Fine. I appreciate the help."

Deano asked, "What next?"

"I don't have a clue."

I hung up the call, shifted the Jeep into drive, and left the cemetery. I wandered for a bit, the top down and the breeze in my hair, much like it was for Amelia right before she died. It all seemed so senseless, but I knew that was wrong. There was a reason and I needed to figure it out. And quickly.

My phone rang and I saw it was Roman.

Before he could say anything, I said, "You hear about Amelia Hedley, Greg's ex-girlfriend?"

"No. What happened?" I brought my would-be employer up to date. "Jesus, Jericho, what the hell is going on?" he asked.

"I don't know, Roman. Not yet. What's up?"

"I got Chambers' phone records. I'm emailing them to you as we speak. I had my paralegal look up the numbers and who they belong to. Let me know if you have any questions."

I thanked him and hung up. A moment later my phone beeped to tell me a new email was in my inbox. I decided I needed to eat something, even if I didn't want to, and drove to Divots.

Mary was off tonight, and it was just as well. I wasn't in a talkative mood. I settled in, ordered and in short order, an Old Fashioned was sitting in front of me. While I waited on the steak, I found Roman's email and opened the PDF attachment.

The first thing I noticed was all the calls he made to Amelia. The phone records showed the length of the calls and none of them were over thirty seconds. No doubt she was letting his calls go to voicemail.

There were several calls back and forth with Lear Electric, several to the pizza place where he ordered his last meal. The one call which stuck out like a huge pink elephant was a call to the courthouse the day he died. The call was placed at 1:46 in the afternoon and it lasted for nearly five minutes.

I quickly memorized the number, closed my mail app, and dialed it. After a couple of rings, a woman answered.

"Circuit court, how may I direct your call?"

I was momentarily frozen. There were a few reasons why Chambers might be calling the circuit court. But calling the courthouse only an hour or so after being at Winifred Scott's house? There could only be one.

The woman repeated her question. I broke out of my trance and asked, "Is Judge Scott in please?"

"I'm sorry, sir, but Judge Scott is currently on the bench. May I take a message?"

"No. Thank you."

I ended the call as my steak arrived and I dove in, finding myself suddenly hungry. I now remembered where I saw the ring and I now possessed a lead to who was behind all this.

Though I realized if I was right, my quarry was going to be hard to bring down.Yet I knew in my heart, the asshole must pay.

29

Agatha swung open the door and showed a look of surprise when she saw who it was knocking. "Mr. Jericho, how may I help you?"

"The gates were open, and I needed to speak to the missus of the house, so I stopped on by. Would you let her know I'm here?"

"Let me see if she's taking visitors. She's suffered a sleepless night and isn't in the best of moods."

"While I'm sorry to hear that, please tell her it's incredibly important."

"Very well. Won't you please come in?"

I walked into the house, and she shut the door and disappeared down the hallway. While she was gone, I strode over to the painting of Colonel Samuel Scott, resplendent in his military greens. And on his left pinky was a matching green signet ring. The emblem of the lion was hard to make out due to the small size of the ring, but it was there.

Agatha returned and said, "She was reluctant, but said she will give you five minutes."

"Will wonders ever cease?"

Agatha let out a very un-lady-like snort and I followed her down the hallway to Winifred's makeshift bedroom. Agatha opened the door and waved me through.

Winifred Scott was where I'd last seen her, propped up in her bed. This time she wore blue pajamas with clouds on them, which seemed to be out of place in the closed-in space. She held a cup of coffee in two hands and was taking a sip when I came in.

She nodded to a chair near the bed, and I sat. She took her time sipping her coffee before resting the cup in her lap and raising one eyebrow.

I took this as my invitation to begin and asked, "I was wondering if you would please tell me more about Colonel Scott."

"And why in the world would you want to know about my late husband, Mr. Jericho? Are you planning on giving up on detective work and trying your hand as a biographer?"

I laughed and said, "No ma'am. It's just that I find what little I know of his story to be both interesting and sad. After all, he died relatively young, did he not?"

"Why do I get the feeling you know exactly how old my late husband was when he died?" I kept quiet and she sighed.

"Very well. I'll give you the short biography then I want you out of here. Do you understand me?"

"Yes, ma'am."

"As long as we understand each other, Mr. Jericho. My husband was born and raised here in Oldham County, though his father, General Wilford Scott sent him to a boarding school in Virginia. Once he completed his primary education, he then went to West Point."

"Where he graduated the top of his class, if memory serves."

"If you know the answers, young man, why are you intruding on my day?"

"Because you know things the internet does not, Mrs. Scott."

She harrumphed at my comment and at least acknowledged the truth of my statement. "That's where Samuel and I met. I am from New York, and we were introduced by mutual friends and hit it off from the start. I was in the early stages of my musical career and once he graduated, he was shipped off to Korea to fight as a brand-new second lieutenant. At the same time, I began to travel the world, playing for kings and queens across the European continent.

"In the early sixties, he came home from Korea, and we married. Thankfully, he stayed stateside during the Vietnam war, and I began to travel less and less to perform." She paused a moment, then said, "I was good, you know."

"I am only sorry I have not had the chance to hear you play."

She held up one of her boney hands, while the other held tight to the coffee cup. "And thanks to my severe arthritis, you never will, I'm afraid."

"My loss."

She glanced at me, and I knew she was looking for a touch of sarcasm but found none. "Thank you, Mr. Jericho. As for my late husband, we lost him in 1978."

"He died in a hunting accident?"

She again wrapped both hands around the coffee cup and stared deeply into the brown liquid. "He loved big game hunting. At one point there were heads of his successes all around the house. Elk, big horned sheep, leopards, and whatnot. When he died, I had them all removed. I found hanging dead animals on the walls to be disgusting, but he was descended from a long line of hunters and boys will be boys."

"He was hunting in Kenya when he died?"

"Yes. He was with a group of people from here in town on a safari near Nairobi. They were hunting elephants. One morning, everyone else was up and ready to go, but Samuel wasn't there. They sent one of the safari guides to wake him up and found the rear of his tent torn to shreds, the insides covered in blood. They think a lion came into his tent in the middle of the night and dragged his body away."

"I am so sorry for your loss, Mrs. Scott. I mean it. Did they ever find your husband's remains?"

"They did not. They did find a solitary male lion near their encampment, and they shot it. Such a majestic beast. What a waste. If he was the one who killed my husband, he was only doing what nature demanded of him."

"That's a rather magnanimous response, all things considered."

She gave me a hard look. "Mr. Jericho, my husband spent years murdering innocent creatures and mounting them in our house. I did not condone what he did. I even told him before he left on that last trip, I found the killing of elephants to be repugnant and one day his cruelty would catch up with him. And it did."

Perhaps it was only the bitterness of age, but it sounded a lot like Winifred Scott was not as upset about her husband's death as I would have thought.

I asked, "And his brother Jacob? Does he share his brother's love of hunting?"

Scott offered a dismissive wave of a hand. "Jacob? Heavens no. To the best of my knowledge, he's never even fired a gun. At least not in the time I've known him, which is almost as long as Samuel."

"Was he also in the military?"

Scott laughed. "No. He never got drafted due to an eye injury he suffered as a teen. He's blind in his left eye. He went to Purdue and majored in mechanical engineering instead and worked for a local engineering firm here in Louisville."

"How long has Jacob lived here with you?"

"He may live on the property, Mr. Jericho, but he does not live *with* me. To answer your question, he has lived on the property since shortly after my husband's death. He felt it was his duty to help take care of me and the house. And considering it was the Scott family estate and with the size of the house, I agreed. He lives in what used to be the servant's quarters out back. We had them upgraded for Jacob and he's lived there ever since. His needs are minimal and most days, we never see each other."

Once again, I was struck by the dismissive tone in her voice, much like when she talked about Jacob's late brother. It made me wonder if this was always the way Winifred thought about her late husband and brother-in-law, or was this an attitude developed over the decades?

She broke me out of my reverie by asking, "Is there anything else you'd like to know, Mr. Jericho?"

"Is Jacob here? I'd love to talk to him if he is."

"I'm afraid not. Jacob left early this morning and I don't have any idea when he'll be back. One moment."

She reached over and pressed a button on a device next to her bed, and I heard a bell ring out in the front of the house. A moment later, Agatha stuck her head in the room. "Yes, Ms. Winifred?"

"Do you know where Jacob went this morning and when he will return?"

"No, ma'am. I don't. He said nary a word to me when he went out this morning. I know he left in a hurry, though."

"Oh," Winifred said, "Do tell."

"Well, ma'am, he fixed a large cup of coffee in one of those thermal mugs and then left it sitting on the kitchen counter. You know how Mr. Jacob is about his coffee in the morning. He would have realized pretty quickly he forgot it, but he didn't come back and get it."

"Thank you, Agatha. That will be all. Will you please show Mr. Jericho out?"

Agatha nodded and I thanked Winifred and followed Agatha to the front door. She opened it for me and before I stepped through, I asked, "What do you know about the death of Colonel Scott?"

"Not a thing. I've been here nearly twenty years and Ms. Winifred and Mr. Jacob never talk about it. If it weren't for that painting on the wall, you'd never know he existed."

"I noticed the cool signet ring on his left pinky. Does Mrs. Scott have it? That's a lion on the ring, correct?"

"Yes, it is and no she doesn't have it. She's remarked more than once over the years she'd have loved to have the ring to pass on to her son, but it must have ended up in the belly of that lion."

"There's no chance he took it off and left it here before the trip?"

Agatha gave me the kind of look you give to people speaking in tongues. "There's zero chance. Ms. Winnie said the Colonel never took it off."

I thanked her and walked to my Jeep. When I got in and started it up, I spent a moment staring at the old plantation style home, with the peeling paint job on the old clapboards, the roof with more than a few shingles sticking up in the air, surrounded by all the trees offering up some measure of shade on a pleasant warm day in May.

There was an undercurrent of something not quite right with the Scott household. The main reason for my visit was to get another look at the painting of Colonel Scott to verify the ring in my coat pocket was the same one he wore on his left hand. Mission accomplished.

There were now two main questions: how Greg Chambers came by the ring, and how did he expect to profit from having it? Did Chambers find the ring somewhere in the house when he was there to do the wiring job for the tub? If so, what did a ring have to do with a man who died a continent away in Kenya?

No matter how he came by it, he had it. Then he makes a call to the courthouse, a courthouse where Judge Scott sits on the bench, then a few hours later he's a dead man. Did Greg Chambers try and blackmail the Scotts' and was killed for the trouble?

In the note to Amelia, he said the ring would be the answer to their prayers when it came to money. Blackmail would fit. And his murderer, did Chambers let him in the house thinking the guy was bringing his big payday? But if it were blackmail, what was he blackmailing them about?

I did a quick three-point turn and left down the long driveway flanked by the old oaks when another question hit me. When Judge Scott came to see me and asked me about the case, was he doing it for the reasons he said, or was he trying to find out what I knew about the ring? The cell phone records showed Chambers spoke to someone at the court-house for nearly five minutes. Was it Judge Scott?

I dialed the number for the courthouse and asked to speak to Judge Scott's judicial assistant. I was transferred and the call went straight to voicemail. I left a message asking for a call back and a meeting with Judge Scott. I hung up the phone and thought a bit.

It was time to start digging into the Scott family and see what dirt could be found just below the surface.

30

Back in the day, finding dirt on someone meant a lot of shoe leather, which is where the term gumshoe comes from. After all, if you walk around a city long enough, you will get gum on your shoe.

Today's detective has it much easier. We are much more likely to get carpal tunnel syndrome than we are bad feet. I fired up my Mac and researched articles on Winifred, Samuel, Jacob, and Ransford Scott.

I found a YouTube video of Winifred playing with the San Francisco Symphony and she was phenomenal. They performed Brahms Symphony No. 1 and I was mesmerized. Her fingers moved as if by magic and now I really did wish she was able to play something for me. Her arthritic fingers had robbed the world of a great talent.

There were articles about her performance years in old

copies of both *Time* and *Life* magazines, and several in over-seas publications. Once she and the Colonel returned to the Louisville area, she served on the boards of both the Louis-ville Opera and Louisville Symphony until health issues forced her to retire from both of them.

I found quite a few pictures of both she and Colonel Scott, but almost none of them together, reinforcing my thoughts that she did not seem overly fond of her late husband. Nothing concrete, simply a hunch.

Another article, this one in the *Louisville Times News-paper*, mentioned the birth of Ransford on May 17th, 1973 and how she planned to balance her performing life and motherhood.

I heard a sound and glanced out the window at what looked like two teenage kids doing circles in the middle of the river on jet skis. At least they were both wearing life jack-ets. The way they were zipping around, they were likely to need it.

I returned my attention to the screen. The *Army Times* went into detail about the disappearance and assumed death of Colonel Scott while on safari in Kenya on the 6th of July 1978, along with a couple of follow up articles reporting no progress in finding the Colonel's body.

Three of the men who were on the safari with him stayed several extra weeks to help in the search, but to no avail.

Their names and their occupations were listed in the arti-cle. Tommy Marksberry was an insurance executive; Henry

Tune, a captain in the Air Force; and Joseph Johnson, a novelist.

I did a quick search of the three men on the Tracers Investigative Research website and found the only one still alive was Johnson. And luckily for me, he still lived in Louisville, down in the Cherokee Triangle area. I made note of his address and phone number for a visit later today.

I heard the woop woop of a siren and glanced out the window. The LMPD River Patrol was now on the scene. I watched as the police officers on the boat waved to the teens who then glided up to the patrol boat. What followed was a lot of talking by one of the two cops on the boat and a whole lot of nodding by the boys. After a moment the patrol boat left and when it was out of sight, the boys both shrugged and headed upriver at a much safer pace.

I laughed and turned my attention to Jacob Scott. He was listed with several mechanical engineering groups, was current on his taxes, and led what seemed to be an ordinary boring life. The man was completely lacking in an online profile. Most of us show up in database searches for any one of dozens of reasons. Jacob? The only reason he showed up in the mechanical engineering organizations was because someone in the two major groups scanned in their newsletters and posted them online. His online presence was even smaller than that of Chambers.

Jacob Scott also appeared to have never been married, a lifelong bachelor. Good for him.

I called Judge Scott's office and once again got voicemail. I left another request for a call back and meeting. I was beginning to feel a little like the judge was avoiding me.

While I waited for the return call, I dug into the life of Ransford William Scott. There was almost too much to find on Judge "Hang 'em High." He got his undergraduate degree at the University of Kentucky and his J.D. from Virginia Law School. He was the top of his class at both institutions of higher learning.

He returned to Louisville where he was a prosecutor in the Commonwealth's attorney's office. After twelve years of putting the bad guys away, he ran and was elected a circuit judge in Louisville and now was ready to step up and take the next rung up the judicial ladder. There were even some who speculated he might have even higher ambitions with U.S. Senator Mitch McConnell getting up there in years.

Judge Ransford Scott, much like his uncle, had never been married. The more I dug into the good judge, the more it seemed he was as close to a choir boy as one man can get just this side of Jesus. Which means I didn't trust him. Occupational hazard. Nobody is that clean.

I read an article from late January on the upcoming Kentucky Supreme Court race, and it listed several of the possible candidates for the highest court in the Commonwealth. Races for the Supreme Court are supposed to be nonpartisan, though everyone knows the party alignment of all the candidates.

One judge, Jane Burke, caught my eye. Where Scott was a conservative icon and ran with the full backing of the Republican party, Burke was a progressive darling and the standard bearer for Democrats. The two clashed more than once or twice in the past over the lengths of sentences handed out by Scott.

Burke came down more on the treatment side of things, when it was an option for drug offenders. Scott? Long jail sentences did better. One was the carrot, the other the stick. I have always favored the stick. If it were up to me, the Commonwealth of Kentucky would mirror federal law and do away with parole. I understood the idea behind rehabilitation. I simply wished more would benefit from the new chances they were given.

A few key taps later and the direct number for Burke's judicial assistant, Sophie Bishop, appeared, along with her email address. I dialed the number. A moment later a woman answered and said, "Judge Burke's office."

"Is this Ms. Bishop?" I asked.

"It is. And to whom am I speaking?"

I introduced myself and asked for a meeting with Judge Burke.

"And what may I say is the reason for your meeting?"

"Judge Scott."

"What about Judge Scott?"

"I have some questions about Judge Scott I think Judge Burke would find interesting."

There was a brief pause, then she asked, "And what do you do for a living, Mr. Jericho?"

"I'm a private detective."

There was another, longer pause, and then Bishop said, "One moment."

I listened to a Muzak version of Bob Seger's *Night Moves* while I waited. After a few minutes Bishop returned to the phone. "Judge Burke can see you this afternoon if you can be here in thirty minutes."

"I'll be there in ten."

I hung up and headed for the door. Time to see the judge.

31

J udge Jane Burke was a tall middle-aged woman with rich chestnut brown hair worn in a no-nonsense style. Her eyes were a piercing blue which offered a bit of amusement when she greeted me. She wore a navy pantsuit, both practical and stylish.

I knew she was born and raised in Louisville, attended the University of Louisville for both her undergraduate and law degrees where she graduated with honors, and served as the editor-in-chief of the law review.

Following law school, she clerked for Supreme Court Justice Ruth Bader Ginzburg before returning to Louisville where she went on to become a partner at Frost Brown Todd. She was appointed to the district court in 2016.

I also know she loved hiking the Appalachian Trail, skiing the mountains of Colorado, and volunteering at the

Humane Society. Amazing what you can learn from a campaign brochure while you are waiting.

She waved me to one of two burgundy colored high back chairs off to the side of her mahogany desk. I sat, and she did the same. Her office was devoid of a wall of law books like you see in most of the offices of those involved in the law. Instead, her office featured pictures of her with several different people, the largest being one with Justice Ginzberg.

She crossed one long leg over the other and said, "Sophie tells me you wanted to talk about Judge Scott."

I offered my best smile and said, "I do."

"And that you are also a private detective."

"I am."

She offered a smile in return. "Are you always this chatty?"

"You should see me once I get a bit of caffeine in me."

"Are you investigating Ransford?" she asked.

"Tangentially. You are familiar with the arrest of Robert King?"

"Yes, he's out on bond and Ransford was assigned as the judge of record for the trial, if memory serves. How are you involved?"

"Justin Roman is King's attorney and he hired me to investigate the case. Find the real killer."

"And you believe King is innocent?"

"I do."

She raised an elegant eyebrow. "And you're telling me Ransford has some involvement? How?"

"Again, tangentially. The murder victim, Greg Chambers, is an electrician and he did some electrical work for Judge Scott's mother the day he was killed."

This time Burke showed actual surprise. "Oh, did he now? Did he hire the electrician?"

"No, his mother did. Would he have to recuse himself if he did?"

Burke said, "It's a gray area. If he hired the guy, he would be best to recuse himself, but it would be up to him. With his mother doing the hiring, it is not a conflict of interest. This ties into Chambers' murder how?"

I shrugged. "I'm not sure it does. I have some questions about his uncle, Jacob. Ever met him?"

She shook her head. "No. I have not." She paused for a second, and then continued, "But why come to me?"

"You are opponents for the Kentucky Supreme Court vacancy. Almost all people running for office do some sort of opposition research. I was wondering if you found any skeletons in Judge Hang 'em High's closet."

"Such as?"

"Has he had affairs with married women? Or married men? Does he like to kick stray dogs? The usual stuff."

She stared at me for a long moment, then said, "We've found nothing like that at all. In fact, he seems to show no interest in dating men or women. There are no scorned lovers in his past, for instance. We cannot find even a trace of a lover of any type, which I do find a bit strange."

"Anything on his family?"

She shook her head. "Not a thing. Should we be looking at them? This uncle, for instance? What makes you curious about him?"

"While I can't go into any great detail, I've found an avenue of inquiry which makes me curious about the death of Judge Scott's father."

"His father died in Africa on a hunting trip, correct?"

"Yes. And the body was never found."

Burke tilted her head a bit sideways, staring at me much like a bird would. "Interesting. And something is making you look at the uncle?"

"It is. It may be something and it may be nothing. Only time will tell."

"Do you plan to talk to Ransford about this?"

"I would if his office returned my phone calls."

"Well, how about I help you out?" she asked.

"What do you have in mind?"

"There's a charity function at the Speed Art Museum on Saturday night. I have a table for eight and one of my guests called today to say they will not be able to make it. I know Ransford will be there. Anybody who is running in this year's election will be there. Why not go as my plus one?"

"Why, Judge, are you asking me on a date?"

She let out a bark of a laugh. "No, Mr. Jericho. I am not. I prefer the other team. Does this bother you?"

"It does not. I like women, too."

"Most excellent. I can't wait to see the look on Ransford's face when we stroll in together. Meet me there at seven. And Mr. Jericho, it's a black-tie event."

"I'll be there with bells on."

She said, "Now that I'd pay to see."

Wouldn't we all.

32

The next day, I met the novelist Joe Johnson at Jack Fry's, an upscale bistro-styled restaurant in the Highlands, not too far from the comedy club. Joe agreed to meet me if I was buying. And since Roman was paying the bill, I told him not only was I buying, but he was free to order the most expensive steak on the menu. And he did.

He was a small man, with thinning white hair neatly combed over a balding scalp, and soft chocolate brown eyes which constantly roamed the room. He came dressed in a blue suit and crisp white shirt, open at the collar. I was similarly dressed in a blue blazer, though I opted for a blue shirt.

Joe tore into his filet like it was the last meal he would ever eat. I went with the pork chop, and it was fabulous. Both of us sipped some Four Roses bourbon. Over small talk, I learned he was the author of twelve bestselling mysteries and retired to a life of leisure in his mid-sixties.

I asked, "How did you come to write mystery novels?"

"During World War II, I was attached as a liaison between the U.S. and the British Air forces. In between the bombing raids, there was a lot of down time, and I helped fill the time by reading Sherlock Holmes novels, often by candlelight. I fell in love with them. The atmosphere, the plot, the characters, all of it. When I got home, I thought, 'I could do that.' The hubris of youth. There is only one Sherlock Holmes."

"You didn't do too bad yourself," I said. "All of your novels were New York Times bestsellers. Not too shabby. Why the retirement?"

He chewed his steak for a moment, a faraway look in his eyes. Then he shrugged and said, "Truth be told, I didn't so much retire as I developed a severe case of writer's block and never got over it. After months and months of fighting it, I gave in and accepted my lot in life."

"I'm sorry to hear that. Sincerely."

He waved away the comment. "Don't be. I had a great run. Now, why all the interest in a long-dead Army colonel?"

"It might tie into a case I'm working on. How well did you know Colonel Scott?"

"Not well. We'd never met until the safari trip. In fact, none of us from Louisville knew each other. I knew who he was, of course, as he was often on the *Voice* society pages.

"If you guys didn't know each other, how did you end up on the safari together?"

"Oh, it was some charity raffle. I don't remember the group name, but we all had made a rather large donation and the grand prize was a trip to Kenya and big game hunting. There were four winners. I really had no interest in hunting but figured why not go. Perhaps I could use the trip in one of my books."

"And did you? Use the trip in one of your books?"

"I decided against it, considering how it all ended."

We were both silent for a few moments, then I asked, "Tell me what you remember about the trip. How did you and the Colonel get along?"

Johnson said, "He was a swell enough fella, though we didn't interact all that often. I was trying to finish up a new novel and I spent most of my time swatting away the bugs and writing. I do remember he didn't talk much."

"Did you notice him talking to any of the other guys?"

"He spent the most time talking to Marksberry. But even then, it wasn't a lot. And he and the other two are long dead. Scott claimed he was suffering from an upset stomach. I do remember that. It's why he retired to his tent early the night the lion got him. He thought he got some bad food on the flight over. Little did he know he was about to be the food."

"And nobody heard the attack during the night? No screaming, no roars from the lion?" I asked.

"Not a soul. I can only imagine the terror of being

dragged from your tent in the middle of the night by such a creature."

"Didn't it seem strange nobody heard a thing?"

"Are you suggesting this is a case of the lion that failed to roar in the night, much like the famous Sherlock Holmes case of the dog that failed to bark in the night?"

"Something like that, yes."

Johnson laid his fork and knife on the table next to his plate, then his elbows, laced his hands together, rested his chin on his hands, and stared at me. "Mr. Jericho, I think it's time you fill me in a bit on what exactly you think happened in Kenya all those many years ago. The mystery writer, whom I believed to be long gone, seems to still be down inside me somewhere and you have sparked my curiosity. Are you claiming Colonel Samuel Scott was not killed by a lion in Kenya?"

"Humor me for a second. If someone wanted to fake their death while on safari in Kenya, how might they do it, Mr. Mystery Writer?"

He now sat back in his chair and dropped his hands to his lap. The brown eyes showed a spark they lacked a few minutes earlier when we sat down. "Well, now. One might go to their tent early, wait until everyone is asleep, and then slash up the tent to mimic a lion attack. Next, I would want to spread some blood around. Lord knows there was plenty of animal blood available if one was inclined to do so."

"And then?" I prompted.

"And then, I'd walk to the closest town and hitch a ride to Nairobi. We weren't that far away. I would have arranged to fly home under a fake passport under a different name to be untraceable. I'd change my looks a bit, my clothes—small changes. Then I'd be able to disappear into the sunset with no one the wiser. Are you suggesting this is what happened?"

"I'm suggesting I have my doubts things in Kenya went down the way everyone thinks."

"What leads you to believe Colonel Scott faked his death?"

"I don't think he did. I think someone else did it for him."

Johnson began to laugh and said, "Oh, my. Sir Arthur Conan Doyle would be so pleased. When you get it figured out, be sure to tell me. I might even break out the old typewriter and give writing another try."

"Then I propose a toast to murder most foul and the men who write about them," I said.

We raised our glasses of Four Roses and clinked them together. The writer and the detective. I was sure this would be the beginning of a beautiful friendship.

33

I left several more messages with Judge Scott's office without a return phone call. I decided it was time to go and speak to Jacob Scott personally.

When I got to the Scott estate, this time the front gates were closed. I pushed the call button on the box and after a moment Agatha said, "Scott residence. How may I help you?"

"Agatha, it's your favorite detective. I'm here to speak to Jacob, if he's home. Would you buzz me in?"

The pause lasted so long I almost pushed the button again, but then Agatha was back. "I'm sorry, Mr. Jericho, but the Scotts are not accepting visitors today."

"Really? Why not? I thought they loved me."

Silence. I waited a bit then pushed the buzzer again. And again. No response. I shifted the Jeep into park, turned up the radio, and prepared to wait at the gate until either they let me in, or someone came out. It was a gorgeous day, and I had removed the Jeep's doors that morning. I was good to go for as long as it took. At random intervals, I pushed the call button on the gate box just for fun.

Turns out it did not take long, as there was an option number three I had not considered, and it presented itself in the form of a Pewee Valley police cruiser. I was singing along with Billy Joel's *My Life*, when the cop car came to a stop behind my Jeep, while its light bar rotated between bright blues and reds.

I watched in my side mirror as the officer got out of his car. He was about six feet tall, well-built, and clean shaven. His black uniform looked to be freshly pressed, both shirt and pants. He walked up to my side of the Jeep with his hand resting on the holster of his gun, but otherwise, he looked relaxed. I kept my hands on the steering wheel.

"License and registration, please," he asked.

His name tag read Bryant. I dug out the requested documents and handed them over. "Pleased to meet you, Officer Bryant. To what do I owe the pleasure?"

"I'm thinking you know exactly why I'm here. The homeowner says you are harassing them. And considering I find you here, parked in their driveway, singing, I would have to say they're correct. Have you been drinking, sir?"

"It's a bit early even for me, Officer. And I'm not really harassing them. The housekeeper, Agatha, told me they weren't seeing visitors now, and I decided to sit and wait until they were. I didn't want to miss my chance."

Officer Bryant raised an eyebrow. "Oh, and what, pray tell, is so important you feel the need to sit and wait?"

"I'm a private detective working on a case, and I wanted to speak to Jacob Scott. I think he might have some information which could shed light on the situation."

Bryant handed back my license and registration and said, "That old bastard? Good luck with that."

"Sounds like you know him. You guys have run-ins with him?"

"Nah. Nothing like that. When I was a teenager, I worked at Beard's Grocery when it was still open. He would come in and be the biggest pain in my ass. It was like the man was born ornery. No matter how I bagged his groceries, he'd complain I screwed it up."

"Sounds like the guy I've met. Any idea who called it in and sicced you guys on me? A man or a woman?"

"Dispatch said a guy called in the complaint. You must have really gotten under his skin."

"One can only hope."

We both glanced up the long drive on the other side of the gate, a gate which remained closed. He continued, "While I don't have any love for Jacob Scott, you can't sit here. He wanted you arrested for trespassing. In fact, he said he'd rather we shot you. How about we agree you will leave and not come back unless you call first and have an appointment?"

I stretched out my hand and said, "Fair enough, Officer Bryant. The fact he called you tells me what I need to know anyway."

Bryant shook it and offered a small nod. "You think he's committed a crime?"

"I remain ever hopeful."

He slipped a business card out of his pocket with his cell phone on it and said, "If he did, and you can prove it, call me. I'd be happy to help."

I took the proffered card and put it in my own pocket. "Wow, he was that big of a prick?"

"You don't even know."

"Beware the checkout boy scorned."

"You bet your ass."

Bryant returned to his car, got in and pulled away with a wave. I returned the wave and backed out of the driveway and followed him, my mind elsewhere. It would seem the family Scott were pulling up the bridges and hiding in their plantation castle. I wondered if Agatha told either Winnie or Jacob about my asking about the ring. It might explain why they were going silent.

There was no doubt Chambers took the ring from somewhere on the property. If Agatha was right and Winnie Scott said the ring vanished with her husband, then there were only so many ways the ring came to be here and not buried in the dust in Kenya.

And if the ring was no big deal, why would anyone care? The fact they did care was as close to an admission that the facts of Colonel Scott's death were not as previously presented. I did wonder what part Judge Ransford Scott played in the current drama. There was virtually no way he was involved in the events in the '70s. He was only a child, after all, when Colonel Scott disappeared.

Though, when you consider the good Judge told me to call him anytime, I needed help and he would provide it, the fact he now refused to take my calls or call me back was also illuminating.

The lack of possible involvement could not be said for Jacob Scott and his sister-in-law, Winnie. Exactly what either of their motives would have been in offing the dear Colonel was not clear. I figured Jacob to be my main suspect. I found it a bit of a stretch picturing Winnie in Kenya pulling off such a thing as making the colonel vanish. She didn't seem to possess the temperament or the physical strength to murder a man then drag him out of the tent and make him vanish.

Jacob, on the other hand, offered up many possibilities. Was this a retelling of Cain and Abel? Was there an animosity between brothers which came to a head? I started to think about how I'd do it, if I was Jacob. And the one thing which kept coming to mind was how much they looked like each other. There was no need to make a murdered man disappear if he was never there to begin with.

My imagination took off with the thought. What if it wasn't Samuel Scott on the trip to Kenya, but Jacob Scott, impersonating his brother? After all, I thought the guy I saw chopping wood was the same guy as the man in the painting in the hallway. What if the man using the charity trip was an imposter? None of the other three men knew Colonel Scott personally prior to the trip, and feigning a stomach bug to cut down on the conversation helped to reduce the chance of saying something and slipping up the deceit.

When I came to a stop sign, I texted Deano and asked him to snag a copy of Jacob's driver's license and send me the photo only, with the name and other personal data removed.

He replied with a thumbs up emoji and a few minutes later my phone pinged with the arrival of the photo. I saved it and then texted it to Joe Johnson and asked if he recognized the man.

In less than a full minute my phone rang. Joe Johnson said, "That's Colonel Scott. A few decades have been added, but that's him for sure. I've dreamed enough about that trip for it to be burned into my memory. So, he is still alive, after all these years. Where did you find him?"

"I do think that's the man you saw, but believe it or not, it's not Colonel Scott."

"Then who is it?"

"I think it's his brother, Jacob."

There was a moment of silence and then Johnson let out a low whistle. "Then you are talking something old school biblical here. Are you talking fratricide, Mr. Jericho?"

"When I find out for sure, I'll let you know. For now, keep this under your hat."

He said he would and then rang off, and I made the rest of the drive home thinking of Cain and Abel, Samuel and Jacob. Cain killed Abel during a fit of jealous rage after both brothers had presented God with offerings, with God preferring Abel's to Cain's. Cain then lured his brother out to the middle of a field and killed him. Was jealousy once again a driving force? Was Jacob jealous of Samuel's career? Maybe.

Did he covet his brother's wife, Winnie? Lust and love were powerful motives. Yet if this was the reason, it seems he fell short in replacing his brother, being relegated to the servant's quarters. There was no doubt Winnie showed no outward affection for her brother-in-law. If that was the plan, it hadn't worked out too well. And was it possible the two of them were in it together? Love didn't have to be the reason for killing Colonel Scott. Money would work, too.

I assumed it was likely Winifred Scott was the one to inherit the Scott estate and all monies the couple possessed. I wondered if anything went to Jacob Scott following his brother's death. Getting a look at the will would be a wonderful thing, if it was publicly available.

Thinking of how the Scott family was retreating behind their walls made me think of yet another Bible story. And like Joshua outside of Jericho, I was going to start blowing my horn and bringing the walls down.

Amen.

34

Judge Burke and I strolled through the crowd, the judge clinging lightly to my left arm as we mingled with the upper crust of Louisville society at the Speed Art Museum Ball.

The museum is the Commonwealth's largest and oldest and is down next to the University of Louisville campus. The museum's biggest claim to fame was the acquisition of Rembrandt's *Portrait of a Woman* in the late seventies. While I can appreciate great art, I can't tell a Rembrandt from a Renoir from a DaVinci. I draw crooked stick people because I can't draw straight ones.

Judge Burke dazzled in a form fitting ankle length backless black dress. The top half was covered with sequins which shimmered and danced in the ambient light. The pattern created a mesmerizing display of a beautiful starry night sky.

Her chestnut hair was gathered and arranged artfully on top of her head and held in place by a couple of silver decorative hair combs which matched the elegance of the dress.

I wore a black Brooks Brothers suit and tie given to me by my first wife when she hoped I might make something of myself. If only she could see me now.

I noticed people watching the two of us as we walked through the museum. There was no doubt the judge and I made a great couple, even if it was an illusion. With that said, we looked damn good.

We stopped often to talk to people and the judge introduced me to the mayor, a senator, and two congressmen, with more than a couple of them wearing surprised expressions since the judge's choice in genders was well known.

Before arriving, I visited the Speed Museum website to find out the cost of a table for eight and it was a cool grand a person. Considering the place was packed, the museum was bringing in quite a haul. At least I wasn't a cheap date.

At the judge's request, I went to the cash bar and retrieved two glasses of white zinfandel. I would rather have a Woodford, but for tonight I was willing to pretend I was more refined.

I handed the judge her glass and we clinked them together and sipped. She said, "I must say, Mr. Jericho, you clean up quite well."

"And Judge Burke, you look like a million dollars. You better be careful, or people are going to think you're a Republican."

She laughed in a way that the knees of most men would have buckled on the spot. It took an effort, but I remained upright. I was about to speak when the judge nodded behind me and said, "It's show time."

Judge Ransford Scott was holding court in the corner of the room next to John Singer Sargent's *Interior of the Hagia Sophia*. It was pretty, with lots of gold and yellow shadings, but the painting's significance was lost on me. Give me a stack of baseball cards any day of the week over modern art.

He was talking to a portly flushed-faced man who appeared to be in his early sixties. His hair was thinning, and his scalp was ruddy as his face. Next to him was a woman as slim as he was hefty, her gray hair curly and cute, and she was at least two decades his junior. Her dress was sleeveless, form fitted, and gorgeous. She also wore a sparkling diamond necklace with matching earrings guaranteed to send any jewel thief into convulsions on sight. They were a Beauty and the Beast kind of couple. The only difference being there was zero chance he would transform into a handsome prince.

Judge Burke leaned toward me and whispered in my ear, "The two talking to Ransford are William and Resina Stalker. He is one of the richest of Eastern Kentucky's coal barons and most likely the richest man in the commonwealth. His wife is a lovely lady, but William not so much. They are Ransford's biggest supporters. And William also believes I am an abomination who will burn in Hell for my beliefs."

"How lovely. Let's go crash their party, shall we?"

Judge Burke slipped her hand once again around my arm and practically purred in my ear, "I think we shall."

When we got within a few feet of the threesome, Judge Scott glanced our way as we approached and for the briefest of moments, he let his guard down. Something cold and reptilian shone in his eyes. It was there one moment and gone the next. The *other* slithered off to where it normally hid, replaced by his normal inviting gaze.

Judge Burke squeezed my arm, and I heard a sharp intake of breath, and knew she had seen it too. Softly she said, "Oh my."

We joined the small group, and the public version of Judge Scott offered a high wattage smile and said, "Hello, Jane. How are you?"

He offered her his hand and she shook it.

"I'm doing well, Ransford. And you?"

"I couldn't be better." He turned to me and repeated the offered hand gesture. "Mr. Jericho, what a pleasure. I didn't know you and Jane were friends."

"Evening, Judge. Oh, Jane and I go way back. At least a week."

Everyone laughed though I could tell the Stalkers had no idea why.

Judge Scott introduced me to the Stalkers, "Mr. Jericho is a private detective, so you'd best be careful what you say, Bill. He may be taking notes."

Smiling, William Stalker said, "I live a life so boring and squeaky clean it wouldn't interest Mr. Jericho at all. Others might not be able to say as much."

He said the last while sneering at Judge Burke. She offered up a smile with about as much warmth as an icicle from the northernmost town in Alaska.

"Oh, come on now, Bill," she said. "I'd tell you to let your hair down and live a little, but we both know that's not possible."

His eyes started to glance upwards to his nonexistent hairline before he caught himself and his face turned so red, I thought the man was going to have a stroke on the spot. His wife turned her head slightly and bit her bottom lip as she stifled a smile of her own. I liked her already.

Sensing the coming explosion, his wife rested a hand on his arm, turned to me and said, "A private detective? That must be exciting."

Her husband snorted before I could answer and said, "They call them Peepers for a reason, dear. I am guessing the most exciting thing Mr. Jericho does is sneaking a look in someone's windows chasing cheating spouses. Am I right, Mr. Jericho?"

I offered a half shrug. "Sounds like you've had some personal experience in the subject. Am I right, Mr. Stalker?"

"Now wait one damn minute you—"

Judge Burke cut him off and said, "Bill, you couldn't be more wrong. He's working on a salacious murder case which is the talk of the town, isn't he, Ransford?"

I had to give the man credit. Judge Burke managed to turn the conversation in the direction we both knew Scott wanted to avoid, but he handled it smoothly.

"That's true. Mr. Jericho is working the Robert King case on the side of the defense and there's a great chance it will land in my court. Our intrepid detective here believes King is innocent."

William Stalker murmured, "Bottom feeder."

I ignored the remark and said to his wife, "Judge Scott has promised to help me any way he can in my investigation. After all, as he says, he wants to get the right person."

Her eyebrows raised in surprise. "Is that true, Ransford?"

He bowed slightly. "It is. Justice must be served but it must be served to the one who deserves it."

"And the help is much appreciated, though I must admit, I've left quite a few messages with your office and I've yet to get a call back. I'm sure it's a simple oversight."

He nodded solemnly. "I'm sure it is. I'll talk to the staff and get back to you."

Judge Burke said, "And, Ransford, I hear the murder victim was at your mom's house a few hours before he was killed. I can't imagine going through that myself. I hope your mother is doing alright."

"What the hell?" exclaimed William Stalker.

Scott said, "He was an electrician and was at mom's house wiring a new hot tub ordered by her doctor." He then turned to us and continued, "Now if you two will excuse us, while I'd love to continue to gossip, we need to get to our table."

With that, the three of them walked briskly away with Bill Stalker talking angrily to Judge Scott in a low tone. Resina turned and glanced over her shoulder, and I would swear she winked at me.

When they were gone, Judge Burke and I stood staring at *Interior of the Hagia Sophia*. She asked, "What do you think?"

"I think Sargent was at least better than the average painter."

She slapped me playfully and said, "Not the painting, smartass. I'm talking about Ransford's reaction when he saw us. Or, more importantly, when he saw you. I don't think he likes you very much."

"I get that a lot."

"And I'm sure Bill Stalker doesn't like the fact his golden boy might be connected to a murder, even if by circumstance. When you drop as much money into an election as he has, you want your purchased judge to be as squeaky clean as possible."

"Wow. That's cynical, your Honor. Does that mean you are for sale, too?"

She hooked my arm, and we began to wander to our own table. "Oh, we are all owned to a certain extent. Anyone who tells you otherwise is lying. Running for office takes a lot of money and the big donors aren't tossing their money around for nothing."

"So not cynicism, but reality?"

"Some people claim prostitution is the world's oldest profession. I think it's politics. Prostitution is what politicians do to get elected. Don't get me wrong, most of us still try and do what we think is right. But that's most of us. Not all of us."

"And do you think Judge Scott falls into the latter group?"

"I do. When Bill Stalker is your main backer, they don't come any slimier. Ransford has chosen to get into bed with Bill and when you become attached at the hip the way they are, the stink will cover you too, sooner or later."

"Stalker's wife seems to be an odd fit," I said.

"Not much longer, if the rumors are true. When they got married, they signed a prenuptial agreement, but unlike most of those, her prenup has an expiration date that's coming soon. If I were a betting girl, the day after she crosses the prenuptial finish line, her lawyer will file the divorce papers."

"It couldn't happen to a nicer guy."

She laughed again and this time there was a touch of devilish pleasure in the sound. "No greater truth has ever been uttered. How about you? Did you accomplish what you wanted by coming tonight?"

"I did. The Scotts now know I won't be going away. If Judge Scott is protecting his uncle, then I need to do what I can to draw them out from behind their driveway gates and office guardians."

"Then I wish you the best of luck," she said. "Especially if you can do so before the election."

"Am I your new opposition research guy?"

"No. You're my bull in the china shop instigator."

"As long as you pay the bill when it comes to the 'you break it you buy it' part."

"I can afford it. Besides, won't having a future Kentucky Supreme Court justice on your side be a good thing for you?"

"It will. If you win."

"Well, there's that. Time to up the pressure, Mr. Jericho."

Yes indeed.

35

"What was it like hobnobbing with the rich and famous?"

Mary sat at my main dining room table surrounded by law books, pencil in hand, while she jotted down notes in preparation to take the bar exam following graduation.

I'd picked up two The Works omelets from a new First Watch restaurant which opened in Holiday Manor recently, mine sans the mushrooms. I don't do fungus. Mary's omelet sat half eaten while I was down to the last bite of biscuit.

"It was quite illuminating. I can tell you Judge Burke and I were photographed more than a few times."

"I know." She said this with a bit of an edge in her voice and I was smart enough to notice.

"Did you now? And just where were you doing your noticing?"

She dropped her pencil to the table and turned to her laptop. She hit a key to bring it to life and then spun the machine around for me to see the screen. It was open to a website and there at the top of the page was a color picture of Judge Burke and me leaning in close, talking, both with a glass of wine in our hands.

Mary said, "This is the blog of a political reporter I follow. Her name is Hannah Freeman. I like her because she's a bit snarky. Anyways, I open today's post and who do I see right off the bat? You and Judge Burke having way too much fun."

I must admit, the picture of the two of us did look pretty good. Under the photo, Freeman wrote: "Considering it is well known the judge is an unabashed lesbian, everyone at the Speed Ball was speculating who the mystery man on her arm might be."

I turned the laptop back around to face her. "I don't know how there could be any mystery. Only like everyone there running for office asked my name and if I'd be willing to donate to their campaigns."

"You two did seem to be enjoying yourselves."

"We did, but it was all for show. Like the caption says, she plays for the other team."

"Or maybe she's bisexual and only pretends to be gay for political purposes. Did that ever cross your mind?"

"Hmm. No. It didn't. Do you think I missed an opportunity?"

She snatched up her pencil and threw it at me. Thank goodness it was a mechanical pencil and not the old school No. 2 kind. It bounced off my chest, and the thin tip of lead broke off with a little snick sound and landed on my side of the table.

I picked it up and gently threw it back. She caught the pencil in midair and stuck it in her hair behind one ear. "Was being the Judge's arm candy at least worth it?"

I told her about our run-in with Judge Scott and the Stalkers and the moment the judge let his guard down. She thought about things for a moment, then asked, "If you really think Jacob Scott is behind the killing of his brother, Greg Chambers, and the others, is it a good idea to keep pushing them so hard? After all, you've already had someone try and kill you when they killed Amelia. What if they try again?"

"I know it sounds strange and counter intuitive to the desire to live a long and happy life, but I'm hoping they do. We need to catch these guys in the act of doing something illegal. What I have so far is not even great when it comes to circumstantial evidence."

She shook her head and said, "It doesn't help if they kill you first. And what if he decides to use a rifle again? You won't even see it coming."

"That's one of the details that's off. Winnie Scott says Jacob's never even fired a weapon. The person who made the shot killing Amelia hit a small target at a good distance. That takes training and lots of it. You don't just pick up a rifle and become a sniper. I've begun to think he has help. A partner in crime, if you will."

Mary tilted her head for a second in thought and said, "You know..."

I asked, "What?"

"You said Jacob Scott was not known to use guns. What about his nephew?"

"Judge Scott?"

She shrugged. "Why not?"

"You think a candidate for the Kentucky Supreme Court is running around shooting people?"

"Hold that thought," she said. She picked up her phone, scrolled through her contacts, selected a number, punched call, and put the phone to her ear. "Hey, Darcy. It's me. Yeah, it's been a while. Look, I've got a friend who is thinking of voting for Judge Scott for the Supreme Court but is worried he might not be strong on the second amendment, and I remembered you did that paper on him last year. Do you know about his thoughts on guns?"

She listened for a bit then said, "Wow. That will put his mind at ease. I never knew that. Thanks for the help. Let's get together soon. Thanks again. Bye."

She placed her phone on the table, and I saw the triumph in her face. "You will never guess who was the best shot on the University of Kentucky Rifle team that won the national championship in back-to-back years."

I felt a shiver run down my spine. "One Ransford Christopher Scott?"

"The one and only."

In a morbid sort of way, it made sense. "An uncle-nephew killer tag team?"

"I'll say again: Why not? It's well-known psychopathy is mostly genetic and can be passed down through generations. Let's say Chambers finds the ring and it leads him to somehow figure out Colonel Scott didn't die in Kenya. Maybe he even finds evidence which points to Jacob Scott."

I nodded. "Go on, counselor. You're on a roll."

"Thank you. And then Chambers learns Ransford is running for the open Supreme Court seat, and he sees dollar signs. After all, if it was to come out that his uncle murdered his father, his chance of winning the open seat would go up in smoke. You said he called the courthouse. Maybe that's when he tried to blackmail Scott. Pay up or I go to the cops."

"And instead of paying up, when either the Judge or Jacob shows up, they kill him instead. It fits," I said. "Chambers' murder always pointed to one of rage. Being blackmailed or you lose a chance at the Supreme Court would be enough to make me angry."

"Do you think Winifred Scott knows what is going on?"

I thought for a moment, then said, "If she does, then she's as cold blooded as the other two and one hell of an actress.

She gave no indication of nervousness or tension either time I spoke to her."

"Does this mean you'll go to the cops with what you know?" she asked.

"Counselor, if you were a cop and I came to you and said the state's top Boy Scout, one of, if not the, most respected judge in the state, is either on his own or with his uncle, responsible for multiple murders, what would you say?"

"Well..." she trailed off.

"And keep in mind, I'm working for a guy the cops want to string up from the highest yardarm. In fact, the case is likely to be tried in Scott's court. Would you believe me?"

She leaned back in her chair, the signs of defeat clear on her otherwise angelic face. "No. You're right. I'd think you were insane and only trying to muddy the waters for your client."

"This does explain something else that's bugged me."

"What's that?" Mary asked.

"I wondered how someone found out about Reggie Davis and Hunter Pavey and knew about Reggie offering to pay me off. I thought it pointed to a cop, but a district judge would have the contacts to find out the same kind of thing."

Mary shuddered. "And to think one of the two also beat that poor girl to death with their bare hands and then stuck your card in her mouth. It's almost like they want you to come after them." She paused for a moment and then continued, "What will you do now?"

"Jacob Scott might be able to stay out of sight and hide behind the gates of the Scott estate, but Ransford isn't as lucky. He's got court every day. I think tomorrow I'll start following him around and see what he does."

"And you'll make sure he knows you're doing it too, won't you?"

"It wouldn't be fun any other way."

I got up, moved behind her, and began to massage her shoulders, much like she did for me the day I got home following my beating. She moaned with pleasure and let out a long sigh.

"The kind of life you lead, will it always be like this?" she asked.

"Pretty much. And if we are going to be together, you will have to accept it. Can you do that?"

"I'm guessing you wouldn't consider a career change? Like maybe becoming a plumber or carpenter?"

"If you'd ever seen me try to use a hammer or screwdriver, you would know better. I'm sorry, but I can't imagine myself doing anything else. Are you okay with that?"

"Okay with it? I guess I'll have to be, but I do know one thing for sure."

I watched her close her eyes and arch her back as my fingers worked hard on her shoulder blades. I felt the tension begin to leak from her body. "And that would be?" I asked.

"When I pass the bar exam, I'd planned on being an environmental lawyer. I think if I'm going to keep hanging around with you, I might want to go into criminal law."

"You think I might need representation?"

"No." She sighed. "If they manage to kill you, I'll want to join the prosecutor's office and nail their asses to the wall."

"If they kill me, have at it. Would you like me to pay you for your services in advance?"

She stood up, turned, put her arms around my neck and kissed me. "Why don't we go to your bedroom, and you can work on the retainer you will need. We might be a while. I don't come cheap."

Thank God my elderly male tax lawyer didn't work this way.

36

Later the next day, I sat in my Jeep in a metered spot down the street from the courthouse with a view of the permitted lot where the people who worked in the building parked. I was between an LMPD cruiser and a beat-up old red Ford pickup truck.

I'd learned the Judge drove a dark green Jaguar F-Type sedan and a quick walk down the sidewalk a few minutes earlier confirmed the car was in the lot.

Thanks to the Kentucky Court of Justice docket website, I knew Judge Scott was presiding over the trial of a man accused of strangling his live-in girlfriend. The trial started at 1:30 p.m. and it was not expected to last long. There was little doubt the guy should have made a plea deal. Taking your chances in Judge Hang 'em High's courtroom was a huge misstep, considering how often he handed down the maximum penalty allowed by law.

While I sat and watched his car, it gave me time to think through the possibilities of his involvement in the carnage swirling around me. Taking on Jacob Scott was one thing. Taking on a well-respected district court judge was something else altogether.

I thought of the evidence I possessed, and it was all weak. The ring proved nothing in and of itself. They would claim it was left in a drawer somewhere in the house and it proved Chambers was a thief.

My thoughts were interrupted by a parking enforcement officer who was headed my way down the sidewalk, checking meters. She was a short plump woman with a ticket pad in her hand. She stopped at the red Ford and began to write. Evidently his meter time expired. She tore off the ticket and stuck it under the truck's windshield wiper.

She got to me and saw my meter still showed over an hour of parking time. She shot me a glance and I said, "Afternoon, Officer."

She nodded at me without saying a word in reply and went on about her business. I shouted, "Nice talking to you, too."

The only sign she heard me was a half turning of her head. Before long she was out of sight, and I returned to my contemplation of the case. Or the lack of one.

When it came to Chambers calling the courthouse, there

were hundreds of people who worked there. Who was to say he was calling Judge Scott? There were dozens of reasons he might call the courthouse.

The fact the Judge was on the UK rifle team also proved only that he was a good shot. So were literally thousands of other residents of the Commonwealth. I knew of nothing placing him anywhere near Zachary Taylor National Cemetery. I had checked the court docket and found he was off the bench by then, but had no clue where he went.

And then there was the issue of what his motive would be. While I was now convinced Colonel Scott was never in Kenya, I had no proof of that either. The cops would never believe Judge Scott was killing people to keep quiet the murder of a man who it was known died in a hunting accident half a world away.

And that brought me back to the ring. There was no way the ring itself would cause this kind of a freak out and the murder of Chambers. The dead electrician had to have had more than the ring to blackmail the Scotts. Yet, if he did, then why didn't he send it with the ring to Amelia for safekeeping? Was the proof at his home and the killer took it with him?

To know a thing was one thing. To prove a thing was something different. All I could do was to pressure the bad guys and get them to make a mistake. Preferably one where I was still breathing when it was all over.

A couple of hours later, I watched as a thunderstorm

began to roll in from the west. It turned the far horizon a deep blue, the kind of blue that matched my mood. The occasional bolt of lightning fell to Earth and the smell of fresh rain filled the air.

My reverie was broken when Judge Scott jogged into view, obviously trying to reach his car before the rain started. He made it with less than a minute to spare. The judge had no more than started his car when the sky opened, and the deluge cut loose.

I started the Jeep and rolled up the windows and when the judge edged his Jaguar out of the lot, his windshield wipers beating furiously and his lights on high, I was two cars behind.

We left downtown and made our way over to Mesh, an upscale restaurant which catered to an upper middle-class clientele. I watched the judge park, and while the heavy rain continued to pound the pavement, he made a mad dash to the front door. No umbrella or raincoat for him.

I gave him ten minutes or so to get settled, and when the storm passed, I got out and followed him inside.

A young hostess greeted me when I walked inside and asked, "Hello and welcome to Mesh. Would you like a table or will you be sitting at the bar?"

"I'm here to meet a friend. Judge Scott. Do you know him?"

"Sure. The Judge is a regular. He didn't tell me he was expecting anyone." She got a menu and said, "Follow me."

We entered the main dining area and I saw Judge Scott sitting alone at a table next to a roaring fireplace. The restaurant sported a look both contemporary and elegant and the judge fit right in. Me? Not so much.

The judge was concentrating on something he was reading on his phone and did not register our presence until we reached the table.

The hostess said, "Judge Scott, your friend is here."

He glanced up as I pulled out a chair and sat down across from him. And once again, I was impressed with his ability to roll with the situation. I hoped I would at least push a few of his buttons and knock him off his game. Instead, if anything, he wore a bemused expression.

He said, "Thank you, Kelly."

She laid the menu down in front of me and left us. I glanced down at the menu and the prices and was happy I was on an expense account.

The judge picked up what smelled like a tumbler of Scotch and took a long sip. He then placed the glass down on the table and said, "Mr. Jericho. I wish I could say this is a pleasant surprise, but it's not."

"And here I thought you'd be happy to see me."

"You know, I thought I recognized your Jeep behind me when I left the courthouse."

We were interrupted by the waitress, and I ordered Scotch as well. When she left to fill my order, I said, "You know what kind of car I drive?"

He picked up his drink and took another sip. "I know quite a lot about you, Mr. Jericho."

"Oh? Do tell."

"When someone inserts themselves into my life, I make it a point to know everything I can about them. You? I already know where you work. I also know where you live, who your friends are, who you're dating. I must admit, Ms. McGill is quite lovely. You are certainly out of your league where the soon-to-be lawyer is concerned. Maybe she'd like to clerk for me. Who knows?"

I felt the cold thing deep inside me begin to rear its ugly head at the mention of Mary's name. I stared at him for a moment knowing he was trying to get a rise out of me. He succeeded.

The waitress was back with my drink. I passed on ordering dinner, and she left us. I decided to hit back with a rhetorical punch of my own.

I said, "Was it you or your uncle who beat Kaylee Lund to death?"

This time, his smile was one of satisfaction and I knew right then, without any doubt, it was him who murdered Lund and he wanted me to know it was him.

He took another sip of his whiskey and said, "Why, Mr. Jericho, that's quite a slanderous accusation. Making those kinds of comments might land you in some deep trouble."

"Being in trouble is a daily occurrence for me. I know it was you who shot Amelia and tried to shoot me. With a bad eye, there's no way your Uncle Jacob would be able to make that shot. Congrats on the NCAA championship by the way."

"Championships. Plural."

"My bad. Championships. Which one of you killed Chambers? Was he blackmailing you from the get-go or did he start with your uncle?"

"Do you realize how completely crazy you sound? Accusing me, of all people, of murder?"

I paused for a moment as a group of teen girls were celebrating a sweet sixteen birthday at a long table near us and the wait staff brought out a huge cake. The birthday girl, a slender girl with long black hair, beamed as the cake was lit and her friends sang her Happy Birthday.

I returned my attention to Judge Scott and the surreal conversation we were having. A sweet sixteen party at one table, a murderer and his hunter at another.

"What I don't understand is why you killed Davis and Pavey. If you were trying to frame me, you did a piss poor job of it. I would have thought a judge could do better."

"I would have no idea what you are talking about. I had nothing to do with the deaths of either man. In my professional capacity, I could only offer a guess as to possible motivations."

"Offer a way."

"Maybe the killer or killers were simply trying to cause confusion for the police. Point them in another direction from the true motive. Perhaps they were simply trying to complicate your life. Maybe they enjoy playing with you the way a cat plays with a mouse before it goes in for the kill."

"And you think you're the cat and I'm the mouse?"

"What I do know is Cutter and the police force think you are involved in the murders of both men. After all, you were even arrested at one of the crime scenes, were you not?"

"And you know as well as I do, I wasn't arrested. They talked to me, and I was cleared of being involved in Pavey's death. Care to try again?"

Scott shrugged. "What's the point? I get the feeling one day soon you will be joining Robert King with a long prison stay in Eddyville. If you don't end up in a pine box first."

Anger flowed through me to the point I wanted nothing more than to leap across the table and slam his handsome face through the fireplace grate and melt it in the fire beyond. I wanted it so bad I could taste it. I also knew it was exactly what he wanted. A public confrontation with plenty of witnesses. There is no doubt it would help the birthday girl remember her sixteenth birthday party.

Somehow, I kept control. Barely. But I managed it. I picked up my Scotch and downed it in one long pull. I sat the glass down carefully, stood and said with a calmness I did not feel, "No matter where you go, no matter what you do, I'll be there. Day or night. I'll be there. Sooner or later, you'll slip up."

He snickered. "You do know threatening a judge in this state is a crime all on its own?"

"I didn't make a threat. I made a promise."

I turned and left the judge to his thoughts and his meal. He was laughing as I did. I knew from this point going forward I would need to be incredibly careful. There was little doubt if he wanted me arrested, he could arrange it. He also could shoot me dead, if he wanted. But I had something now I did not have before.

Certainty.

His responses to my questions made it clear to me he and his uncle were involved in the deaths of Greg Chambers, Amelia Hedley, Kaylee Lund, Reginald Davis, and Hunter Pavey.

And I was certain what I was going to do, too. It was Niccolo Machiavelli who said, "If an injury has to be done to a man it should be so severe that his vengeance need not be feared."

I would bring the storm to Ransford and Jacob Scott. And when I did, there would be no fear of vengeance.

37

I sat at a front table at Karem's Grill and Pub in Norton Commons, a mixed-use neighborhood designed to resemble old town America, with homes and stores sharing the tree lined streets. In fact, the firm hired to design the town for the developers were the same ones who created the town for the Jim Carrey movie, *The Truman Show*.

The benefit of Karem's for me, besides the great food, was sitting at the table near their front window offered up a great view of Judge Scott's two-story brick townhome a little way down the street. Memorial Day was only a few days away and the judge was getting into the swing of things with an American flag in a stand attached to the wall and a Stars and Stripes wreath on the door.

Thanks to the unit next to his being for sale, I knew the townhome cost him a bit north of half a million dollars with close to three-thousand square feet of living space. A lot of room for an avowed bachelor, though I suppose it was a great investment.

Night was in full swing, and a conveniently placed street-light made sure I kept a full view of both his front door and the alley leading to his garage. While it did not guarantee he would not be able to give me the slip, it made it harder.

True to the promise I made him at Mesh, I had spent the last few days following him from place to place. Thanks to his regular court schedule, I was able to catch some shut eye during the day but made sure I was waiting outside on the street each day when his car left the parking lot. I even got to know the meter cop. Her name was Ruby Johnson, she has three kids, two in college, and she even once noticed the meter was nearly out when she got to me and coughed loudly enough for me to realize she was there and to put more money in the meter before she wrote me a ticket.

Each night the judge would go to different restaurants to eat. It would appear something the judge and I shared was a lack of cooking skills. I made sure to follow him inside each time. I would find a spot at the bar where I could see him, and he could see me. The first couple of times he saw me he would raise his glass and toast me from his table. I never returned the gesture.

Though it was obvious I was now begging to get under his skin. Tonight, instead of eating alone, he met with a fit and trim dark-haired man of about his age. They met in the parking lot of Malone's, one of the city's better steak houses. The new guy drove a Tesla Model X Plaid and they ran north of a hundred-thousand dollars. Must be nice.

The car sported Virginia plates and I sent the plate numbers to Deano. He responded with a DMV photo and a name: Benjamin Downey. Sr. Downey was fifty-three years old, and a quick Google search informed me he was a tax lobbyist with a white shoe law firm in Washington D.C.

When I went inside and found a seat at the bar, Scott and Downey were in a booth with the judge's back to me. I made sure to stare a hole through him and after a bit Downey noticed me doing so and gestured with his fork in my direction. When the judge turned around, I winked at him.

I was able to see his jaw muscles working from where I sat. When he turned his attention back to Downey, the two men bent low over the table for a moment and shared a quiet conversation, with the judge occasionally pointing over his shoulder in my direction with his thumb.

I was on my second Old Fashioned when the judge got up and came and sat next to me at the bar while Downey watched from the booth. There was no smile this time as the judge took his seat.

"You realize," he said, "This is harassment."

"What is?" I asked.

"You know what. Following me like you are doing is harassment."

"Then call the cops. Let's sit down and talk to them. We can both tell them why I'm following you around. Who knows, they may even take me seriously. Stranger things have happened. Then how will your campaign for the Supreme Court go?"

I took out my phone, unlocked it and continued, "You want to call 9-1-1 or should I?"

Scott shot Downey a quick glance and now he was the one trying to control his temper. He stood and bent low so only I would hear him. "You will soon regret yanking my chain, Mr. Jericho. Very soon."

He returned to his booth and he and Downey finished their meals. At one point, Downey took out a phone and made a call. While he talked, he glanced around the judge to stare at me. I was too far away to hear what was said, but after he ended the call, I understood the word he said to the judge: done.

The judge nodded his head and gave Downey a thumbs-up. The waiter brought the bill, and the judge paid it. The two men stood and left the restaurant. They passed near me, and I noticed both men wore a smirk. The judge even gave me a wink. Whatever anger he felt from my presence was gone.

Now, staring out the window at Karem's, this change in mood bothered me. True, there was no telling what made a psychopath feel something from one moment to the next, and I was quite sure Judge Ransford Scott was a psychopath.

There's usually a reason they act like they do. It made me wonder who Downey called.

My reverie was broken by the ringing of my phone. I saw Mary's name and when I heard her voice, fear hit me like a sledgehammer.

The strain in her voice was unmistakable as she whispered, "Someone's hunting me."

I jumped up from the table, dug a twenty out of my wallet, and threw it down as I ran for the door. I said, "Where are you? What's happening?"

I barreled through the door and hit the sidewalk at a dead sprint for my car. As I passed by Judge Scott's door, he opened it and stepped outside, a drink in one hand and a cigar in the other. He raised his glass to me as I went by.

He knew. He sent them. Only Mary speaking stopped me from beating the man to death where he stood, consequences be damned.

In my ear, Mary said, "I'm in the boathouse near your condo. I was walking to your place from work when I heard someone say, 'I see her.' A guy was talking on the phone and was behind me. I saw a second guy on a phone near the sidewalk to your place. He was also holding a phone. And a gun." She continued to speak in a whisper, "I ducked down and slipped over the hill to the boathouse and the door was unlocked. I'm hiding inside."

I made it to my Jeep, threw open the door, and dove inside. In seconds, I roared down the street toward home. In my rearview mirror Judge Scott still stood on his stoop. Laughing.

My Jeep picked up the Bluetooth from the phone and I said, "Did you dial 9-1-1?"

"Yes, but they are at least ten minutes away." There was a brief pause and then she said, "They're outside. I've got to turn off my phone. They may see the light."

And she was gone.

38

I pushed the Wrangler to its limits, the Jeep meant for rugged driving not Speed Racer type of use, and made it to the boathouse parking lot in six minutes. The blue and whites were not there yet, and I braked hard and slid the Jeep into an empty spot on the hill overlooking the boathouse.

I reached over and retrieved my gun from the glovebox, a Colt 1911 M1A, thumbed the hammer back, and exited the Jeep, my gun up and ready. The parking lot was about half full of cars which belonged to the people who lived on their houseboats this time of year.

I scanned the area looking for the two men but did not see them. Adrenaline coursed through my body like wild horses charging across the plains, and my heart pounded in rhythm with them. I edged my way toward the boat house which sat at the opposite end of the pier from Divots.

The only lights on at the restaurant were a security light over the front entrance, and one over the metal stairs down to the boat house. It was a moonless night and while the side of the building was visible, the light failed to reach the mouth of the structure which loomed like the entrance to a deep mountain cave. The lights inside were off.

The boat house is where Teddy kept a TRU-X 241 Jet Boat and several jet skis, along with equipment he used to help maintain the restaurant. I made my way slowly down the row of cars, my gun hand constantly tracking from one spot to the next as I walked the edge of the embankment, the river to one side and the cars and the parking lot on the other.

From somewhere up the Ohio River, a barge horn sounded, long and mournful. Otherwise, it was quiet. The night sat heavy, and the temperature was cool here by the river.

I was halfway to the steps when I heard a sound behind me. I spun and came within a fraction of a second of putting a bullet into the brain of Detective Emit Brown who appeared out of the darkness between two cars.

I pointed my gun toward the sky as he raised his hands, palms out to me and shouted, "Jesus, Jericho. Don't shoot me. Jesus."

I snarled, "Dammit, Brown, there are people here trying to find my girlfriend. I could have shot you."

Before he was able to respond, it was as if my words brought the shooters to life. It is amazing what the brain notices in a fraction of a second when your life's on the line.

For instance, in the faint light, I saw there were two men, one black and one white. Both men wore black T-shirts, black jeans and dark shoes. The black guy stood a bit over six feet tall, with short cropped black hair. The T-shirt showed off the arms of a guy who worked out. A lot.

The white guy was several inches shorter, with a bald head and wiry frame. It was a good bet this guy never worked out a day in his life. But neither of them was going to beat us to death. Both held a gun, and they were raising them to shoot Brown in the back.

All this I noticed from one breath to the next. And unlike what happened with Amelia, this time I did have time to act. I shouted a warning to Brown and then dove, wrapped my arms around him, lifted him off the ground, and took us both over the side of the embankment toward the river. The two men both fired, and the sound of shots whizzed by me, one close enough I thought I felt a breeze.

As we fell, I twisted and shoved him away to get some separation between us, and we both rolled down the hill. I ended up on my back, my head almost in the water and my feet pointing back up the hill. I raised my Colt toward the top of the embankment and in my peripheral vision, I saw Brown doing the same with a Glock. How the man managed to get his gun out while rolling down the hill I did not know and did not care. He came to a stop flat on his stomach, his gun held in a two-handed grip, aimed at the parking lot.

When the two men reached the edge of the embankment, searching for the two of us, we both cut loose. I hit the bald man in the chest, and he propelled backward out of sight. Brown put a perfectly placed shot in the middle of the black man's forehead.

From a prone position. Shooting uphill. In the near dark.

The guy's head snapped back, then he fell to his knees like someone had just pushed the off switch in his brain, which the bullet, in effect, did. He then fell forward and slid halfway down the hill before coming to a stop a few feet from where we were, his lifeless eyes staring right at us.

We both laid there, breathing hard for a moment. I turned to Brown and said, "Nice shooting, Tex."

"Yeah. You too. Think you killed your guy?"

"Considering I'm shooting a .45 there, should be an exit wound in his back the size of an orange, unless he was wearing Kevlar. Why don't you check while I go find Mary?"

Like the men before her, I no more said her name than there was a ripple in the water next to the boathouse and Mary broke the surface of the water and swam into view while Brown made his way cautiously up the hill to check on the bald guy.

"What the hell?" I asked.

She tread water for a moment and said, "They came inside looking for me, so I hid my phone under a jet ski and slipped into the water and swam out to the riverside of the building where they couldn't see me."

"Are you okay?" I asked.

"Yes. How about you guys? I heard you shout something, and I peeked around the corner of the boathouse in time to see you two sliding down the hill and the shootout. Are you both okay?"

"I am."

I turned in time to see Brown holster his gun. He said, "I'm fine. These two assholes aren't. This one is gone, too. No Kevlar."

I returned my attention to Mary. "Do you need help getting out?"

"No. I'll swim back into the boathouse and get my phone and dry off. I'll be back in a bit."

She disappeared once again beneath the water, and I made my way up to stand by Brown. Baldy stared up at the night sky, seeing no more than his partner did. Brown seemed to be considering something, then said to me, "When you grabbed me and we went over the hill, I couldn't help but notice you turned me, so you were between me and the shooters. If not for you acting quickly, I'd be like this guy." He gestured to the dead man lying in the parking lot.

"Pure luck," I said.

He considered that for a moment. "Yeah. Maybe. Maybe not." He paused another second or two, then said, "Were they here to kill her or you?"

I laughed. "How do you know they weren't here to kill you, Detective? After all, with your sunny disposition, I'm sure you've angered a few people."

He laughed. A pure, honest laugh. "Well. True that. I do tend to tick off people."

We both heard sirens getting closer. The calvary coming after the bad guys were already down. I said, "I'm only giving you grief. I think they were here for me. They set a trap they knew I would run straight into. I think they wanted Mary to know they were after her, knowing she would call me. They knew she went into the boat house, but instead of trying to find her, they laid in wait for me."

"Sounds about right. Someone sure has a bug up their ass where you're concerned." He paused a beat and then asked, "You ever kill anyone before?"

I shook my head. "Nope. Hell, I've never even shot anyone before. You?"

"Not since I saw combat with the Marines. You think you'll have any trouble now that you killed a man?"

"Considering the man in question was planning on killing me first? No, I won't."

"Yeah. Me either. You get what you ask for. And these two were asking to be dead."

"Which begs the question: I know why I was here, but why were you here? Without you coming up behind me, they'd have likely shot me before I knew they were there."

"Because something happened late today, and we needed

to talk. Now it's even more important. Looks like we are each other's God damned guardian angels. Life sure is funny."

"Amen, Brother Brown."

"Let me call Tugbe. This is going to turn into a cluster fuck of the highest magnitude. With us both discharging our guns and killing people, the Public Integrity Unit will be involved. Neither of us will be getting much sleep tonight. And, Jericho?"

"Yeah, Detective?"

"When we sit down and talk, we need to come clean with each other. About all of it. Both sides. Agreed?

I grunted in reply and nodded my agreement as the two patrol cars rolled up and four cops got out. Detective Brown, badge out and held high, went to meet them.

For my part, I let out a long breath and turned to watch for Mary and thought about Judge Scott. He knew the guys were here, no doubt in my mind. Things were ramping up and Brown was right: it was time I brought him and Tugbe into the fight.

Up to now Ransford and Jacob Scott were theoretical threats. Now they had crossed the line, and much like the two dead men laying on the bank of the Ohio River, they were going to get what they earned: retribution.

39

Detectives Tugbe and Brown, along with Deano, sat at my dining room table while Mary caught up on some much-needed sleep. After all, all of us except Deano, had spent the night at police headquarters giving our statements on what went down with the two assassins.

Lucky for Brown and myself, Divots' security camera, installed after my beating several weeks ago, recorded the attack and backed up our statements.

Despite this, we were both required to surrender our weapons, and Brown was on desk duty until the investigation by the Public Integrity Unit was completed. The shoot was righteous, but there was a process and Brown was sidelined until it was over.

At my suggestion, we all got together at my place and

Deano picked up carry out Mickey D's for the four of us. Various types of McMuffins and huge cups of coffee were spread over the table as we filled up while we talked.

With most of the food now gone, Tugbe said, "Things have escalated, and quickly. You shoot a civilian, that's bad enough. But to be willing to shoot a cop, too? Someone is going to suffer the wrath of God on Earth. And that will only happen if we work together."

I nodded and said, "I agree, Detective. And I have things to share. But first—" I looked at Detective Brown. "You said you were there last night because something happened earlier in the day, and we needed to talk. What happened?"

Brown wiped his mouth with a napkin, balled up his sandwich wrapper and tossed it into a takeout bag. "Late yesterday, I had another meeting with Commonwealth's Attorney Alexandra Cutter."

"And?" I asked.

"She's called me in to talk several times since the case began. I must admit, I was feeling kind of special. There was talk of me moving over to the Commonwealth's Attorney's office, helping them out with investigations if we were able to wrap up this King thing."

"And now you don't feel as special?" Deano asked.

"Not particularly. During our meeting yesterday, Cutter wanted to know what new evidence we had on the King investigation. I told her not only did we not have new evidence, Tugbe and I were starting to have doubts about King's guilt."

"I bet that went over like a lead balloon," I said.

"Worse. She all but came out and suggested I should 'find' new evidence implicating not only King, but you, in the murder. And it was hinted that the person who did find such evidence would be greatly rewarded."

Tugbe said, "Emit called me as soon as the meeting was over. The fact the Commonwealth's Attorney would even hint at fabricating evidence to put King away raises all kinds of questions."

Brown said, "But she's smart. She never came out and said the words, but talked around it, making it obvious what she wanted."

"Okay," I said. "And you came to see me why?"

"I came to your place looking for you to warn you. I saw your Jeep fly by me, and I walked down to the parking lot to talk to you. Turns out you needed the warning."

Deano asked, "You think Cutter sent the goons?"

Before Brown could answer, I said, "No. I know who sent them. Time for me to update you and the fine detectives on what I've found out."

I reached into my pocket, pulled out the envelope with the ring, and dumped it in the center of the table. "Gentlemen, you are now looking at what I believe started this whole mess."

I spent the next few minutes explaining everything I

knew about Chambers, the Scotts, Amelia, and what I believed to be a blackmail scheme gone wrong. I gave them chapter and verse on the conversations I had with Judge Scott at Mesh and Malone's, and how he came out on his porch at the same moment Mary called me.

"He knew what was going on because he set it up. As for Greg Chambers, little did Chambers know he was trying to blackmail two psychopaths."

Brown picked up the ring and turned it this way and that. "And this is all we have to connect the Scotts to the murders? This and a phone call by Chambers to the courthouse?"

I said, "Even less than that. Winifred Scott could say she found the ring in a forgotten drawer, and her husband wasn't wearing it when he went overseas, or it's not even the same ring."

Tugbe held out a hand and Brown dropped the ring in his palm. "There has to be more than the ring. Chambers would know the ring by itself wouldn't be enough. You say you think Jacob Scott killed his brother, pretended to be him, went to Africa, and then disappeared?"

"I do," I said.

Tugbe said, "Despite how fantastic that sounds, let's say you're right, considering it's the only thing which makes sense to me. That means not only did Chambers find the ring, then he found the body, somewhere at Winifred Scott's place. As you pointed out, if it was just the ring, there are plausible explanations to explain it still being in the house."

"Agreed," I said. "Did you guys ever find the missing cell phone or laptop?"

Brown said, "No. Neither one. We did get access to his Gmail email account, but there was nothing there of any interest."

Deano drained his coffee cup and then asked, "What type of phone did he have?"

Tugbe replied, "An iPhone 11. AT&T service. Why?"

"Well," Deano said, "If you found a dead body wearing a ring, and you were going to blackmail someone over said body, you would want more than the ring. You'd take pictures of what you found, just in case they moved the body afterward. If you could get access to his iCloud account, you may find them there if his phone was backed up before he died and depending on the encryption used."

Tugbe took out his own phone and typed in a few notes. "I'll do that, but the process will take quite some time and the way things are going, we may not have it."

I said, "The body would have to be somewhere close to the house. Chambers was installing new electricity in the room Winnie is using for a bedroom. There wouldn't be a need to go far from the house."

Brown said, "Makes sense to me. Unfortunately, we don't have enough to get a warrant to tear the place apart."

"Agreed," I said. "Deano, did you get a chance to run Downey through the system?"

Deano said to Tugbe and Brown, "When Jericho told me

about the phone call Downey made, I asked the techs at my company to dig into his life and we found some interesting information. In addition to being a partner in Lancaster & Ivory Attorneys at Law, Mr. Downey Sr. has also brushed shoulders with some New York City mafiosos. In his early days, he represented several lower members of the Gambino crime family in real estate deals."

Tugbe asked, "Did Chambers get caught up in any illegal activity?"

Deano shook his head. "He didn't. They were suspected of laundering money, but he kept his part in the deals straightforward. They went to jail, but he did not."

"Too bad," I said.

Tugbe said, "If anyone might know how to reach two assassins on short notice, he might be the guy."

I said, "Interesting information. What about the two shooters?"

Brown picked up a manila folder lying beside him, opened it, and slid out several sheets of paper. Reading from them he said, "The black guy is, or shall I say was, Zeke Grant. He was thirty-two years old and originally from Scottsdale, Arizona. He did several stints in Rikers Island on extortion and assault charges, then a three-year sentence in Eddyville for nearly beating a man to death in Hopkinsville. The other guy was Vondell 'Viper' Pierce. He was a week shy of turning forty from eastern Kentucky and spent several years as Grant's roomie at Eddyville for shooting a guy during a bar fight."

"Upstanding citizens, they were not," said Deano.

Tugbe said, "And they have one other interesting thing in common."

"What's that," I asked.

Tugbe said, "They were both sentenced by Judge Ransford Scott to lighter sentences than the prosecutors were asking for."

"Wait," I said. "Judge Scott sentenced them? Judge Hang 'em High gave both guys light sentences? He never does that."

"Correction," Brown said. "He *rarely* does that."

Deano said, "Considering they were in town only a few hours after Downey made a call, if we think he was involved, were they already here in town?"

Tugbe nodded. "Yes. They checked into the Holiday Inn East four days ago. They were booked for two weeks. They were planning on being here a while."

I asked, "Were either gainfully employed?"

Tugbe said, "Both were currently employed by Evergreen Builders, Inc. The company was incorporated in Bowling Green."

Deano raised a finger. "Hold up a sec." Deano picked up an iPad and scrolled through some information. "I remember that name. Evergreen Builders Inc is owned and operated by none other than Benjamin Downey, Jr."

I said, "How much you want to bet Downey, Sr. was calling Downey, Jr. while eating with Judge Scott at Malone's?"

Tugbe said, "And once again, a father calling his son, which I'm sure he does often enough, is not out of the ordinary. There's not a judge in town who would issue a warrant for Downey's phone considering the target is another judge without unassailable evidence."

Deano asked, "Did you find phones on the bad guys? Anything in their car?"

"No phones, no I.D., no nothing. We only know who they were because their prints were in the system. We did find their rental car. Nothing in it to incriminate anyone. And nothing in their hotel room either. They share an apartment in Bowling Green, and I have the locals doing a search of their place as we speak."

Brown said, "So what we have is a huge steaming pile of shit we can't act on. Judge Scott has certainly covered his tracks well. What do we do next?"

I said, "I'll keep doing what I'm doing: pissing them off. And the next time they try to kill me, you guys take them down." I could see Tugbe was going to object, but I cut him off first. "I know you want me to leave it to you guys, but—" I gestured with my head at the bedroom door. "They've made it personal. It's one thing to threaten me—I can take it—but you bring in people who have nothing to do with what's going on? You endanger Mary? All bets are off, Detective."

Tugbe thought for a moment then made a reluctant nod of his head. He said, "I can't condone what you may or may not do. Officially."

"But unofficially?" I asked.

Tugbe offered up an evil smile and said, "Motherfuckers must pay."

Brown let out a short bark of a laugh and said, "It's about time you started coming round to my way of thinking and doing things."

Deano said, "Now what?"

"Emit is riding a desk for the next week or so. I will go back and reinterview Winnie and Jacob Scott under the pretense we are doing it with all the people Chambers spoke to that day," Tugbe said. "I will do the same thing at Lear Electric to show we are being even handed in case they pitch a fit to the chief. When we do, we will get a better feel for where Chambers was in the house, maybe get an idea of where Colonel Scott might be buried if your theory is right about Africa."

"Works for me," I said. "Coming after me the way they did was a mistake. Now we know for sure they were involved, even if we can't prove it yet."

Deano said, "And I'll tear even deeper into Downey's life and see what I can dig up. The fact the two assassins worked for Junior gives us another leverage point. Jericho's right. They screwed up."

"Do we want to know how you're going to do that?" Tugbe asked.

"No. You don't, Detective," Deano replied.

"Fair enough." Tugbe picked up the ring. "This is now evidence," he said. "I think I'll use it to push my own buttons at the Scott household."

"Give it your best shot," I said.

Tugbe and Brown stood and gathered up the rest of their things and headed for the door, with me in the lead. I opened the door for them and the two detectives stepped outside.

Once on the sidewalk, Tugbe turned to me and said, "I know I don't have to tell you after last night, but they are playing for keeps. You hesitate, and you're dead."

"Believe me, detective. They aren't the only ones playing for keeps."

I watched the two men get into their car and drive off. Deano joined me at the door and said, "I'm going to head to the office and set the crew to crawl up Downey's ass. In the meantime—" He pointed up the street a bit. "I've got guys watching the front and another pair in a boat on the river watching your place from there. You and Mary are safe to rest up a bit."

I offered Deano my hand and he took it. I didn't say anything in reply as I knew I didn't have to. Deano left and I closed the door and turned to find Mary sitting at the dining room table. She was dressed in one of my Kentucky pullovers, her long legs crossed with one foot beating time to a tune in her head.

"Morning, Sunshine," I said. I bent low and kissed her.

She smiled and said, "I want a gun."

"Okay. Do you know what kind?"

"Am I allowed to have a flamethrower?"

"I'm afraid not."

"In that case, I'll leave it up to you."

"Have you ever shot a gun?" I asked

"Yes. I dated a guy in high school, and he loved to go to the gun range every weekend."

"I'm guessing it didn't work out?"

"Nope. I was a better shot, and he couldn't handle it. His redneck buddies kept making fun of him and he broke it off. Would you be able to handle it if I was better than you?"

"Damn straight. If you are better than me, then you'd be the best shot in Louisville. I'll ask Deano to get you one. At least we'll both be armed."

"Bonnie and Clyde?" she asked.

"I'd rather have a different ending, if you don't mind."

She stood, took my hand, and started for the bedroom. She said, "Then why don't I start making you feel better now for the butt whuppin' you're about to suffer when we go to the gun range?"

"If this is what you're going to do every time you beat me, I'll be missing on purpose."

She snickered as we entered the bedroom and shut the door behind us.

Annie Oakley, get your gun.

And she did.

40

I sat at Divots eating a club sandwich and thought about things. I needed a way to force the Scott boys into more mistakes which didn't end up with me dead, preferably. What I needed was more information. I sent a text to Officer Bryant of the Pewee Valley police force and shortly thereafter, he sent me a thumbs up emoji.

I was thinking of what to do next when Teddy Ferguson dropped into the booth across from me and sat a bottle of Johnnie Walker Blue and two glasses on the table between us. When I looked up, I noticed the restaurant was quiet and a quick glance showed it was empty and there was no wait staff in sight.

Teddy said, "I was wondering when you were going to notice. I've posted outside we are closed for the next thirty minutes, and I told the crew to take a break outside. We won't be disturbed while we talk."

He screwed off the top of the whiskey, poured a double into both glasses, recapped the bottle, and then nudged one of the glasses in my direction. I picked up my glass and took a sip, the Blue offering a smooth burn going down.

I asked, "Why the privacy Teddy?" Though I thought I knew.

He sipped his own whiskey and then nodded to my phone, lying on the table next to my club plate. He said, "Let me see your phone for a moment."

I hesitated for only a moment, then slid my phone across the table to him. He flipped the phone over so he could see the screen, held down the power button until the option to turn the phone completely off appeared. He then powered my phone completely off then handed it back to me.

"Want to check me for a wire?"

He laughed, but it was an evil laugh. "Nah. Not needed. I just wanted to make sure there would be no recording of our talk."

The word I would use to describe Teddy's mood was serious. Normally a bombastic, boisterous type of guy, ready to bust your chops when given the chance, this afternoon he sat still, his hooded eyes even a bit more closed.

"What do you want to talk about?"

He took another sip of his drink, then said, "I want a name."

I knew what he was asking, but I played dumb anyway. "You need a dog name? Or are you getting a cat?"

He set his glass down on the table with an exaggerated slowness, a slight clunk as the heavy tumbler met the wood. "Not tonight. Don't fuck with me, Jericho. Someone was going to kill a girl who is as much a daughter to me as my very own flesh and blood. They were going to put her down. I know you are a damn good detective. I know you know things. I want a name."

It was easy to see how the man sitting across from me was a major player in the mob in Boston. I considered myself impervious to intimidation but the look on Teddy's face alerted me to the fact I needed to be careful in what I said next. It was if it were shark week, and I was just dropped into the ocean wearing a bloody steak around my neck.

There was part of me who wanted to take on these guys all on my own. The reason they came after Mary was because of my actions. My decisions. And, to me, it was a matter of honor that I be the one to deliver justice to each one of them. I wanted each to spend a long time in jail. Teddy's brand of justice was likely to be a lot quicker and more permanent.

With that said, building a case against Judge Scott that would hold up in a court of law was going to be difficult if not impossible. There was no way to prove motive. I had no evidence putting either Ransford or Jacob Scott at any of the murder scenes. I was like a blind man in a dark room looking for a black cat.

Judge Ransford Scott believed he was the apex predator in this equation. I decided it was time to introduce him to someone who had been one a hell of a lot longer and was likely to be a hell of a lot meaner.

I spent a few minutes giving Teddy the same rundown I gave to Tugbe and Brown. I left nothing out. While I talked, Teddy sipped his whiskey and kept quiet and never interrupted me.

When I was done, he said, "Judge Fucking Scott. You're sure?"

"No doubt in my mind. But, Teddy?"

"Yeah?"

"He's mine. You don't touch him. That's not negotiable. Understand? You want to go after the rest, have at it, but not the Judge."

"You giving me orders, Jericho?"

"When it comes to Judge Scott? You bet your ass. He's mine."

Teddy stared me down for a bit, then offered up a half shrug of his shoulders and drained the last of his whiskey. "I can live with that."

He poured another couple of fingers for himself and then did the same for me. He stared into the depths of the liquid for a few moments, then said, "I get out of the life. Come down here to make a new start. Be with my kid and try and relax a bit."

He paused a moment, and I didn't say anything. Out the window, I watched as a speed boat pulled up to the gas pumps, a young twenty-something guy wearing a Bengals hat backwards behind the wheel. He motioned to one of the workers he needed fuel and one of Teddy's guys nodded and began to gas up the boat. Normal life outside. Dark recesses of the human psyche being discussed inside.

Teddy began again, "And yet here I am. Dealing with crooked motherfuckers who are running around killing people." He drank the rest of his whiskey in one long pull and then set the glass down again. He stood up and glared down at me. He asked, "And you say Downey, Jr. is the one who employed the hired guns?"

"He did. There is no doubt about it."

Teddy nodded and said, "Then get out. I'll let you know when I know something that can help you. It's time I get back to earning some money."

I finished off my own pour of Jonnie Walker Blue, stood up, and headed for the door. Before I could open it, Teddy said, "And, Jericho?"

"Yeah, Teddy?"

"This conversation never happened. And when you go out, take the sign off the door, please."

I met his gaze for a moment then offered a short nod, opened the door, stepped into the sunshine, and removed the taped closed sign from the door. There was already a line of people outside waiting to go inside and I held the door open for them.

Life at Divots returned to normal. People were laughing, smiling and enjoying life. All was good with the world. For me? Not so much.

I was snapped out of my thoughts by a text from Officer Bryant. While Teddy did what Teddy was going to do, I would keep doing what I could do on my end.

And when the two ends met? Justice.

41

Bryant was sitting in a red Pontiac Trans-Am outside the Kroger store on La Grange Road. The parking lot was packed, and people were out, busy doing their weekend grocery shopping.

I pulled in next to him so our driver's side windows were facing each other. He said, "The housekeeper went inside about twenty minutes ago. She was carrying around six empty cloth grocery bags so I expect she will be a bit."

"I appreciate the heads up."

"I've been cruising by the Scott place more than usual, trying to see what I can see. I think Jacob Scott has noticed."

"Oh?" I asked.

"Yesterday I went by early in the morning. As you know the street they live on is a lonely stretch of road. There's not much traffic. When I went by, he stopped and watched me.

When I went back an hour or so later, he was sitting in his truck under an old oak tree. I got the feeling he was watching the road to see who was coming and going. I've never seen him do that before."

"I'm not surprised. They are on high alert."

"So I've heard. Word is some guys took a run at you the other night and you and a plain clothes detective took them down."

"All true. The detective was Emit Brown. Better them than me. Like I told you, I'm dealing with some bad people and the fact they tried to kill me shows I'm getting close."

He offered a short nod and said, "Well, at least you're dealing with two less of them. Let me know if I can be of any other help."

The young beat cop shifted the Trans-Am into gear and left. I got out, locked up the Jeep, and went inside to find Agatha. It didn't take long. I found her with a nearly full cart in the frozen food aisle looking over the frozen fruit. I walked up as she snagged a bag of blueberries and dropped them into the cart.

To say she was less than happy to see me would be an understatement. Before I could open my mouth, she began to wave her hands back and forth in front of her as if conjuring a spell to keep me away.

"No, no, no. I can't talk to you. No way. It's not going to happen."

"It's good to see you, Agatha."

"I can't talk to you, Mr. Jericho. I just can't."

She started to push her cart past me, and I let her get a few feet before I said, "Agatha, they're killing people."

This brought her up short and I watched her stiffen as if every muscle in her body was cramping. And then the moment passed, and she deflated like all life had suddenly left her body. She stood there with her head bowed, not moving. I walked and stood next to her, resting my hands on the edge of the grocery cart.

I said, "You don't seem surprised."

She didn't say anything at first. She just continued to stand there with her head down. Her hands gripped the handle of the grocery cart hard, like she thought it might fly away. Finally, she said, "Look, Mr. Jericho, I don't know anything. I don't."

I said, "Let me ask you two questions and then I'll let it go. Fair enough?"

She sighed and said, "Fine. Ask."

"The day Greg Chambers came to work on the electric for Winifred, where did he go inside the house?"

This question seemed to surprise her. Even with her head down, I saw her eyebrows come together. I'm not sure what she thought I was going to ask her, but this was not what she expected. She answered, "In the house he mainly worked in Miss Winnie's new bedroom."

"And nowhere else in the house? Did he do any wandering around?"

"No, sir. He came in the front door, down the hallway, and into her room. He spent a few minutes in the kitchen eating his sandwich but that was pretty much it inside the house."

"And outside the house. Where did he go?"

"Well, it wasn't so much outside as it was under it. He got real dirty when he had to go through the crawlspace under the house to run the extra wiring for the hot tub. Miss Winnie was none too happy with him walking in and out with his clothes covered in dirt."

"And nowhere else?"

"No, sir."

"Where's the crawlspace access?" I asked

"Near the steps out the back door. I don't know how anyone can crawl around under houses like that. All of them snakes and bugs and stuff. You couldn't get me to do that for all the money in the world."

"I hear you. Thank you, Agatha."

"Are we through, Mr. Jericho?"

"We are. And you don't have to worry. I won't tell the Scotts you and I talked. You have my word."

I took a step back, but she didn't move. She stood there for a moment, then she finally looked me in the eyes. I saw her swallow hard, and she asked, "Bad things are happening, aren't they?"

"Yes. They are. I notice you didn't argue with me when I said they were killing people. Is there something you want to tell me?"

I watched an inner struggle play out across her face, her jaw muscles working. But in the end, she simply said, "No. There's not."

With those words, she started on her way the checkout lanes at the front of the store. I called after her and she turned to face me. "Agatha, I like you. I really do. So, here's some free advice. Drop off the groceries. Finish your day. Then find an excuse to not come back for a few days. Do you have somewhere you can go?"

"I've a daughter down in Atlanta. My grand baby has been sick. I can tell them I've got to go down and help her."

"Good. Then do it. I don't know about Winnie, but Jacob and Ransford Scott are bad people who have done some bad things. And Hell is coming for them. Don't let it get to you, too."

A hand covered her heart, and her breathing was coming out quickly. "Are you trying to scare me, Mr. Jericho?"

I walked up to her and rested a hand gently on her arm. "Yes. I am. I don't want anything to happen to you and I'm worried if you stay there, it will. I want you to take me seriously."

Tears welled up in her eyes, but she nodded and said, "Thank you. I'll head on down to visit my daughter first thing in the morning."

"I will sleep better knowing you will be okay."

"How will I know when it's safe to come home?"

"Don't worry. You'll know. This will all be coming to an end soon."

She sniffled a bit and then said, "There is something. I'm not sure what it means but Miss Winnie and Jacob were in her room, and I was bringing her dinner. When I got to the door, they were shouting at each other. I heard her say, 'How could you do such a thing? You've ruined us all.'"

"Anything else?"

She shook her head. "No. I knocked on the door and they stopped. I could tell Miss Winnie was upset and so was Mr. Jacob. They were both red-faced. I sat the tray down and then left. That's all I heard."

"How did they react to you interrupting them?"

"They didn't say anything at the time. But later, Mr. Jacob came into the kitchen and found me on my phone, sending a message. He demanded to know who I was talking to. I told him I was texting my daughter. He didn't believe me and made me give him my phone so he could make sure. He's never done anything like that before."

"And you think he was worried you were telling someone about the argument?"

"I do. There's no doubt about it. And you think this means something?"

"Like you said, bad things are happening. Make sure you get out of town."

She thanked me again and then went to pay for the groceries. I watched her go and it seemed to me she had aged decades during our conversation, her pace slow and a bit uneven. The world she'd known for years was coming to an end and she knew it.

After she was out of sight, I got my phone out of my pocket and called Deano. When he answered, I said, "I think I know where Colonel Scott may be hiding."

"Tell me, "He said.

And I did.

42

Mary, Deano, and I met in a back booth at Divots for lunch the next day. We shared a meat lovers pizza and a pitcher of Bud. After the waitress dropped off our drinks, Deano pulled a green backpack he'd brought with him closer, unzipped the top, removed a pink holster, and slid it across the table to Mary.

She picked up the holster and set it in her lap and lifted the snap cover. I watched as she slid the gun out.

Deano said, "It's a Sig Sauer P365. The magazine carries ten more rounds. The paperwork for the gun is folded inside the holster. You'll need to register it."

"What type of load?" she asked.

Deano said, "Remington Golden Sabers."

She lifted an eyebrow. "The +P brass jacketed hollow points?"

He said, "The one and only."

"No safety?" she asked.

He shook his head no. "Not on this model. Point and pull. And it comes with the Trijicon RMRcc red dot sight."

She re-snapped the holster cover and put the gun in her purse. "Are you suggesting I need help hitting the target? Because I don't."

Deano asked her, "I wouldn't dream of it. You don't have a sister by any chance, do you?"

She offered Deano the kind of smile Helen of Troy was rumored to have used to launch a thousand ships and said, "I am a one and only, I'm afraid."

He looked at me and said, "You are so punching above your weight with this one."

I raised my glass, and we all clinked them together. "And don't I know it."

We sipped for a bit and then Deano turned serious. "You think Colonel Scott is buried under his house?"

I said, "Yes, I do. It's the only thing that makes sense. According to Agatha, Chambers didn't go anywhere else, on the property and only in limited number of rooms in the house. If he found something, it was likely under the house."

Mary said, "That's one cold-hearted son of a bitch if he buried his own brother under the house where his widow lives."

"Agreed," I said.

Deano said, "And yet there is still no probable cause to get a warrant to search the property to see if you're right."

I said, "And that's if there's even any evidence still there to find. Let's say Chambers found a skeleton under the house and then tried to blackmail the Scotts with the information. If I were them, I'd be removing any evidence in case things went south."

Mary said, "Someone still needs to look. We need to know for sure. Even if what was left of Colonel Scott was moved, there may be some other type of evidence there."

Deano said, "The main problem is figuring out how. It sounds like Winifred Scott never leaves and now neither does Jacob Scott. Do they have any dogs?"

I shook my head no. "None that I saw, and I was there a couple of times. They don't impress me as dog people. You must have at least some bits of warmth to you to want a dog. Frostbite has more warmth than they do."

Deano said, "Then we only have to worry about the two-legged variety of animal."

Mary said, "True, and at least one of them is much better than average with a rifle. If they see you coming…"

Deano slipped an iPad out of the backpack and opened it. He tapped a few times and pulled up Google Maps. He typed in the Scotts' address, adjusted the view, and then laid the iPad on the table between us, scooting the pizza out of the way.

He said, "It'll be hard sneaking up to the house if anyone

is watching. Their house is surrounded by fields. There are trees but they are all nearer the house."

I said, "Agreed. Most of them line the driveway. There aren't a lot of them close to the back of the house."

Deano said, "Normally, I wouldn't worry about the property being watched, but with them bringing in outside help to hunt you guys down, they may have hired some guys to watch the perimeter. Did you see any cameras when you were there? Ring doorbells?"

I shook my head. "I didn't see any, but then again, I wasn't looking that closely."

I saw Deano glance over my shoulder, and he said, "Heads up. Copper coming."

He scooted over and Detective Tugbe slid in next to him. He was dressed in a powder blue suit and tie and looked like the epitome of the dapper detective. I pointed to the pizza, and he said, "Do you mind?"

"Go ahead. It's why I offered. Join us for a beer?"

"Yes, please."

I motioned to the waitress for another glass and when she brought me one, I topped it off for him. He thanked me and had a long drink. When he sat the glass down, he said, "I can't tell you how badly I needed this."

We waited while the detective wolfed down a slice of pizza, all the while making small pleasure noises. When he finished the slice, he wiped his mouth with a napkin and said, "I stopped by the Scott house today. With Emit on desk duty, I took a junior detective with me, Anthony DeSeno. Good kid."

"And?" I asked.

"At first, Mrs. Scott didn't want to let me through the gates. She said she wasn't taking visitors. When I said I would go down to the courthouse and ask Judge Scott to personally come to the house and join me, she relented."

I asked, "Winifred answered the gate buzzer? That's not normal."

"She did. Seems her housekeeper had to leave overnight for Atlanta. Her granddaughter is sick."

I thought to myself, *Well, good for you, Agatha.*

I said, "And once you got inside? Learn anything?"

"Not much. Winifred Scott claimed not to know much, due to the fact she was in her bed when Chambers was at the house."

I said, "Like we thought. Deny, deny, deny."

Deano said, "And if they were looking for the ring, they know the you guys have it. If they were circling the wagons before, they will be doing even more so now."

"Did you get to talk to Jacob Scott?" Mary asked.

"He wasn't in the main house or the guest house, and Mrs. Scott didn't know where he was. While I was talking to the lady of the house, I had Detective DeSeno go outside and look around, but he didn't find him."

I asked, "Did you look around outside as well? And if you

did, did you happen to see a crawlspace access under the house?"

"I did," Tugbe said. "How'd you know about it?"

"Agatha told me," I said.

Tugbe laughed. "And let me guess; you were involved in Agatha leaving town?"

"Guilty as charged, Detective. With things heading toward a conclusion, I didn't want her to get caught in the crossfire, so to speak. And it doesn't hurt to put the Scotts off kilter a bit. I got the feeling Agatha did most everything for Winifred."

"I figured as much."

Tugbe sipped his beer and we all sat in silence for a moment. I was about to say something when the waitress came over and said, "Mr. Jericho? Teddy would like it if you would stop by and see him in his office for a minute."

I said, "Sure." She left and to the others I said, "I'll be right back."

Teddy's office was near the rear of the boat, a few steps past the bathrooms. I rapped my knuckles on the closed wooden door and Teddy yelled for me to come in.

Compared to King's office, Teddy's was a sparse affair. A battered oak desk was covered with papers. If they were in any kind of order, I couldn't tell. There was a large black swivel chair behind the desk and several folding chairs in front of it. Teddy sat behind his desk. Instead of the usual golf shirt and, this time he was dressed all in black.

"How squeamish are you?" he asked.

"Why, are you going to try and make me eat your cooking?"

"Funny. Real funny. Answer the question."

"Not overly. Why?"

He stood up, picked up a black windbreaker from the back of the swivel chair and put it on. When he did so, I saw the Glock stuck in the back of his pants. He came around his desk while he zipped it up, the gun now concealed.

I asked, "Are you expecting trouble?"

"Not anymore I'm not." He paused a second then asked, "Mary, your buddy, and the cop still out there?"

"They were when I came back here."

"Make nice with them for a few more minutes, then lose them. Make up any excuse you want. You'll be gone for a bit. Once you ditch them, drive to your condo, park, and then go inside."

"And then?"

"Wait. I'm not sure how the timing will go. When I know, then you'll know. I don't want to have to try and find you. Go home and stay there."

We stared at each other for a moment, and I took several deep steady breaths. The fact he asked if I was squeamish, the change in clothes, and the gun pointed to a very bad day for somebody. And I thought I knew who. I had given Teddy a name and Teddy was the kind of guy to act on the information. The question for me was, did I care?

And deep down inside, I didn't. The thing hiding down there wanted payback for what they did to Amelia and to Kaylee and for what they tried to do to Mary. They set the rules. And they would pay the price.

"Tik-tok, Hot Shot. Are you in or out?" Teddy asked.

"I'm in. I'll head home shortly."

"Good. Don't lollygag."

I turned to go and said, "Who the hell uses the term lollygag?"

He laughed but didn't say anything as I left his office. I made my way back to the booth and took a seat. Three faces looked at me expectantly. I said, "Teddy was grilling me for information."

Tugbe glanced over his shoulder down the hallway to the closed office door. He asked, "And you told him what exactly?"

I offered a half shrug. "Nothing he didn't already know. I told him to let the cops handle it."

Tugbe glanced at the door once more but didn't push it. "I need to get back to work. I wanted to let you know they now know we know. You know?"

I said, "Yes'em. I know. Happy hunting, Detective."

Tugbe got up and left and when he did, Deano asked, "And what did Teddy really want?"

I said, "He may have a lead and the two of us will need to go check it out."

Deano said, "You want backup?"

I shook my head no. "I won't need it. If I'm not safe with Teddy Ferguson involved, then I'm not safe anywhere."

Mary kissed me and said, "Teddy won't let anything happen to you."

"Agreed," I said. "What will you do?"

"Well, since we are hanging around cops these days, I think I'll go register my new toy. I work tonight, so I'll see you back at your place after my shift's over."

We walked out together and each of us got into our own cars and left. I made it to my condo with no issues and turned off the Jeep. I sat there for a moment and looked around. There were no cars I recognized. At least not at first. At the far end of the row of condos I thought I saw what might be Tugbe's unmarked. Trust but verify, Detective? He was smart enough to know Teddy wasn't after a simple update.

I got out, locked up the Jeep, and went to my front door. I unlocked it and went inside. I closed it and relocked it and then stood there unmoving. I figured that would be a good thing to do considering there was a man standing there with a gun in his hand.

43

Like Teddy, he was dressed all in black from head to toe in comfortable looking clothes and the same style of windbreaker. He was of average height and from the little hair I could see sticking out of a midnight-colored knit cap, his hair was curly and brown. A clean-shaven face framed a hawkish nose and dark blue eyes.

I held my hands out to my side so he could see I was not holding a weapon. He nodded to me and then walked up next to me, nudged the curtain covering my front window to the side with the barrel of his gun, and glanced outside.

"Anyone follow you?" he asked.

His deep bass voice did not seem to match his size or look. I said, "Detective Tugbe. He's parked down the street and watching my front door. After my talk with Teddy, he suspects something's up."

He nodded and said, "Not a worry." He waved toward my couch. "Take a seat."

I did, and he sat in an armchair across from me. His gun disappeared inside the windbreaker and his hand came out empty. He crossed his legs and placed his hands in his lap.

I said, "And we are waiting for?"

"The signal to move."

"And you expect that when?"

"Not likely until closer to nightfall."

"You do know that's a few hours away, right?"

He offered a smile and no comment.

"Okay. And your name is?"

"Call me Bob."

"Is that your real name?"

Another smile. Another no comment.

I said, "I'm guessing there's no point in asking where we're going or who we'll be seeing?"

Another smile. He sure smiled a lot. He must be a happy guy.

"The way you said 'call me Bob' makes me think you're from around Boston. Am I close?" This time, instead of a smile, I got a shrug. I asked, "How far back do you and Teddy go?"

"Who?"

He even said it like he meant it. I decided asking more questions was pointless and gave it up. I heard a lawnmower kick up outside as the lawn guys began to mow the grass around all the condos.

We sat there for several hours doing nothing more than listening to the workers outside and staring at each other. At one point, a guy came close to my door using a weed eater, but that was it. Before long, the sounds of the lawn guys faded and then stopped all together and quiet settled over my place.

The man was comfortable with the silence and so was I, since I didn't have a choice. Once, my phone rang and he told me to let it go and not answer it, and I did as he asked.

Without warning, he stood up and said, "Let's go." A man of few words.

"Did they send you the message telepathically?"

"Buzz of my phone. Speaking of which, leave yours here."

"What if I want to play Wordle later?"

"You'll survive. Do it."

I tossed my phone on the counter, and we walked to my rarely used kitchen and to my back door. Bob cracked it and glanced around. Once he was sure there was no one around, we slipped outside onto my patio. Bob turned the inside lock and pulled the door closed behind us quietly. All the condos in my row sat thirty feet or so above the river, which kept us safe from all but the once in a century flooding.

The man moved through my yard with a familiarity which unnerved me a bit, to a seldom-used path which led down to the river's edge. It was steep and in the early evening gloom, we walked with care. I followed behind him down the path to a waiting two-person motorboat. He hopped into the spot next to the single engine motor and I dropped into the seat in the front.

He pushed a button and the little engine came to life, the sound soft on the water. He gently turned the throttle and pointed the motorboat in the direction of the Indiana side of the Ohio. When we closed in on the far shore, he made a hard right and headed upriver. This path made sure to keep us out of view of Divots and anyone who might be watching in the growing darkness.

I asked, "Do I get a life jacket?"

Bob simply snickered and ignored me.

The river was quiet as city lights came to life behind us. I could just make out the Bell of Louisville, the more than century old steamboat, as she left her dock for a trip on the Ohio on a warm late spring night.

Once we were clear of anyone at Divots hearing us, Bob opened the engine and we increased speed, bouncing over the small river waves. The moon was out and nearly full and the moonlight bathed the river in a silver glow. It was the kind of night that made me wish Mary was with me on the river and not Bob. Then again, considering what the night might hold, maybe not.

After about a half hour, the shape of several large barges and the tugboat pushing them downriver toward us came into view. The barges were nearly black in the moonlight and as we came up next to them, I counted four of them. All four were covered, their contents hidden from view.

Another thing I noticed was the tug was running with minimal lighting. Normally on the river at night, they are well lit to alert other craft in the area they were there. Not tonight.

Bob swung the little boat up next to the tug which was barely moving, almost floating at the speed of the river. I saw the side of the boat was covered in huge truck tires. That's one way to keep the huge barges from banging into the side of your boat. A rope ladder was visible between two of the tires. Bob pointed to the ladder and said, "Up you go."

I grabbed the rungs of the ladder and climbed quickly to the deck. When I did, I turned to see if Bob was coming too, but instead of climbing up behind me, he goosed the engine a bit and continued upriver.

I turned and glanced up at the tugboat tower which rose nearly thirty feet above me. I knew there was someone there controlling the boat, but from this angle they were out of sight.

I started to wonder what I should do next when a man stepped out of the shadows. Like Bob, he was also dressed all in black which matched the color of his ebony skin. He was on the short side, perhaps five-foot-six-inches in height, with a bit of a paunch around the middle.

I stuck my hand out and said, "I'm Jericho."

He ignored my hand and said, "This way."

His accent sounded more Midwestern than anything else, but it was hard to tell. He walked a few feet, opened a door, and disappeared inside without waiting to see if I followed. I did. He didn't have to duck his head to walk through. I did.

A short hallway led to some stairs going down. He descended them with me right behind him. We came out in the engine room and, even with the tugboat barely moving, the noise was incredible. I saw two yellow engines with the Caterpillar name on the side, the individual piston heads looked as big as my head.

We walked between them and a bunch of other mechanical parts and dials whose function I had no clue about. When it comes to mechanics, I'm the guy you see getting ripped off in the car repair commercials. I know how to change a tire and that's about it. There was a reason I'd become a private detective.

At the far end of the engine room, he opened another door and stepped through. This time he waited for me to pass through after him and then he shut the huge metal door and the engine noise reduced to a dull hum.

He moved down another small hallway with a couple of doors on each side. Two of the doors were open and through one I saw a full kitchen and dining area, complete with a huge refrigerator, sink area, and a table and chairs with enough room to seat six people. The room was empty.

On the other side was a sleeping area with two bunk beds and a bathroom, though I guess these guys called it a head. I never understood why. It was also empty. He stopped by the last door on the right which was closed. He held up a finger for me to wait and then opened the door, entered, and closed it behind him.

While I waited, I moved to the other closed door and listened. I thought I heard muffled talking but wasn't sure if it were people talking or maybe someone watching television. No way to tell.

I turned around when the door behind me swung open and Teddy and the little guy stepped out. The small man once again closed the door then retraced his steps back to the engine room. Teddy was still dressed in black but there were several patches of darker color on the jacket. I didn't have to guess what it was due to the faint smear of blood along one side of his jaw.

Without offering a greeting, Teddy said, "Here's the deal. You walk through this door," and he pointed with a thumb over his shoulder, "You're committed. You will take what you see and hear to the grave. How soon you find yourself six feet under depends on how good you are at keeping your mouth shut."

I glanced past him to the door. It seemed I was being offered the same kind of choice Nemo was offered in the *Matrix* movies. Red pill or blue pill. Go through the door and know the truth of what lies beyond or walk away and go home, none the wiser, but perhaps better off for having done so.

In my case, there wasn't really a choice. I'd made my decision before I even got in the little two seat motorboat. The people I was up against were evil. They weren't saints. And when it came right down to it, I was an ends justifies the means kind of guy.

I stepped around Teddy and opened the door into a nightmare.

The room was a larger version of the bunk bedroom. Perhaps the sleeping quarters of the captain. There was a huge bed in the middle of the room, with a bathroom in one corner. A desk area and TV were off to one side.

I saw this through the plastic which covered every surface of the room. It was taped to the walls near the ceiling and then again at the base of the wall. The plastic was also stretched from one side of the bed to the other. There was not a single surface not covered by plastic.

The reason for this preparation lay stretched out on the bed. A man who might have been in his late twenties was lying on his back on the bed. A rope ran from one wrist, under the bed to the other side, then tied to the other wrist. The same for his feet. The rope pulled tight enough to cause deep grooves in the bed.

He was naked except for a pair of blue boxers. Bruises covered nearly all his body and it seemed to me at least one leg was broken by the bulge pushing up on the skin. The man's face was beginning to swell to the point where I wondered if he could even speak. In addition to the beating, there were cuts here and there from his chest down to his ankles. A chair stood off to one side, duct tape hanging off the arms.

The likely cause of the man's torment was standing next to the head of the bed. A large man of Asian descent stood quietly. He was built like a light heavyweight boxer. The muscles in his arms bulged but with the tone of a fighter, not a weightlifter.

He was around six feet tall with a smooth bald head and was dressed in all black like everyone else. When I came into the room, he watched me but said nothing. He simply crossed his arms and stood still.

I felt the bottom of my stomach drop away with the brutality of the scene. I expected something bad, but this? Teddy moved to stand next to me and as if he read my thoughts, he said, "Mr. Benjamin Downey, Jr. was not too keen on giving up the information I wanted. I offered him the easy way and he chose the hard way."

"Jesus, Teddy."

Downey lifted his head from the bed, and it seemed the effort took nearly everything he had to do it. He croaked, "Help me. Please."

I took a step in his direction but came up short when Teddy placed a huge meaty hand on my chest, stopping me.

"Before you feel too much sympathy for this man, you should know that in retaliation for you and the cop killing two of his men, he planned to kidnap Mary and do to her what we are now doing to him. Then they were going to mail you bits and pieces of her before they finally killed you, too."

"And you know this how?" I asked.

Teddy nodded to the corner of the room where Downey's clothes were piled on the floor. On top of them sat his cell phone. "He and his father use WhatsApp to communicate. My associate here convinced Junior to give me the password. The instructions from this old man were quite detailed."

Teddy continued in a tone of voice one might use to discuss the weather. "It also seems both Senior and Junior have done this kind of thing before. I scrolled back through their conversations and there are two other people they tied to beds, tortured, and then killed. They took pictures of the victims throughout the process. These are sick fuckers."

I heard Downey begin to whimper on the bed as he struggled weakly to break free of the ropes. One part of me felt incredible sympathy for him. No human should ever experience this kind of thing. It was inhumane. We were the higher species on the planet and yet we still held the capability to do this to each other.

Another part did not. If Teddy was right and they had done this to others, then wasn't this the ultimate case of karma extracting revenge for the victims? If you swim with sharks, don't be surprised when you get bitten?

I didn't know. One thing I knew for sure was I would never sleep easily again after seeing him this way. This was not the kind of thing one could easily forget. I considered myself more on the hardened end of the scale. But this? I wanted revenge for the fallen. In my head this meant life in prison or maybe a bullet to the head. Not this.

I took those thoughts and feelings and locked them away. I would deal with them later. Right now, I need information. I asked Teddy, "Did he implicate the Scotts?"

"In the murder of Chambers and all the others? He doesn't know anything about that. You were right in that his father called him and asked him to put the two assassins on you and Mary. Killing Mary was a bonus. You were the main target."

"But no mention Scott asked his dad to do it?"

Teddy shook his head. "No. Evidently, his father has done things for Judge Scott in the past, but it was all need-to-know stuff and Junior here didn't need to know. But the call from his father making the request matches the time when you were watching the Judge and Senior having dinner."

Teddy reached inside his windbreaker and removed several sheets of note paper and handed them to me. "An added bonus. Turns out the Downeys have been involved in more than a small amount of criminal activity. They have secret online accounts where they store all the information. Mainly blackmail and extortion."

I glanced at the paper and saw web addresses, account numbers, and passwords in Teddy's barely legible handwriting. He said, "Hand this stuff over to Monroe and let his tech geeks get copies of it all. Then find a way to anonymously hand it over to the Feds."

I folded the papers and then stashed them in the back pocket of my jeans. I stared a bit at Benjamin Downey, Jr. I knew how this had to end. There was no way Downey was going to see the sunrise. And if this is what they planned for Mary, then screw him.

Maybe we were all headed to Hell. Downey, Teddy, the hired thugs, me. All of us. My belief in Heaven and Hell was a bit loose. I considered them, but not often. I considered myself to be, overall, a good guy. On the side of the righteous, the defender of the helpless.

What did it say about me that I was able to witness what was going on in this room and be okay with it? Was I deluding myself into thinking I was one of the white hats? Did I care?

Not enough, it seems.

I asked Teddy, "What happens to him next?"

Teddy said, "There's a large barrel up top and the guys are already mixing concrete to fill it once we dump Junior here inside. There's a spot on the western side of Louisville where the Ohio is over one-hundred and sixty feet deep. You can guess the rest."

The whimpering on the bed turned into screams and Teddy nodded toward the door and we left the room. The screams were abruptly cut off when Teddy closed the heavy metal door behind us.

Teddy led the way topside, and we both were silent while we made the trip. Once on the tug's deck, he said, "Like I said, these are some sick fuckers, Jericho. I don't take pleasure in what is going on down there, but he earned every second of what he's going through."

I kept quiet.

"And, thanks to how we came by the torture and murder information, there's no way to send the stuff to the cops directly. In this case, I'm the judge, jury, and executioner. You can use the other information to bury Senior."

I nodded and tried to turn my mind to other things. "A tugboat? How are you involved in a tugboat?"

"My old friends from Boston are hip deep in all ways to move things: truck, rail, and river. I made some calls to bring in a few professionals and found out this tug was near Louisville. The crew knows how to keep their mouths shut and there aren't many better ways to get rid of the evidence than in deep water."

I heard the return of Bob and the motorboat before I saw him. I said, "I thought you were out of the life?"

He laughed and said, "There's 'out of the life' and then there's out of the life. Once you're a made man, Jericho, there really is no way to be completely out of the life. Well, other than a casket."

"Are they going to want something in return for helping?"

"Yeah. They are. They want you to use the information in

your pocket. Downey and his group were kind of in competition with my old crew in the Northeast."

Everything connected to everything else.

There was a soft whistle and Teddy said, "Time to go home, Hot Shot."

I made my way down the ladder and retook my seat in the motorboat. Bob guided us back to Divots and my condo. I sat there thinking about the night. Teddy didn't have to warn me again to keep my mouth shut as now that I'd been there and did nothing, I was a co-conspirator in what was surely going to end up in murder.

The world will soon be without Benjamin Downey, Jr., and it would be a better place for his absence. I cleared my mind and tried to relax and enjoy the short trip. Bob swung onto a private dock a few hundred yards from the one at Divots, the boat coming to a stop by a short wooden ladder.

Bob said, "You walk from here. We don't want anyone seeing you returning by boat."

I climbed out and up to the dock. Before I could even turn around, Bob was off without any more conversation. What a night. The moon was now almost directly overhead as I trudged down to my place. I glanced at my watch and saw it was almost midnight and knew Mary would be over soon. I was dog tired but seeing her would be a great thing after a night like tonight.

I made it to my front door and was inserting the key into

the deadbolt when I felt a gun placed to the back of my head. A man said, "Where's my son, you son-of-a-bitch?"

And my night just kept getting better.

44

I turned around with a calmness I didn't feel as Benjamin Downey, Sr. pressed the muzzle of his gun against my forehead. If I survived this encounter, I was going to have to have a long talk with myself. First Reggie got the drop on me, now lawyer boy managed to do the same thing. My awareness of my surroundings was sorely lacking. One day it might get me killed. Maybe tonight.

The normally dapperly dressed lawyer looked anything but in the faint glow of a nearby condo light. His suit looked as if he had slept in it, his hair was mussed, and I smelt the faint air of whiskey on his breath. The hand which held the gun trembled slightly. I got the feeling using one was not something Downey often did. And why should he when he had access to hired killers?

I said, "I'm sorry, but you are?"

The man practically growled as he used the gun to press me back against the door to my condo. "You know who I am. You saw me with Ransford."

"Oh. Yeah. Now I remember you. Maybe. You didn't make much of an impression."

He blinked a couple of times. I think he was offended, though through the mask of anger and fear which permeated his whole being, it was hard to tell.

"I bet I'm making an impression now, aren't I, asshole?"

"I must admit, you have my attention. I don't even know your name. What makes you think I know who your son is?"

The lawyer in him fought for a moment over what to say. Once a lawyer, always a lawyer. He knew I had to know by now the assassins sent to kill me worked for his son's company, but if he said as much, then it was a form of admission, and he did not want to say so. His brows furrowed a bit. He was stuck.

Then he said, "I'm Benjamin Downey. You're trying to tell me you don't know who I am? Or who my son is?"

"Sorry, dude. I don't have a clue. The fact you hang out with Ransford Scott shows you have a poor choice of friends. But I've never heard of you. Or your son. If he's missing, I'd try the cops."

"That's not possible. I can't go to them. And you do know who my son and I are. Don't lie to me. Ransford said you were too smart by half. He said you were going to figure things out once..."

His voice trailed off and I knew he was going to say, *once Tweedle Dee and Tweedle Dum assassins failed in killing me.* His inner struggle continued as the need to know about his son and admitting to being involved in a plot to commit murder held him up.

"Come on, why would you think I would know where your son is? I don't know him and, as far as I know, he doesn't know me. I think you've got the wrong guy."

I tried to keep him talking. My gun was tucked nice and safe in the holster on my waist. It would take me a couple of seconds to withdraw it and by that time, even the shaky-handed Mr. Downey would be able to blow a hole in my head. And I liked my head the way it was, thank you very much.

I thought briefly about Junior, his fate and my earlier thoughts about how karma had caught up to him. I was forced to admit, karma was a bitch. I knew one day karma would likely pay me a visit, too. However, I never thought it would be in a few hours.

"What makes you think your son is missing?"

"We were supposed to meet for dinner at Captain's Quarters, down on the river. He loves to watch the boats go by. When I arrived, his car was there, and I parked right next to it. When I went inside, he wasn't there and no one had seen him. His phone goes straight to voicemail. He's gone."

I thought to myself, *if you go sit in my backyard and watch the river, your son will be going by in an hour or so on one of the boats he loves to watch.* What I said was, "And you think I'm involved how?"

"You know how. And I'm tired of waiting. Tell me where he is, or I'll blow your fucking head off."

I laughed when he said this and, if possible, he got angrier.

"What's so funny, asshole?"

"You can't shoot me."

"And why not? All I have to do is pull the trigger and I'll splatter your brains all over your door."

"First, if I do know where your son is and you shoot me, you'll never know, will you? He will be lost to you forever. As far as shooting me, yes, that's all you need to do. But to pull the trigger, you have to first click off the safety. And from my up-close view, I can see it's still on."

Downey was holding what looked to be a Glock 19. I wouldn't swear I had the exact model, but it was for sure a Glock. And what people who own one know, a Glock doesn't have a safety. It's a point and shoot kind of gun. I was bluffing hoping Downey was one of the uninitiated who didn't know much about guns. This was based on his years as a white shoe lawyer, his soft looking hands, and manicured nails. Men like him hired people to do the dirty work. They didn't do it themselves.

I was lucky. He didn't know there wasn't safety. He turned

the gun a bit sideways to glance at where a safety would be if it had one, and the muzzle moved from pointing directly at my head. The moment it did, I snapped up with my arm and used the back of my hand to swat the gun further away from me and then hit Downey with a vicious headbutt.

When you headbutt someone, you must be careful to do it in a way where you don't injure yourself, as well as the bad guy. You want to use the area a couple of inches above your eyes, the crown of your head. It will hurt a bit, but you will live. The other guy? It can be devastating.

Downey and I were around the same height and my headbutt caught him flush on his nose. I heard it break and a fountain of blood poured out all over his expensive rumpled suit. He dropped the gun, his knees wobbled, then buckled and he landed ass-first on the sidewalk path which led to my front door.

I bent, scooped up the Glock, and tucked it in the back of my jeans. Downey covered his nose with both hands to try and stop the bleeding and moaned. He finally managed to croak out, "You broke my nose."

"Considering you were planning to shoot me, I think you got off easy. I should put a bullet in your brain where you sit. That's what you deserve."

And then Downey began to cry. Not silent tears kind of crying, but big heavy mouth breathing kind of crying. I must admit, it put me off a bit. Out of all the reactions I expected, this was not one of them. What I wanted, with the adrenaline running full speed inside me, was a continued confrontation. No such luck.

Like I had for his son, I started to feel sorry for the guy. But then, just like his son, remembered what Teddy told me about how the two of them took pleasure in torturing and killing people and any fleeting sympathy I felt disappeared into the night.

I said, "Get up. Now."

Downey first turned over onto all fours and then did as I asked. When he made it to his feet, he looked at me and I saw hate in his tear-filled eyes. I didn't care.

He said, "You're a dead man walking, Jericho. Count on it."

When he spoke, I saw blood bubbles around his broken nose.

"You know, Benjamin, threatening a man who just laid you out and has your gun is not a wise thing." I stepped up close to him and in a quiet voice said, "I see you near me again, I'll kill you. You come for anyone close to me again, I'll kill you."

I'm not sure what he saw in my eyes, but his own widened a bit and he turned and stumbled off. I watched him walk over to a gray BMW X5, open the hatch, and reach inside. I slipped his Glock out of my jeans and held it down close to my side in case he was going for a backup gun, but there was no need.

Downey got a towel out of a gym bag, pressed it to his

nose, then got in behind the wheel and left. He never looked back at me the whole time. I heard movement to my left and saw Mary step out from behind my Jeep where she'd been crouching.

She held her new gun in both hands, the muzzle pointed at the ground, but when Downey was out of sight, she returned it to her purse. She came to me and hugged me. She said, "I'm glad you were able to handle that. The man's hands were shaking so badly I was afraid if I yelled for him to drop his weapon he'd startle and pull the trigger. Same thing if I just shot him."

"I appreciate your situational awareness. How long were you there?"

"I saw you walking down the road in front of the condos. I wondered where you were coming from. I wasn't far behind you when the guy jumped you. That was Downey Sr.?"

"I went for a stroll. And yes, it was. He was looking for Downey Jr. It seems Junior has disappeared, and he thought I knew where he was."

"Do you?"

"Why don't we go inside?"

She nodded and, after checking to make sure no one else was going to jump us, I led her into my condo. She flipped on the lights and this time there was no Bob waiting. The night was improving.

We sat on the couch and I put my arm around her. She

leaned her head against my shoulder and asked again, "So. Do you know where his son is?"

"Maybe. But I don't think it's something you and I should talk about."

She said, "Teddy?"

"Again, I think there are some things best left unsaid. What I will tell you is Teddy takes your wellbeing very seriously. And heaven help anyone who might threaten you. I would leave it at that. Fair enough, counselor?"

"Will I have to worry about Downey Jr. going forward?"

I didn't answer, which was all the answer she needed. She sighed, stood, took my hand and pulled me up. "Let's go to bed. I'm tired and I know you must be, too."

I didn't argue. She was right. I was exhausted. We weren't in bed for more than a few minutes and Mary was fast asleep, her breathing smooth and even. The easy sleep of the innocent. Me? I laid there thinking of tugboats, plastic, and water. I thought of Downey Sr. and the pain and desperation he showed at the disappearance of his son that was genuine.

All because an electrician found a ring and tried to blackmail the wrong person. A guy who believed he'd found a meal ticket to a better life, but who instead toppled dominoes which were still falling. Counting himself, there were now six people dead, on both sides. Good guys and bad guys, going down for the count, and I couldn't help but think there was going to be more.

When I finally started to drift off to sleep, images of the Scotts' house were filling my mind, and the crawlspace, dark and foreboding, beckoned to me. Even though I'd never seen it, it called to me. And I knew I was going to have to make the same journey Greg Chambers made several weeks earlier.

The only question was, would I suffer the same fate?

45

Deano and I sat eating omelets at the Waffle House on Lyndon Lane. I ate a fiesta omelet and he opted for the vegetarian without the cheese. Wimp.

I'd awoken tired and restless. If I dreamed more of the Scott house, I didn't remember it. Mary had showered and then left to study for her bar exam, which was coming up in a few days.

I'd used a burner phone to send the information on the Downey accounts to a burner phone Deano kept for just these kinds of situations. An hour later, he suggested we meet at Waffle House and here we were.

Deano said, "We've imaged all the stuff in the hidden folders the Downeys set up. And I've got to tell you, there's a lot. These boys have been up to no good for years."

"Any mention of Judge Scott?"

"There is. Seems Bill Stalker is not the only person funding Scott's Supreme Court bid. Tens of thousands of dollars have been laundered into his campaign account by an Eastern Kentucky organized crime group with ties to everything from coal to marijuana to state politics."

"And they were using the Downeys to gain access?"

Deano forked some egg into his mouth and said, "Yep. And then there's the stuff Teddy's old gang is interested in. Downey Sr. has continued to work for his old mafia buddies. When the Feds go through this stuff, the Downey's are going away for the rest of their lives."

I didn't bother to mention to Deano that Downey Jr. wouldn't have to worry about the Feds. "When will you transmit the data to them?"

"Already done. I have a contact in the FBI and he received an 'anonymous' delivery about a half hour ago."

"Your guys are quick. Well done."

"Teddy made it easy for us." He sipped his coffee and then continued, "You plan to visit the Scott house tonight? Are you sure that's wise?"

"We are to the point where I don't see I have much choice."

"Well, if you wait a bit, the Feds will lower the boom on the Downeys. I'd be willing to bet they'd flip and give up Judge Scott. Then Tugbe and Brown can get a warrant and search until they find the proof we know is there."

"All true, but how long before that happens? And with the walls closing in, how long before the Scotts make another run at me? Or Mary? I don't think I can afford to wait."

"Fair enough. So how do you want to do this?"

I told him.

"And if it goes south on us? What are the rules of engagement?"

I said, "Execute with extreme prejudice."

"You know Tugbe and Brown won't be overly happy with us."

"Probably not but they can get used to disappointment. I want this over with. One way or the other, it ends now."

"Damn straight."

We fist bumped and I paid the bill, leaving the waitress an extra-large tip. Karma. I was trying to yank it back in my direction. Would it pay off? It couldn't hurt.

46

In the darkness, I crouched down on my stomach, about fifty yards from the back door of the Scott house, waiting and watching. Deano's voice was low, but clear, as it came through an AirPod in my left ear.

"You're good."

Deano's company used drones for many different things. One of them was night surveillance. Prior to my approach to the house, Deano set up a mini command post in a field just out of sight of the house. He launched the drone and sent it hundreds of feet in the air and used a night camera to monitor the grounds. He checked for dogs and possible cameras and, as I suspected, found neither.

I also contacted Officer Bryant and found out he was working the night shift, getting off at midnight. I hooked him up with Deano and he was watching the road leading to the Scott house to warn us if anyone showed up unexpectedly.

About a half an hour earlier, Deano's eye in the sky caught Jacob Scott going into the main house and nothing had moved since. It was approaching midnight and my luck held as it was a cloudy night and the moonlight was hit or miss, keeping me hidden in shadows. Like Teddy and his men, I was dressed head to toe in black: black shirt, jeans, shoes, and socks. I'd even smeared some dirt over my face as well. Jericho, detective ninja.

There was a light on in the kitchen, but the light barely reached outside, and I knew it would be hard to see me right up until I found the crawlspace. I wasn't able to see it from where I hid, but Tugbe said it was to the left of the back steps. Easy enough. Unless someone walked out the back door and looked down, they'd never see me.

I got up and sprinted for the kitchen door. I made it with no problems and knelt next to the steps. A bit off to one side, I saw the crawlspace, a darker patch against the rest of the house. It was covered with lattice work, and I worried about making noise removing it, but a closer examination showed it was simply leaning against the opening, not wedged in. If Chambers removed it, he never put it back properly.

I lifted it away and sat it next to the hole. I dropped to my knees and looked under the house. The darkness was complete. I wasn't even able to see more than a few inches. I removed a small flashlight I brought for the occasion, thrust my hand into the crawlspace, and thumbed it on. I'd covered the light with a bit of gauze to reduce the brightness in case there were any creases in the floorboards where the light might be visible.

The floor joints were ancient in appearance and spider webs hung down in several places. I fought the primal urge to turn and run, inhaled a deep breath, and squeezed my way through the opening. I barely fit. In fact, I had to corkscrew my body to do it, one arm raised high above my head, the other down by my side. Chambers' smaller frame was a must for anyone who needed to fit into spaces like this and still be able to work.

Once under the house, I took a moment and figured out where I was in relation to Winnie's new bedroom and began to crawl in that direction. I knew it was a good distance from the crawlspace opening. I used the flashlight to swipe the cobwebs out of the way as I crawled. The place smelled of mold and dirt. I was halfway to where I wanted to go when my hand brushed something, and a rat snake darted off further under the house.

I nearly bit my tongue trying not to yell out. I knew rat snakes were harmless and, in fact, were great to have around your house as they kept the rodent and bug populations down to a minimum. But there's knowing a thing and knowing a thing when you are under stress.

I made it another few feet when I realized I heard voices. I inched ahead with deliberate slowness, not wanting to make a sound the people above me might hear. I realized the people were in Winnie's bedroom.

Then I saw it. What Greg Chambers had seen. What set all the events in motion. I felt such a rush, I momentarily forgot the people talking in the room above me.

Partially buried in a slight depression was a skeleton. Most of the clothes it wore had long since rotted away, but the collar, thicker than the rest of the clothes, was still there and a colonel's clusters were visible, glinting in the faint beam of the flashlight. From where I was, I saw a skull, an arm, and one long boney hand extended in my direction. The index finger seemed to point right at me which once wore a green signet ring with a design of a lion.

I slid out my phone and, making sure the flash was off and the sound turned off, snapped a few low light photos of the skeleton. It was then Deano spoke again in my ear. He said, "Officer Bryant says a car is headed your way. He thinks Judge Scott is driving. Time to get your ass out of there."

I was about to do what he said when the voices above me increased in volume. I heard Winnie say, "It's over, Jacob. You fools have ruined us all. There's no point in running from this anymore."

I switched off the flashlight and listened.

Jacob said, "If you keep your mouth shut and let Ransford handle things, then there won't be a problem."

Winnie offered a cruel, harsh laugh. "Handle things? Jacob, the police have the ring. How is it a police detective has the one thing you and my son were unable to find? Despite all the pain and suffering you left in your wake. It won't take them long to start piecing together what you did. And why. And with Mr. Jericho pushing them..."

Jacob said, "Don't you worry about him. He won't be a problem for much longer."

"Oh, Jacob. You old fool."

In my ear, Deano said, "Judge Scott is parked and out of his car and going inside the house. He's carrying what looks like two suitcases he got from the trunk of his car. I can't tell what they are from this angle. But you are clear to leave. Repeat, clear to leave."

I didn't dare respond. I knew he was right. I should get out of there without hesitation. I now had proof Colonel Scott never made it to Africa. In fact, he never left his house. We had them. All we needed to do was to give the photos to Tugbe and he could nail their asses to the wall.

But I was frozen in place. I was like the fly on the wall, although in this case, I was the mouse under the floor. No one knew I was there, and I wanted to hear what Ransford, Jacob and Winifred Scott had to say to each other. I ignored Deano and stayed where I was.

A moment later, I heard a door open, and Judge Scott entered the room. Jacob said, "Ransford, talk some sense into your mother. She wants to call the authorities and confess it all. Tugbe coming here with the ring has her spooked."

"Mother, the police are no longer your concern. And,

Uncle, it's not Mother's fault," Judge Scott said. "It's your fault for burying my father here under the floor. That was stupid."

Jacob laughed. "He loved this bloody house so much. He could damn well spend eternity here."

Judge Scott said, "It was still stupid."

Jacob said, "We can salvage the situation. You can—"

Judge Scott cut him off, "I'm afraid not, Uncle. It would seem my friend Benjamin Downey was arrested late this afternoon and his son is missing. The federal charges against him are many, and in the end, Downey will break. He's a weak man. I knew I should have killed him the moment the hitmen failed. He will be trading us in to save his own skin. I've seen enough of it in my court to know how this will end."

Winifred said, "Then what are we going to do?"

Judge Scott said, "I'm going to leave the country. I've set up another identity in Argentina for just such a purpose. I'm hopping on a private jet the moment I leave here. New name, new passport, new everything. I have enough money stashed in an account there to live my life in the luxury I've become accustomed to."

Jacob said, "And what about us?"

Judge Scott said, "You? I guess you will be spending eternity here too."

I heard Jacob Scott yell, "No!" right before two shots rang out, and the sound made me jump. A large body hit the ground and I assumed Jacob Scott was no longer with the living.

There was a brief pause and then Judge Scott said, "Goodbye, Mother."

If she said anything in response, I didn't hear it. There were two more shots and then it got quiet. In my mind's eye, I pictured ole Judge Hang 'em High shooting his mother and uncle twice each to make sure they were dead.

I then heard the judge leave the room and I turned to begin my way to the crawlspace exit when the judge returned to the room. There were two small thumps, as if he was sitting something heavy on the floor. A moment later I heard him walk back and forth across the room.

I didn't have to wonder long what he was doing as gasoline began to leak down between the floorboards, the smell strong in the enclosed space. Holy hell. He was going to burn the house down. And he had soaked the floor between where I was and where I needed to be. I crawled as quickly as I could toward the exit, no longer worrying so much about being quiet. I heard a woosh overhead as the judge must have struck a match to the room.

Instantly, the floorboards above me roared into flames, the almost two-hundred-year-old wood frame house going up like the dry kindling it was. Smoke rolled out and began to fill the crawlspace. I resisted the urge to cough and pulled my shirt up to cover my nose to try and help, but I lost the battle.

The heat was incredible, and I worried my hair would catch on fire. I beat down the panic and forced my way through the smoke. By the time I made it into the fresh nighttime air, I was hacking up a lung. I rolled onto the ground and began to stand when I heard the kitchen door open and Judge Scott say, "Well, well, well. This is the night that keeps on giving. I thought I heard someone."

I stood hunched over a second, my back to him, then slowly stood up and turned to face Judge Scott, my hands held out to my sides. He stood there, a gun pointed at my chest, his Cheshire Cat grin visible in the flames now leaping up to the second floor of his childhood home.

He motioned his head to the side, indicating we should move away from the flames. I did as he suggested, and we walked a few yards away. The flames bathed his face in an orange glow, giving it a demonic sheen. I would guess that wasn't too far from the mark considering the man just murdered his mother and uncle. He lowered the gun and held it down at his side, knowing he could shoot me easily before I reached my own gun.

I asked, "Was it you or your uncle who killed Greg Chambers?"

Judge Scott said, "Why not. I'll answer a question or two. You'll be dead in a few minutes anyways. It was me. He thought he could blackmail me. Me of all people."

"Why not just pay him?"

"I was going to. I even had the money with me. If he'd taken the money and kept his mouth shut, it would have ended there. But no. That wasn't good enough. Once I got to his place, he decided he wanted more. The dumb ass ordered pizza to celebrate and then turned his back on me, believing he held all the power. I lost it. His hammer was right there so I grabbed it out of his tool belt, and I bludgeoned him to death."

I said, "I know you killed Amelia. Which of you killed Kaylee?"

"That was Jacob. He was trying to find the ring. Chambers told me he hid it where we'd never find it. Once we learned about the girlfriend, we figured she might know where it was, but she disappeared. Gone with the wind."

"And when you couldn't find her, he beat her roommate to death trying to find her?"

"Exactly what he did. Turns out, Amelia lit out and didn't even tell her roommate where she was going. The roommate died for nothing it would seem."

"And Davis and Pavey? I'm guessing they were both you."

He bowed his head slightly in response. "Guilty as charged, Detective."

"And why did you kill them? You had to know their deaths wouldn't stick to me."

"Like I told you at Mesh: it was just to mess with you and to send the police on wild goose chases. And besides, after killing Chambers, I found I liked it and wanted to do it again. Why not remove two more vile human beings from the city I love?"

I asked, "Did your mother know about Jacob killing your dad? Has she known all along?"

Judge Scott shook his head. "She only figured it out when Tugbe showed her the ring. She said she didn't recognize it to buy time and talk to Jacob. But in the end, she was willing to throw it all away."

"And that was worth killing your mother and uncle? What the hell, Ransford?"

"Loose ends. Jacob told me Mother was going to spill the beans to Tugbe. She was old and near the end of her life. She didn't care if it ruined the family name. She wanted to die with a clear conscience. After all, all the murders were carried out by Jacob and me. She believed she would be viewed as blameless."

I asked, "Did Jacob tell you why he killed your father originally?"

"They got into a fight over a game of Gin Rummy. Of all the stupid things. Can you believe it? When the fight got heated, my father told Jacob to leave the property and never return. They'd never liked each other."

"A card game? Seriously?"

"As God is my witness. My mother was gone on a tour of Italy at the time and my uncle decided to kill my father, tear up the dining room floor, and bury my father there where he would be each time we ate dinner. He then went to Africa pretending to be my father and I think you know the rest."

I said, "I can see you killing your uncle. Maybe. But your own mother? Jesus, Judge."

"I was raised more by nannies and boarding schools than I was by my own mother. Good riddance."

"You're a sick puppy, you know that?"

"I won't argue the point."

"You won't get away with it. You know that, right? You're going to prison for a long time."

"It won't happen. With you dead, there won't be anyone to tell them what happened and by later tonight, I'll be on my way to Argentina. I've covered my tracks quite well. They will never find me."

"They won't have to take my word for it. I think your own words will be good enough."

I swiveled my hips around a little and nodded with my chin to my front jean pocket where the edge of my phone was barely visible, the black case blending in well with my clothes. "The moment I heard you behind me, I FaceTimed Detective Tugbe and slipped my phone into my pocket with the lens out. He's been listening and watching your whole confession. And whatever private plane you were going to take? By now, all flights by private jet will have been put on hold. You are so toast."

I watched first surprise, then anger, then resignation, then bliss cross across Judge Ransford Scott's face.

He said, "Bravo, Detective. Bravo. You got me. I told Ben you were smart. I should have listened to my own advice and shot you the moment you crawled out but I wanted to see your face knowing it would be me to kill you. I wanted that satisfaction. At least I still get to do that much."

I nodded and said, "Before you try, take a quick glance at your chest, right where your heart would be if you had one. I'll hold still while you do."

He did and his eyes went wide when he saw the red dot I'd been staring at for the last minute or so. It hovered right over his left breast.

I said, "I know someone almost as good as you are with a rifle."

He snarled and raised his gun to shoot me. He wasn't quick enough. Before his arm was halfway level, the rifle round hit the Judge right where the red dot aimed. The impact took the judge off his feet, and he was dead before he hit the ground.

By now, the house was fully engulfed in flames, and I wandered a good distance away, as the heat was too much to handle up close. I heard sirens in the distance and knew both the fire department and cops were on the way.

I pulled my phone from my pocket to see the face of Detective Tugbe staring back at me, none too happy to see me. I turned up the volume and heard him say, "You will have a lot of explaining to do, Jericho. Jesus. You were almost killed."

"True. A couple of times. It seems God loves me."

This got a snort out of Detective Brown who I guessed was driving the car.

Tugbe asked, "Did Monroe take the shot?"

"He did. He'll be here too."

Tugbe said, "Don't move. We'll be right there."

I offered up a small salute and ended the FaceTime call. I sat down in the grass and watched the house burn and incinerate the bodies of Jacob and Winifred Scott, along with the skeleton of Colonel Scott.

I made a quick call to Deano. "The calvary is almost here. You might as well come on over. Oh, and I'll be telling Mary you needed to use the laser scope to hit your target."

He snickered and hung up. I put my phone away.

I knew there was something profound about how this ended, some great metaphor about life I should consider, but I was too tired to even think about it. The threat was over. The bad guys were down. And the good guys lived to see another day. That would have to be profound enough.

47

Teddy clinked a knife against the side of his champagne glass and the group of people there to celebrate Mary becoming the Commonwealth of Kentucky's latest lawyer all grew quiet.

Teddy said, "A toast. To one of the hardest working people I've ever met in my entire life. And one of the best, too. To Mary McGill, attorney at law."

We all raised our glasses and the room filled with cheers. I sat with Mary at the head table with Teddy, Deano, and Mary's parents, Christina and Terry. Deano made small talk with Mary's parents who were obviously proud of their daughter.

Teddy said to Mary, "And I hear further congratulations are in order. I hear you've been accepted as a law clerk to Judge Burke and will be moving with her if she wins a seat on the Kentucky Supreme Court. Something she's likely to do with Judge Scott out of the picture."

She kissed him on the cheek. "Thanks, Teddy. I owe you a lot. More than I can ever repay." She turned to me and said, "Teddy doesn't want people to know, but he helped pay my tuition. My parents don't make a lot of money and he didn't want me to have a lot of student debt."

I leaned forward to look at Teddy. "You old softy. Next thing you know, you'll be the one rescuing seal pups and saving the whales."

"Kiss my ass, Jericho. What I want to know is will you still be coming here now that your favorite waitress is moving on? You leave and I may be out of business."

I laughed and said, "Don't worry. While it won't be the same without Mary behind the bar, I don't plan on learning to cook. I'll still be here."

Mary said, "Teddy, just make sure he's waited on by a male waiter, please." She stood up and said, "I'll be back in a minute. I want to go thank the other people who are here."

When she was out of ear shot and Teddy was sure no one else could hear him, he asked, "Are you in the clear on all the Judge Scott stuff? Are you worried they will bring any charges against you or Monroe?"

I shook my head. "No. Thanks to my FaceTime with Tugbe and the photos of the skeleton, it was as good as having Judge Scott confess on the witness stand. And Judge Burke pulled a few strings to make sure it stayed that way."

Teddy said, "It never hurts to have a judge on your side. Better than having one trying to kill you. And I'm guessing you had something to do with Burke offering Mary a job?"

"Nope. Not a thing. She got that all on her own. It never hurts to finish first in your class at law school and score a near perfect on your bar exam. Mary had her choice of jobs and she wanted to clerk for Burke and Burke wanted her."

Teddy winced a bit. "I'm not sure I'm happy with her deciding she wants to go to work for the Commonwealth attorney's office when she's done clerking. It feels like she's going over to the dark side. Speaking of which, I hear Commonwealth's Attorney Alexandra Cutter pitched a fit when she was forced to drop all the charges against King."

"And she's not likely to get reelected because of it. She staked her career on the prosecution of Robert King. After charging the wrong guy and being so closely associated with Ransford Scott, her popularity is taking a nosedive. She's being roasted by every newspaper and news program in the country. This has made national news."

He said, "Does this make you and King pals now?"

"I'd rather be pals with a pissed off polar bear."

We both were silent for a bit as we watched a radiant Mary glide around the room, taking the time to talk to everyone, a smile beaming on her face.

Teddy asked, "What's next for you?"

"I'm taking Mary on a vacation to Hawaii. I haven't had a

vacation in years. It's overdue. In fact, I was going on vacation when King hired me to investigate Chambers' murder."

Teddy's look sobered up and he said, "You know, if you turned King down, a lot of people would still be alive. Ever think of that?"

I sighed and said, "Yeah. I have. But in the end, the murderer would have gone free if I had. It breaks my heart what happened to Amelia and Kaylee, but I don't regret getting the right guy. It would be like me asking if you regretted what happened to Downey, Jr."

"Fair enough."

Teddy got up, clapped me on the shoulder, and went to check on the wait staff. I sat there and watched Mary. She was dressed in a mid-thigh length white dress, her blonde hair free and flowing over her shoulders. An Amazonian Goddess come to life. She was talking to an older couple I didn't know, the seventy-something man going on and on about something or other. Mary listened with rapt attention, like he was the most important man in the room. Then she glanced at me and gave me a wink.

Considering all the carnage left in the wake of Ransford and Jacob Scott and their cronies, and considering a man like Robert King, a man who deserved to be in jail many times over was celebrating being a free man, it would be easy to view the current state of humanity with less than a favorable eye.

Then Mary winked at me.

And I knew it was going to be all right.

ACKNOWLEDGMENTS

In 1998 my short story, *Leaves of Departure*, was published in the May issue of Kentucky Monthly Magazine. In the bio accompanying the story, I mentioned my next project was going to be a detective novel.

Years later I pitched two novel ideas to a group of publishers: the detective novel and a supernatural thriller. Hydra Publications signed me and decided they wanted the supernatural book first, and with the release of *The Hand of God*, the world of Victor McCain and Samantha Tyler, was created.

The detective novel was pushed to the back burner and over the next thirteen years I released seven more books, six in the world of Victor and Samantha, and a book of humor.

But the detective novel was still rolling around in my brain. And last year, twenty-five years after its conception, Final Judgement: A Jericho Novel, was finished.

I grew up reading the novels of Arthur Conan Doyle, Agatha Christie, and any other mystery novelists I could get my hands on. Today, my favorite reads are by Lee Child, John

Sanford, Nelson DeMille and Michael Connolly. To finally have my own mystery novel out in the wild, a life-long dream has been realized.

For me, writing a novel is not a solo affair. I have a group of people who help me from brainstorming ideas to editing to beta reading. I would like to thank James Caffee, Teresa Collins, Bill Noel, and Ed Woods for their input and suggestions.

A huge thanks goes out to one of my real life Jericho inspirations, Jim Griffin, the owner and driving force behind Big Sky Solutions, LLC, a private investigative firm. If you need your own Jericho, call Jim.

I would not be able to write anything without my wife, Karin, who red pens everything I do. She helped to make sure Jericho was spelled correctly. Oh, and the rest of the novels, too.

Thanks to Starbucks Store # 2464 in Prospect, where I finished the book. I spend more time with my extended family at Starbucks than anyone else, and you guys are truly fam.

And thanks to you, dear reader, for making my career as a novelist possible. I hope you enjoy Jericho as much as you do Victor and Samantha. The game is afoot.

ABOUT TONY ACREE

Tony Acree is an award-winning publisher, novelist, and screenwriter. He lives near Louisville, Kentucky with his wife, twin kids, three female dogs, three female cats, and says the way the goldfish looks at him, he's sure she's female, too.

www.ingramcontent.com/pod-product-compliance
Lightning Source LLC
Chambersburg PA
CBHW072053020726
47501CB00003B/575